MURDER MOST HOLLYWOOD

A CAROLYN NEVILLE MYSTERY BOOK 4

JOHN DUCKWORTH

Murder Most Hollywood
Paperback Edition
Copyright © 2021 John Duckworth

CKN Christian Publishing
An Imprint of Wolfpack Publishing
5130 S. Fort Apache Rd. 215-380
Las Vegas, NV 89148

www.cknchristianpublishing.com

Paperback ISBN 978-1-63977-095-3
eBook ISBN 978-1-64734-534-1

MURDER MOST HOLLYWOOD

*To Dad, who performed on Broadway
and in the pulpit.*

PROLOGUE

STILL FEELING DIZZY, I PARKED IN MY USUAL SPOT NEAR THE
Oasis Gardens. I'd never walked this stretch after dark alone,
but didn't have much choice.

No panhandlers, no street preachers. Nothing but feeble
street lighting and the occasional *hrrrretch* of spitting in the
alley.

I could hear a car approaching behind me, but it was at
least a block away. Turning, I watched the headlights grow
bigger. The make, color, and model were a mystery, even
when I squinted.

The engine revved. There was a thump as the vehicle
jumped the curb and starting riding the sidewalk.

I started running.

The thumps came faster as the car sped up. No time to
look over my shoulder.

My breath came in gasps. Somebody was trying to run
me down.

A park opened up on my right. Grass, trees, a garbage
can, swings.

I could hear the unseen driver bearing down on me, only

a few yards between us. Thought I smelled gasoline, but it could have been my imagination.

I looked around for help. Nobody.

The street was deserted, or seemed to be.

The beams of the headlights lit the sidewalk at my feet. I cut to the right, into the dark.

God, get me out of here.

There was a pain in my side. I hadn't run like this since I was a teenager. Mikki would be so proud. Maybe she'd mention it at my funeral, except she wouldn't know how fast I was going when I died.

I just missed colliding with a streetlamp, then nearly tripped over an abandoned bicycle.

The glowing eyes of a cat or raccoon or something zipped past.

Maybe I can make it.

The headlights lurched to the left. The car couldn't follow this far. I could hear it bumping into the distance.

I kept running, but stumbled and fell headlong into the sand next to a playground slide.

Panting, I hugged the ground and waited for someone to slam a car door and appear with a gun. But there was only silence.

CHAPTER 1

"I CAME AS SOON AS I COULD."

Standing just inside the door of Room 344 at San Diego's Scripps Mercy Hospital, I peered into the darkness. I could barely see the familiar silhouette of Harrison Yoder's bushy white beard and bulbous nose.

But he was no Santa Claus.

Oscillating lines sped across the monitor like fireflies. A tiny red valentine pulsed along with his heart; little yellow lungs showed he was breathing. No alarms beeped. I relaxed a little.

"My God, Carolyn," he said with a faint chuckle. "No need to look quite so earnest. I'm not dead yet."

I set my purse on the floor and sat in the chair by the bed. "Good. I'd hate to think I blew half this quarter's travel budget to fly here for nothing."

"Not my fault you work in Manhattan. You should move Pendleton Publishing out here."

I shook my head. "Not my call. Editors aren't allowed to change anything more important than a paragraph indentation."

He turned toward me. "Did you bring the agreement?"

"Yes, but I haven't signed it yet."

"Second thoughts?"

I sank back in the chair. "I'm still on first thoughts. I don't know if I can do what you're asking."

"You're the *only* one who can. I don't trust anybody else." He coughed, long and phlegmy, reminding me I hadn't just imagined his lung cancer.

"How about one of your fellow lawyers? Or a grandson with a YouTube channel?"

He cleared his throat. "Grandkids aren't speaking to me, thanks to my ex-wife." He paused. "Carolyn, of all my books, *Winchester Creek Homecoming* is the most personal. I spent most of my career as a B-team John Grisham, but I only put my heart into this one."

"But—"

"I'm lucky anybody wants to make a film out of it. But I won't be around to see they do it right. The docs give me a month at most."

I watched the lines on the monitor march left to right.

He turned toward me. "Don't suppose you've got a cigarette, do you?"

"Are you kidding?"

"Gallows humor."

"I don't know the first thing about Hollywood," I said.

"Well, *I* do. Writers get no respect, and the sausage factory turns everything into crap. That's why I need you."

I groaned.

He coughed again. "I haven't asked much, have I? Considering everything, I mean."

I leaned forward. "Considering what I owe you?"

"Well, I wasn't going to put it that way."

I looked at the floor. "You never have. But it's always been the elephant in the room."

"I was happy to do it. You always went to bat for my books, so I went to bat for you."

It had happened seven years ago. A certain fiancé had broken off our engagement. After calling in sick and crying for two days straight, I got myself together enough to eat Pomegranate Dark Chocolate Swirl ice cream by the pint and binge-watch *The Office* on DVD.

By the time I got back to work, I'd missed a meeting with Harrison. He'd flown all the way from California. My boss took a tennis ball from the pail on his desk and flung it at me, demanded I apologize to Mr. Yoder, and gave me 48 hours to shape up. Two hours later, my mortgage check bounced. I'd been paying my grandfather's home health care nurse for the last year. All I had to do was hang in there for the next 30 years and not spend anything.

When I called Harrison that day, I took a deep breath and started to explain what had happened. About 25 words in I choked. There was a long silence while I looked around for my bottle of Poland Spring water, which was nowhere to be found.

Finally he spoke. "Carolyn, are you all right?"

I knew it was unprofessional, but it all came out. I managed not to get weepy, but my voice had more vibrato than the Bee Gees.

"Hmm," he said when I'd run out of steam.

"Sorry to unload," I said.

"No problem."

Long story short, he insisted on giving me a loan. Nothing huge, but enough to cover my condo payments for six months.

He never brought it up again. It took me four years to pay him back.

Yeah, I owed him. Not just for the money, but for giving a rip.

I looked up. "Okay. I do have Stephen."

"Who's Stephen?"

"My senior editor. The kid knows everything about showbiz, or thinks he does. And he's even more opinionated than I am."

"Is that possible?"

I closed my eyes. "If we came out here for a month or so, my boss would have a fit. We've got a publishing program to run."

He coughed again. "I'd reimburse your company, pay whatever it takes to hire temporary help. I've got the cash. It's not going to my ex, that's for sure."

I listened to the monitor beep. "We're talking about a lot of money. *Winchester Creek Homecoming* isn't going to be a Marvel blockbuster. And I hear the director is a jerk."

"It's a labor of love—for me, anyway. I'd like to die knowing it won't be the next *Cats*."

I opened my eyes. "How am I supposed to make sure it isn't? Why would anybody listen to me?"

He shrugged. "You're a lot prettier than I am. I look like that fat old guy who wrote *Game of Thrones*."

We stared at each other. Finally I threw up my hands. "I'll bring it up to Hunter."

He snorted. "Is that idiot still there? You should have replaced him by now."

"Well, life's not fair."

He nodded, then adjusted the oxygen cannula in his nostrils. "You're telling me."

I cringed. "I didn't mean to compare your illness with—"

"Hey, at least Hunter Thicke isn't your fault. I've been smoking since I was fourteen. Knew it wasn't good for me but I did it anyway."

"I'm the same way with doughnuts."

He patted my hand. "So, will you sign the agreement?"

"After I talk with Hunter. And Stephen."

"Good."

We listened to the oxygen hiss. His clear plastic tube ran to a contraption on the wall that bubbled the gas through water. The digital readout said 26.9, whatever that meant.

He stared up at the ceiling, blinking. His eyes were shiny.

"I've been thinking a lot lately," he said.

"I'm sure you have."

"The folks where I grew up seemed pretty sure what they believed and where they'd go when their time came. I just couldn't buy it. Couldn't wait to get out of there."

He paused. The water bubbled. "Never been a religious man. I know you have some inclinations in that direction."

"I do."

He swallowed. "Pray for me, will you, Carolyn? Maybe not right now, but sometime?"

I reached over and took his hand, the one without the IV in it.

Right now seemed as good a time as any.

* * *

Hunter Thicke didn't like what he was hearing.

I could tell because his eyes were squeezed shut and he literally had his hands over his ears. "What is this, *The Wallabys?*"

"Excuse me?"

"That old TV show. A big family in ugly clothes lives in a shack on a mountain."

"You mean *The Waltons?*"

"Whatever. So Harrison Yoder is like John-Boy. He gets his Indian Chief pad, writes down his story by candlelight, and you're going to turn it into a movie."

"It came as a surprise to me, too," I said, shifting in my chair. "It's just that—"

He put his hands down, then used them to slick back his black hair. "And your senior editor's going to help because he doesn't know anything about making movies, either."

"Sounds crazy, doesn't it?"

"And stupid. I can't afford to send you two to La La Land. I need you here, losing money on the *other* projects you keep proposing."

I leaned forward. "Harrison's going to pay for it. He's made a nice profit for us over the years, and his books will sell long after he's gone. It's only right to grant his dying wish."

"Is he actually dying yet?"

"Well, not exactly. They're giving him a month or so."

He rolled his eyes. "Then you're jumping the gun. Let's wait a month, then talk about it. Maybe he'll have a miraculous recovery."

I folded my hands in my lap, trying to look harmless. "When's the next board meeting?"

He consulted Calendar on his iPhone. "Friday the sixteenth."

"I'll bet they'd love to hear one of our properties is headed for the big screen. The last time that happened, you got a nice bonus, didn't you?"

His eyes widened. "How'd you know that?"

"You announced it in Acquisitions."

He frowned. "Oh. Just wanted to encourage the rest of you to do likewise."

"Of course. We'll be rewarded for going the extra mile, usually with a coupon for ten percent off lunch in the cafeteria."

"Well, not anymore. But we have rubber wristbands printed with the words KEEP TRYING." He reached in the drawer of his desk and pulled one out. "Blue for guys, pink for gals."

I pretended to smile. Hunter would have been a great motivator in 1954.

"All right," he declared. "Let's do it. On one condition."

I raised an eyebrow. "Which is?"

"*I* should be the one to go to Hollywood. We need a firm hand on the steering wheel."

My mouth fell open. "But your . . . hand is needed here. Stephen and I are expendable."

He leaned forward and lowered his voice. "I haven't told many people about this, but I follow the entertainment industry. I even subscribe to *Variety*."

"Really."

"That's where I found out who's doing this picture. The director's been in and out of rehab. The producer's mostly known for risking the lives of his cast and crew."

I frowned. "How so?"

"Cuts corners. Last year one of his extras got electrocuted because he wouldn't shut down during a lightning storm. The family sued for reckless endangerment—and won."

"I'll wear rubber boots."

He looked out the window, where construction workers were air-hammering the street in front of an ancient souvenir shop. "But you're right," he said with a sigh. "I'm indispensable. I should stay here to keep the board informed."

"A wise decision, as always."

He kept staring out the window. "I've always wanted to direct. I loved what Martin Scorsese did with *It's a Wonderful Life*."

"I think you mean Frank Capra."

He stood up, hands in his pockets. "Reminds me of a story. Ever heard of Tyler Perry?"

I thought for a moment. "Director. Writer. African-American."

"A renaissance man. Did it all. Dressed up like a fat old lady in the Madea movies. Then I saw a thing he made for Netflix called *Fall from Grace*. He had a little part in it. But his beard was terrible. Looked like they'd pasted clumps of rabbit fur on his chin. The plot made no sense."

He paused. I waited for a point, knowing there was only a 35 percent chance of getting one.

Finally he nodded out the window. "I figure Mr. Perry had complete control, but it was still a disaster. And you're no Tyler Perry."

"You're telling me."

He turned to look me in the eye. "Be careful what you want, Carolyn, for you may not get it."

I rose to my feet. There was only one thing I wanted—to pick up a carton of orange chicken at Panda Express on my way home, call Mikki Flaherty, and ask her why she never stopped me from getting into messes like this one.

* * *

Mikki was speechless, a state she reached only at times of national crisis or acute laryngitis. Finally she spoke.

"*Hollywood? Are you kidding?*"

I looked around my kitchen, trying not to notice the pile of dirty dishes in the sink. "Do I sound like I'm kidding?"

"I don't know. You do that dry humor thing, like Stephen Wright."

"So do you think I should do it? The movie?"

"Why *wouldn't* you? Practically everybody would kill for the chance to do that."

"*I* wouldn't. I've always been happy to be an editor and complain constantly about it."

There was some kind of noise in the background. "Just a minute," Mikki said. "I left my toe shoes in the dryer." She put the phone down. I could imagine her prancing off in her untucked shirt and leggings, skinnier than any woman had a right to be.

A minute later she was back. "Okay. I've had time to think about it, and I haven't changed my mind. You should definitely seize the day and sign the contract. You'll never have a chance like this again."

"I hope not."

She made an exasperated noise. "I see it's time for your weekly affirmation. Do you want the secular one or the Christian version?"

"Don't want an affirmation. They wear off sooner than cheap eyeshadow."

"Am I the only one here who has any ambition? I remember when you told me you wanted to do something that would make the folks back in Montana proud."

"Idaho."

"Right. Do they have movie theaters there?"

I sighed. "Yes. They even have streaming. And GrubHub."

"Then this is your moment. You have that whole thing about quality. You could turn this film into something your grandchildren could watch, and *their* grandchildren."

"I'll never have grandchildren."

"There you go again. You just haven't met the right guy yet."

"Let's not go down this road right now. I just need to know that I won't make a fool of myself."

There was a pause. "What do you want, a guarantee?"

"Sure."

She grunted. "Remember when I auditioned for the *The Nutcracker* three years ago?"

"Yeah."

"I had the flu and threw up the minute I got on stage. Another dancer slipped on it and sprained her ankle."

"And still you got the part."

"No, I didn't. And the other dancer hit me with a chair."

"So how is this inspirational?"

"I kept going. I didn't give up."

"And now you dance at church."

"Not *just* at church. I've got a nursing home gig coming on St. Patrick's Day. Sort of a Celtic thing."

I shook my head. "Other than my boss, this is one of the worst pep talks I've ever heard."

Another pause. "Well, can you at least get me a part in the movie?"

I closed my eyes. "Mikki, this isn't *West Side Story*. It's about a boy growing up in Appalachia in the 1940s. He loses his mother. His father goes to prison. He has to raise his brothers and sisters by himself. He becomes a writer and—"

"They have dancing in Pennsylvania."

"Appalachia. Mountains. Poverty. Overalls. And fiddlers."

"There you go. Barn dances, stuff like that. Have you got a choreographer?"

My eyes were still closed. "Not my department. I'm supposed to keep the author's vision intact."

"Have you read the script?"

"Not yet. But I know the book like the back of my Spanx."

"I tell you what. Pray about it."

"I did."

"And?"

"Nothing."

"Then I'll pray, too. No fasting, though. My nutritionist says if I get any thinner I'll have to register my shoulder blades as concealed weapons."

"Deal."

"Check in with me again in a couple of days, okay?"

"I promise."

"I'll send you my head shot and resumé."

"Already got 'em. Bye."

Opening my eyes, I put the phone on the placemat. Talking with Mikki was always enlightening, except when it wasn't.

I ambled to the living room, got my laptop off the coffee table, and went on YouTube. I recalled what Hunter had said about Tyler Perry. Clicking on a clip from *Madea's Family Reunion*, I proceeded to watch the master at work. He seemed to be playing nearly all the parts. As the old family patriarch, he broke a lawnmower with a wrench. He said the word *carburetor* over and over. The film was obviously not set in Appalachia, but there were a porch and a screen door. And it looked like they'd recycled some of that *Fall from Grace* rabbit fur.

Having thus become an expert on motion picture arts and sciences, I yawned and clicked on a 22-minute clip of Jimmy Kimmel highlights and fell asleep during an interview with Mariah Carey. When I woke up, the laptop was asleep and I was drooling on the sofa.

It was clear what I had to do.

Wiping my chin with my sleeve, I stumbled past the stack of dishes and made my groggy way to bed.

My epiphany would have to wait until morning.

CHAPTER 2

STEPHEN WALKED INTO MY OFFICE THE NEXT MORNING, looking like an electrified ginger cat was sitting on his head. The kid probably hadn't combed his hair in a week. I guessed that was a thing if you were of a certain age, which he was. His cinnamon beard was just unshaven enough to be visible, and his gray sweater vest might have fetched a dollar or so at Goodwill.

He yawned. "You wanted to see me?"

"Know who Harrison Yoder is?"

He squinted. "Harrison Ford's Amish brother?"

"I thought you were familiar with our backlist."

He stood up straight. "I am. But you have to give me the *title*."

I picked Harrison's book off my desk and held it up. "*Winchester County Homecoming*."

"Oh, yeah. The one about the non-Beverly Hillbillies."

I put the book down. "They're not hillbillies. They're . . . mountain folks. Ozarky. They play zithers, or autoharps, or whatever you call them."

"Whatever."

"Harrison is dying of cancer. He's an old friend of mine. They're making a movie out of his book, and he wants me to go to Los Angeles and keep the Hollywood types in line."

He burst out laughing. "You?"

"Is that unthinkable?"

He tried to look a little more respectful. "I mean, writers are on the bottom of the showbiz totem pole. Just above editors."

"But I owe him a big favor. And I figured you, with your vast knowledge of the entertainment industry, could help me out."

He scratched his stubbly chin. "Guess I do have a feel for it. Took a film course at UCLA. Read *Adventures in the Screen Trade* and *Story* and watched every episode of *Inside the Actors Studio*. I know all the Easter eggs in the last three *Star Wars* movies."

"Oh, that should do it."

"You don't look convinced."

"I'm not. Fortunately, Harrison's contract requires the production company to give one or more of his representatives access to the set."

A grin spread across his face. "Fantastic! When do we go?"

"In a few days."

He sat down across the desk. "Okay. Have you ever seen *For Your Consideration*?"

"Is that a movie?"

"Not just a movie. A Christopher Guest movie. The guy who did *Spinal Tap* and *A Mighty Wind* and *Waiting for Guffman*."

"Oh."

"So *For Your Consideration* is about making a film called *Home for Purim*. It's set in the south in the 1940s. Catherine O'Hara, Harry Shearer, Fred Willard, Parker Posey, Eugene Levy."

I frowned. "Isn't that a comedy?"

"Exactly. The director doesn't get the south, the 1940s, or how the Jewish stuff fits in. But he plows ahead anyway and the film starts getting Oscar buzz by mistake."

"How does that help us?"

"It's rural. Porches and stuff. Old-time dresses."

I sighed. "Maybe *The Grapes of Wrath* is a better example."

He snapped his fingers. "Dustbowl. Black and white. Henry Fonda. Have you heard my impression of him?"

"No. I'm not sure it's normal for people your age to know what he sounded like, much less imitate him."

He launched into Fonda's fervent, sibilant speech at the end of the movie, the one about how he'd be there in spirit wherever there was injustice. It sounded more like Jack Nicholson but I didn't tell him.

"That's great. You do Christopher Walken, too?"

"Everybody does him."

"*I* don't."

"Of course not. I could see you doing Cher or Celine Dion. If you didn't mind wearing a wig."

"Never happen." I paused. "What do you know about getting directors to stick with an author's vision?"

He thought for a moment. "You know William Goldman?"

"Not personally. Besides, he's dead."

"Wrote *Butch Cassidy* and the *Sundance Kid, All The President's Men,* and *The Princess Bride.* Said writing for movies is really complicated. Even though he got two Academy Awards, he got no credit line for some of the stuff he worked on. Screenplays are usually written by committees."

"Fascinating."

"They say writers are the most mysterious part of moviemaking, but the most disposable. They're always griping about not getting credit."

"Like editors."

He looked around as if on the verge of divulging a secret. "I'm . . . wondering if you'll have any say about who's *in* the movie."

I shook my head. "I think it's already cast. The big parts, anyway."

"Oh, it wouldn't have to be big."

I stared at him. "Are you asking what I think you're asking?"

He shrugged. "Maybe."

"You want to be *in* the movie? I thought you were above that sort of thing."

He looked away, clearly sorry he'd brought it up. "I didn't spend all my time in college studying English. I was in *1776*. Played Caesar Rodney, the guy with cancer. I spent the whole show with a cloth wrapped around my head. Lost ten pounds for the part."

"That's dedication. But I don't think—"

"It wouldn't have to be a major role. Not even a speaking part."

I sighed. "We'll have to see what we can do. It's up to the director."

"Don't want to complicate things for you."

"Wouldn't be the first time."

He looked at his fingernails. "I bet you'd like a role, too. Maybe a Southern belle or a wench or something."

I rolled my eyes. "This isn't a Civil War picture. Or the Middle Ages. And no, I have no ambitions for a career on the stage."

"You mean the *sound* stage. That's where they—"

"Shoot the picture. I even know the difference between exteriors and interiors."

He leaned back in his chair. "Yeah, this is gonna be fun."

I looked out the window. It would be so much easier to leave him here.

But I didn't have the patience to handle Hollywood alone.

* * *

I've never been one to keep a diary or journal, and I'd never venture to blog. But if I were forced to record the highlights of the next day, they'd go something like this:

6:30 a.m.: Kicked out of bed by siren wailing an insufficient distance from my condo.

6:45: Breakfast of stale donut and flat Martinelli's left over from New Year's Eve, which was three months ago.

7:00: Car dashboard says CHECK ENGINE LIGHT. Smell of burning rubber. Make mental note to put duct tape over dashboard indicator lights.

8:07: Arrive at office. Can't get in. Hunter's admin says he had all the locks changed due to his suspicion that someone stole the football trophy from his desk, and the locksmith forgot to leave the envelope of keys due to sudden attack of diarrhea.

9:40: Keys found. Locksmith reported alive. Pile of unread manuscripts on desk; I move them to Stephen's office. He looks sullen, like so many of his generation.

10:00: Meeting to review marketing plan for new motivational book by Willow Hayly. We see her via Skype. Looks skinnier than ever. I want to throw my laptop at the screen.

12:15: Lunch with agent representing a recently failed presidential candidate. I nod my head at him a lot and explain that most people won't even read books by the winners. My salad has no dressing.

3:29: Hunter stops by. He is introducing everyone to the new outside consultant assigned to increase productivity. He seems unable to remember the man's name. The man reminds me of something called a naked mole rat that I saw on the National Geographic Channel, only wearing a blue suit.

5:35: Try to start my car. Still smells like burning rubber. Forgot duct tape. Drive three blocks before car makes a sound like tap-dancing wooden shoes and stops. Call AAA, which takes just over an hour to show up and tow the car away.

6:45: Walk out of Enterprise car rental with a bright orange Kia. Can't figure out how to turn on the wipers, which is good because it's raining too hard to see anything anyway.

9:00: See on the news that producer Oskar Pulaski has once again been sued for negligence. Name sounds familiar. Google Winchester County Homecoming.

Uh-oh.

During the next commercial, my phone rang.

It was Ned Tudor, Harrison Yoder's lawyer. I'd met him once. He was big, bearish, affable, with a yellow bow tie and a folded handkerchief in his breast pocket.

But now he sounded tentative, regretful.

A chill came over me.

"Ms. Neville, I'm sorry to say that Harrison took a turn for the worse last night. He's gone."

I swallowed. Tears sprang to my eyes. I hadn't been there. Probably no one had.

"Ms. Neville?"

"Yes."

"I realize this is a shock, but Harrison wrote a letter a few days ago that he wanted me to read to you. I could just mail it or I can read it now if you like."

I hesitated. I wasn't sure I could hear it without breaking down. But the day was already a total loss. It might as well end this way.

"Go ahead."

He cleared his throat and began.

Dear Carolyn,

I'm sleeping a lot these days. Probably the pain meds. Things seem pretty clear at the moment, so I thought I'd write you this note. I'm asking Ned to deliver it.

I think I'm nearing the finish line. Tough to get enough air.

Sounds a little grisly, but I'm ready to go now. Ready as I'll ever be, anyway. Especially knowing you're going to protect my most cherished work. What more could I ask for?

Thanks. I owe you one, probably two.

Be careful on that movie set.

Harrison

I couldn't say anything.

"Ms. Neville?" The lawyer said gently.

"Yes."

"I'll send you the original of the letter."

"Thank you."

"Anything I can do for you at this point?"

I sighed. "I don't think so."

"Then I'll say goodnight."

"Goodnight."

I sank back into the couch, feeling the tears on my eyelashes.

I put down the phone and got up slowly. I wanted that frozen entree and some mindless TV, but it could wait.

Walking into my office, I proceeded to slide out a drawer

of my file cabinet. I pulled out the agreement Harrison had wanted me to sign.

You're going to protect my most cherished work.

"I'll try," I said wearily, and wrote my name on the bottom line.

CHAPTER 3

WELCOME TO LOS ANGELES, SAID THE SIGN.

Los Angeles International Airport was surprisingly grimy, covered with tarps and riddled with detours. Giant electronic screens flashed photos of palm trees. A half-completed monorail-style People Mover that reminded me of Disneyland and Seattle loomed overhead as we hiked toward Baggage Claim.

Stephen pointed toward a neon LAX sign. "It's so laid-back here."

I raised an eyebrow. "Are you kidding? This is one of the world's busiest airports. And don't get me started on traffic. The freeways are constipated."

"Where's the HOLLYWOOD sign?" he asked.

I looked around. "Not here, obviously."

We passed a tuxedoed pianist tickling the ivories of a concert grand. I'd never heard such a lush version of "Hotel California" before.

After baggage claim, we rented a basic black Volkswagen Jetta at Budget. Stephen wanted something smaller and self-driving, but when it came to royalties Harrison Yoder had been no J.K. Rowling.

Stepping out of the Budget office into the sunshine, Stephen pulled a pair of aviator sunglasses from his pocket. It suddenly occurred to me that he'd finally gotten a haircut. Maybe his thespian aspirations had an upside after all.

Our destination was the Oasis Gardens Motel in North Hollywood, a two-star place I'd picked out of thin air. It was cheaper than most, and I had no idea how long we'd be here. It had been hard enough to decide which outfits to pack and how many. All I knew about showbiz clothes was what I'd seen on the Oscars. I didn't have anything resembling the cantilevered, flouncing monstrosities those people were always hauling onstage.

"Is it rush hour?" Stephen asked as we crawled south.

"It's always rush hour."

The GPS app on his phone seemed confused about where we were and where we wanted to go. When we finally passed the HOLLYWOOD sign on the right, we figured we were on the right track.

"Wow," Stephen whispered. "That's got to be the most famous sign in the world."

"Except for the Golden Arches."

The further south we got, the more blackened trees we saw on the hills. Last year's wildfires had taken a startling toll, leaving Stephen with few botanical specimens to identify, an irritating habit that occupied him during most of our travels.

We saw billboards for most of the Hollywood landmarks —wax museums, TCL Chinese Theatre, Ripley's Believe It or Not, even the Museum of Selfies. Stephen wanted to check out Hollywood Boulevard, but our motel appeared on the left before we could get there.

The Oasis Gardens looked like it belonged on the withering end of the Las Vegas Strip. On the sign a dirty neon crescent moon rose behind the requisite palm tree. A rundown tattoo parlor, Ozzie's Fleshtones, flanked the motel on one side; a vaping shop called Fog of War stood on the other. According to a poster in the window, the latter was featuring a new flavor—Cotton Candy Grape.

Stephen shuddered. "Where did you find this place?"

"Online."

"Did you read any reviews?"

"Of course. At least one said they had no bedbugs."

"But the neighborhood—"

I signaled and pulled into the parking lot, which wasn't exactly full. "Don't worry. If it doesn't work out, we can find somewhere else. Maybe."

With a grunt he stuck his phone in his pocket.

There was another fake palm tree in the lobby, next to a rusty, bone-dry fountain. I expected the guy at the front desk to be hunched over, maybe even resembling the Crypt-Keeper from the old comic books. But he was in his early twenties, blond, square-jawed, wearing a gray sweatshirt that said HUNTINGTON BEACH and looking like he'd just auditioned for a soap opera.

"Hey," he said, looking up from the copy of *Backstage* magazine he was holding. His smile showcased a substantial investment in orthodontia and whitening. Despite that, Stephen removed his sunglasses.

"We have a reservation," I said, and gave my name.

He consulted a written list. I couldn't remember the last time I'd seen a front desk with no computer.

"Got it," he said. "You guys here on business or pleasure? I mean, if you don't mind my asking."

"Definitely business," I said. "Pleasure to be determined."

Stephen looked around, nibbling on the earpiece of his shades. "Movie business," he added.

The desk clerk brightened. "Really? What are you working on? I mean, if you don't mind my asking."

I flashed Stephen a warning look, which he ignored. "Feature film. Based on a book we published. We're here from New York."

"Righteous."

"Producer is Parthenon Arts."

He nodded, but looked like he'd never heard of it.

"Is it cast? Because I've got a head shot I can—"

I held up my hand. "Thanks, but we don't control that."

He sagged a little. "Maybe next time, huh?" He reached under the counter and took out a large black-and-white photo of himself with a short resumé pasted to the back. "Keep me in mind, okay?"

"Will do," Stephen said, putting his glasses back on.

The young man gave us our key cards—actual brass keys, not cards. I wasn't surprised.

The elevator being out of order, we took the stairs. My suitcase thumped the carpeted steps all the way up. Fortunately, there were only three floors.

Room 305 smelled like bleach, which I took as a good sign. Nothing visible to the naked eye crawled on the orange bedspread. The TV worked, displaying an old episode of *The Rifleman*. Chuck Connors reminded me of the desk clerk but more earnest. And armed.

There was a knock at my door. When I opened it, there was Stephen.

"This place is gross," he said, his sunglasses now pushed up above his hairline.

"It is not."

"I bet if you shined an ultraviolet light on the blanket and floors you'd see all kinds of disgusting stuff."

"Have you got an ultraviolet light?"

"No."

"Then don't worry about it."

"There's no room service."

"Also good. We can't afford it."

"Where are we going to eat? I haven't had anything since La Guardia."

I pulled out my phone and did a brief search. "There's a Chipotle six blocks from here."

He frowned. "Don't they have any of those places with caricatures of movie stars on the walls?"

"What, like the Brown Derby? You've got the wrong neighborhood."

"*Somebody* does," he muttered. "But let's go."

Business was brisk at Chipotle. The smells of onion and cilantro hit us the second we walked through the door. All the servers looked like aspiring actors and actresses, flashing toothy smiles and genetically superior cheekbones. Fortunately, our burritos and guacamole were prepared too quickly for Stephen to let it slip that we were remotely connected to the entertainment industry.

"Wonder whether anybody's been discovered here," he said when we sat down. "A whole bunch of celebrities used to work in restaurants. Jennifer Aniston. Chris Pratt. Jon Hamm. Russell Crowe."

"Russell Crowe? I have a hard time envisioning *that*."

"Amy Adams worked at Hooters when she was 18."

"Where do you learn all this stuff? And more importantly, *why*?"

He peeled the foil from his burrito. "Oh, like you don't know any useless information. You probably know Maxwell Perkins' shoe size. And the name of Agatha Christie's dog."

"*Dogs*. Lots of them. She had one named George Washington. Another named Bob. Even dedicated a book to him."

"I think that proves my point."

"I don't know Maxwell Perkins' shoe size."

"But you'd *like* to."

There was a long pause. We chewed.

"When do we get to meet the director?" Stephen asked.

"Tomorrow, I hope."

"How should I convince him to cast me?"

"That's your problem."

There was another long pause.

"You really cared about Harrison Yoder, didn't you?" he asked.

I looked down at the table. "Yes, I did."

"I think he picked the right person to protect his book."

I looked up. He was scanning the room or pretending to.

"Are you all right?" I asked. "That sounded like a compliment."

"Oops. My bad."

"I'm glad you think I'm the right person."

I wished I could be so sure.

* * *

Next morning the sun rose like a fever blister in the smog, highlighting the dust that floated in Room 305. Still no bedbugs.

After grabbing a sack of Sausage McMuffins and coffee from the world's second greatest icon, we drove past Paramount Studios on Melrose. Stephen gaped at the mission-style adobe buildings, surrounded by still more palm trees.

"We have to take the tour," he said.

"Maybe later."

He took out his phone. "They shot *Chinatown* here. Seventeen Martin and Lewis comedies. All the Bob Hope and Bing Crosby movies."

"You're an old-fashioned guy, aren't you?"

"And *The Ten Commandments*. You should be interested in that. Very religious."

"In a manner of speaking, yes."

We passed an archway and the front gate, where a guardhouse kept gawkers from mingling with the titans of the silver screen. Soon, though, the architecture grew less majestic and more miserable. The palm trees looked like they hadn't had a drink since the days of the pyramids, and the Mercedes on the street were replaced by unwashed Mitsubishis.

"It's around here somewhere," I said.

He kept poking his phone. "I have the feeling our film isn't going to be a *Star Trek*. Not even the worst one, *Star Trek V*. Not even a *Deep Space Nine*."

"*Winchester County Homecoming* isn't a special effects movie. It's about down-to-earth people, real emotions. It's got heart."

"And a shoestring budget."

"I don't know what the budget is."

He scratched his chin. "Still, you can do some amazing things with a little money. Take *The Blair Witch Project*. Or *Rocky*."

"We don't have to worry about the money. We're here to do quality control."

"Without really having control."

"Something like that."

The scenery continued to deteriorate. We were starting to see vacant lots. Worse, there was a guy selling paintings on velvet out of his van. One was of Elvis. The rest could have been anybody.

Finally, on the right, a concrete edifice with grimy, Greek-looking pillars appeared. The words PARTHENON ARTS were chiseled in the gable.

Stephen picked up his phone again. "Wikipedia says the

Parthenon is a peripteral octastyle Doric temple with Ionic architectural features."

"The *real* Parthenon, maybe. This looks more like a high school production of *A Funny Thing Happened on the Way to the Forum*."

"Wasn't that set in Rome, not Greece?"

"Whatever."

We pulled up to the guardhouse, which didn't look nearly as shiny as the one at Paramount. It was more like a toll booth on the road to perdition. One of the windows had been replaced by plywood and the railroad-crossing-type gate was broken off in the middle. I could see what looked like a warehouse about 50 yards behind it.

I pulled up to the striped arm and stopped. A wrinkled, white-haired woman in a too-big khaki uniform and peaked cap slowly made her way out of the booth and frowned in our direction. A clipboard was in her hand.

"You got an appointment?" she asked. When she wasn't talking, her jaw kept moving as if she were chewing tobacco, which seemed entirely possible judging from the stains on her chest.

I tried to smile. "Carolyn Neville and Stephen Ames."

She squinted at her list. "How do you spell that?"

I spelled it.

"Don't see it here."

"We're here to see the set of *Winchester County Homecoming*."

"This ain't Paramount. We don't do tours."

I squeezed the steering wheel and counted to ten. "We're not tourists. We're supposed to observe the shooting on behalf of the author."

"Nobody told *me*."

"The director's Larry Shapiro. He must know about us. If you could just—"

Suddenly the unmufflered BRRRAAAAAAPPP of a motorcycle exploded behind us. I glanced in the rearview mirror and saw a 30ish guy with no leather jacket or helmet straddling what looked like a Harley Davidson. His T-shirt was red, no lettering, and his arms were as furry as the close-cropped black hair on his head. I could practically smell the hormones.

Behind him, arms wrapped around his ribs, sat a younger-looking woman, Asian, wearing a green jumpsuit and Yoko Ono sunglasses.

The driver shook his fist at the guardhouse. "Hey, Elaine!" he yelled over the idling engine. "Let's get this show on the road!"

The old lady straightened up. "Mr. Testaverde." She waved them through, but frowned mightily as they putt-putted past the gate.

I leaned out the window. "Now, if you could—"

"Yeah, I know, I know." She tottered back to the booth, picked up a phone, and made a call.

I looked at my watch. We were going to be late. We'd never get a second chance to make a first impression, and in this case we were going to have a hard time making an impression at all.

The old woman put down the phone and waved us through. If she knew how to smile, she was determined not to show it.

With a nod I eased the car past her.

"All right!" said Stephen, rapping his knuckles on the side window. "Hollywood, here we come!"

"Curb your enthusiasm," I mumbled.

"Great show. They didn't shoot it here, though."

I would have squeezed the steering wheel again, but figured it was pointless.

* * *

The office of Oskar Pulaski, producer, was empty. It was also surprisingly unimpressive. The stink of cigars fought the smell of Lysol; photographs marched across every wall, mostly pictures of Oskar and his slowly receding hairline meeting deceased stars like Robert Goulet, Kitty Carlisle, and Ernest Borgnine.

"Oh, man," Stephen said, stepping up to examine the gallery. "Can you believe this? It's like a *Who's Who* of character actors. William Schallert, Whit Bissell, Margaret Hamilton, J. Pat O'Malley, Agnes Moorehead, Jack Elam . . ."

I shook my head. "You're like *The Man Who Knew Too Much*. Only you know too much about too little."

He whirled as if to defend himself, but stopped and stared over my shoulder. "Oh, hi," he said.

I turned to face a short, obviously dissatisfied woman who looked like an iguana who'd had a lot of work done at the Beverly Hills College of Plastic Surgery. She wore a tailored white pantsuit that had apparently been tailored for someone thinner. Her drooping eyelids and puffy eyebags were a matched set. Squinting through a pair of huge glasses, she raised her chin and cocked her head to one side.

"Help you?" Her voice sounded as if she'd smoked all those cigars herself.

"Carolyn Neville and Stephen Ames," I said, extending a hand.

Unsmiling, she touched it limply. "From the publishing company."

"Yes. Is Mr. Pulaski in?"

"Not yet. Sit down if you want. No coffee yet."

Stephen raised a hand. "Do you have any mineral water?"

She looked at him as if he'd soiled himself. "Too spendy. Oskar knows the value of a buck."

"Oh."

"The man is a genius. And I say that after following him around for twenty-three years."

Stephen stuck his hands in his pockets. "Judging from these pictures, he's worked with some of the greats."

"Yeah. Not recently, maybe, but that's how it is. Hollywood grinds you down, but he keeps going. Like a cockroach. And I mean that in a good way."

"He and the director must be quite a team," I said.

"Larry Shapiro?" She looked away. "Don't get me started."

I raised an eyebrow. "Well, then, Jackson Dunn."

She nodded. "Now, there's an actor. Don't know how Oskar got the guy, but this picture wouldn't have happened without him. Nobody in his right mind would bankroll a movie like this. Maybe it's a tax dodge."

I cleared my throat. "It's not *Avatar*. But—"

"It's *Green Acres*. *Petticoat Junction*."

"Hix Nix Stix Flix," Stephen said.

I turned to him. "What?"

"Back in the old days, there was an article in *Variety* about how audiences didn't like films about rural stuff anymore. That was the headline."

I gave him a warning look. "Whose side are you on?"

He shrugged. "Just stating a historical fact."

There was a knock at the doorframe. The hairy guy and the girl from the motorcycle stood there. He towered over her as she smiled.

"Hey, Annie," he said, eyeing Pulaski's assistant. "Larry here yet?"

"No."

He looked at us. "Who's this?"

The woman sighed as if introducing us would involve donating a kidney. "They're from New York. Here to represent the author."

Since she clearly didn't recall our names, I did the honors. The hairy guy didn't seem interested in revealing his identity but his girlfriend stepped forward and shook our hands. "Leilani Malala," she said. "Script supervisor. He's Axel."

"Testaverde," he added. "Property master." He gripped our hands without much enthusiasm. "Annie, let us know when Oskar gets here."

"He *is* here," called a voice from the hall. It had a thick accent, probably Polish, definitely aristocratic. "Hung over, I think, but here."

A tall man, maybe 75, wearing a black suit, black shirt, and no tie entered. His silver hair was brushed back. He had the posture of a commanding general, imperious, condescending. Three or four rings flashed when he gave a dismissive wave.

"Oskar, these are the publishing people," his assistant said, as if she'd tried to get rid of us but couldn't.

He looked down his Roman nose at us, in more ways than one. "I see. Try not to get in the way, will you?" He managed to smile without conveying a single degree of warmth.

He turned to his assistant. "Traffic was atrocious. I want a table read in half an hour."

She picked up a pad and began to write. "I haven't seen any actors yet."

He frowned. "If they aren't here in thirty minutes, start making calls. If they're not here in forty-five, heads will roll."

Spinning on his heel, he marched out.

"Let's go find Larry," the prop guy told his girlfriend, and they left, too.

The assistant put down her pad. "Welcome to Hollywood," she said.

CHAPTER 4

"You know what a table read is, right?" Stephen whispered.

I nodded. "The actors sit around a table and read the script for the first time. I'm not a pop culture ignoramus, you know."

It took two tables in this case, the kind you might find at a potluck in a church basement. Stephen and I sat in folding chairs at the periphery, like fifth graders waiting our turn to enter a dodge ball game.

This was the one and only sound stage at Parthenon Arts, a sort of airplane hangar fitted with overhead lights, most of which were off at the moment. There were two sets, replicas of a ramshackle Appalachian home, inside and out. This was the Winchester abode, a two-story log cabin full of quilts and primitive furniture and a potbelly stove. On the porch sat a pair of rocking chairs and a washboard. It looked like a museum diorama—a county museum, not the Smithsonian. The fake trees in the background reminded me of the little ones on model railroad layouts, only bigger and phonier. I hoped the camera would keep them out of focus.

Oskar, his assistant, and the director conferred at the head of the table as the actors began to file in. There were about 15 of them, none in makeup or costume. Lots of jeans and sweatshirts. I didn't recognize anybody at first, except for one young woman I thought I'd seen in a toilet paper commercial.

But then the last actor arrived, a 50ish man with wavy brown hair grayed at the temples, eyes that crinkled when he smiled, and wire-framed glasses. He wore khakis and black slacks and went around the tables, shaking hands or touching the shoulders of each cast member.

"Jackson Dunn," Stephen whispered, his eyes wide.

I pulled a small pad from my purse to take notes, trying not to look so starstruck. Like millions of other people, I'd seen Dunn in at least a dozen major movies. He was an everyman, like Jimmy Stewart or Tom Hanks. His nose was just big and crooked enough to keep him from being mistaken for a Brad Pitt or Ben Affleck, but his sincerity and self-deprecating sense of humor made him a favorite of talk-show hosts and soccer moms.

When all the seats were filled, Oskar rose from his chair. "Ladies and gentlemen, welcome to Winchester County." There was a smattering of applause.

"For those of you who haven't had the pleasure of working with him, let me introduce our director, Mr. Larry Shapiro."

The man at his side rose. He was slight, dressed in denim, his curly gray hair mashed under a New York Mets baseball cap. His eyes seemed a little too big for his head, and his expression alternated between a crooked smile and extra-strength anxiety. The actors, beginning with Jackson Dunn, stood up and gave him an ovation.

Shapiro clasped his hands and rubbed them together

nervously. "Please, sit down. We're running behind schedule, and I can't afford overtime."

There were a few chuckles and a major scraping of chairs as the cast complied.

"You're wondering how a neurotic Jew from the East Coast can understand a story about a bunch of Gentiles from the Catskills," he continued.

"I think he means the Ozarks," Stephen whispered.

Shapiro put his hand to his forehead as if taking his temperature. "All I can say is that, as the great Stevie Wonder pointed out, people are the same wherever you go. As he failed to mention, they're generally total hypocrites and will stab you in the back for a few bucks. In other words, they'd be perfect studio executives."

There was a burst of laughter. Oskar did not join in.

Shapiro looked down at him. "Present company except-ed," he said.

More laughter. Oskar looked at his watch.

The director cleared his throat. "Before we start reading, I'd like you to introduce yourselves and tell us one thing about your character or your place on the crew. Don't tell us anything else about *you*, though, because, as you can prob-ably guess, I don't care."

They proceeded to go around the table, saying their names and dropping tidbits like, "I'm Arky Winchester's cousin and I went deaf in the war," or, "I'm Sarah Stubb and I'm carrying the Reverend Boxer's baby."

When it was Jackson Dunn's turn, he looked down at the table. "I'm Harmon Winchester. My character's based on the author, and my fondest wish is to move to the big city and become a famous writer."

Seeing Harrison in my head, I sighed.

Next was a teenage boy, blond, slender. "Zach Tippitt. I

play Harmon as a kid. Jackson's promising to teach me how to play poker between takes." More laughter.

There followed three younger child actors, two girls and a boy, whose parents kept an eye on them from the cheap seats. Then came several men and women who'd undoubtedly been chosen for their gauntness or fatness or just plain strangeness. Nearly all the players were white which was probably right for postwar Appalachia but bound to upset somebody.

The last actor to speak was a 60ish woman I'd seen somewhere before, maybe in a TV series. She reminded me of Mikki, with a lithe dancer's body and blonde hair pulled back so tightly she probably didn't need Botox. "Gabriella Padgett. I play Harmon's mother. Strong woman, salt of the earth. Although I'll need a lot of prosthetics if I'm going to look older than Jackson."

There were more snickers, and the introductions moved to those of us on the sidelines. We did our best to overcome the distance with our outside voices.

"Ansel Mueller, cinematographer." His hair was wild and white, and he wore a safari jacket with plaid pants.

"I'm Edie, and I'll be doing your makeup."

"Guy Fong, lighting."

"Jim Oakley, stunts." Mid-30s, Will Rogers haircut, wiry, trace of a Texas drawl.

Finally it was our turn.

"Carolyn Neville. Here on behalf of the author."

"Stephen Ames. Same." He paused. "And just let me say, this is . . . really cool."

Awkward silence.

"Okay," Shapiro said, picking up his copy of the script. "Here's my take on the story. Boy meets world, boy loses mama, boy gets screwed up, boy turns into man who remembers mama, everybody's happy."

I frowned. From that description, I couldn't tell whether he understood the book or not.

I raised a hand. "Isn't Harmon's character development a lot more complex than that? Doesn't he—"

"Excuse me," the director said. "Who are you again?"

"Carolyn Neville."

"Well, Ms. Neville, all will become clear as we move forward. So let's move forward, okay?"

I sank into my seat.

"That's telling him," Stephen whispered.

The actors opened their scripts. We opened ours.

"And go," said Shapiro.

Jackson read the first line, a voice-over. "I still go there every autumn, when the oaks wrap themselves in gold and the first woodsmoke rises from the chimneys. It reminds me of the days when I had so much to learn about the world, and had yet to realize how many teachers I would need." He sounded so wistful, so world-weary, it gave me goosebumps.

"I smell People's Choice Award," Stephen whispered.

Things went fine until we got to a scene in which a young auto mechanic was supposed to roll out from under an ailing Ford Model A and deliver his diagnosis to Harmon's father. There was silence. Cast members looked around.

Leilani thumbed through the papers on her clipboard. "Where's Dennis?"

More silence.

Finally the director slapped his hand on the table. "Wherever he is, he's fired." He paused. "Let's get a stand-in. How about—"

Suddenly Stephen was on his feet. "I'll do it!"

Shapiro squinted in our direction. "Who said that?"

"I did."

The director sighed. "Whatever."

Stephen clambered down to the table and took the last

seat. "Page seventeen," Leilani said, flipping there and pointing at the script.

"Take it from the previous line," the director ordered.

"How much to fix her?" the actor playing Harmon's dad asked.

Stephen gripped the script in both hands. "Probably at least twenty dollars, Mr. Winchester." To my surprise, he didn't sound like himself. There was a trace of an accent I couldn't identify, but it sounded authentic somehow.

"I know that's a lot of money," he continued. "But you can pay me in chickens if you'd rather."

The actor playing Harmon's father rubbed his chin. "Young man, I can't spare a chicken. How about some Borax to get that oil off your face?"

Stephen shook his head. "You got any comic books? I'm partial to Superman."

"Never heard of him. Two dollars and an antler-handled throwin' knife. Take it or leave it."

"I'll take it."

The scene was over. Smiling, the script supervisor patted Stephen on the shoulder.

The director sat back in his chair. "What's your name again?"

"Stephen. Ames."

"Take Dennis's place. We'll work out the SAG stuff later."

Stephen beamed.

"I think you're in another scene or two," Leilani said. "Congratulations."

I didn't feel goosebumps this time. But my gorge was rising.

He'd be impossible to live with now.

* * *

The reading was over in just under two hours. Jackson Dunn slumped, exhausted, as he talked to someone on his phone. The woman who played his mother lowered her forehead to the table. A few cast members ran for the bathrooms.

Oskar, Shapiro, and the cinematographer huddled in a corner, sipping coffee and looking satisfied. The makeup woman took the pudgy face of a child actor and turned it side to side, frowning at him.

Stephen got up, stretched his arms, and headed toward me. He'd done his three scenes as if he'd been doing this all his life. He was probably as surprised as I was.

"What did you think?" he asked. His glazed-over eyes were a little unsettling.

"I didn't know you had it in you."

He sat next to me. "I can't believe what just happened."

"Me neither."

"I've been discovered."

"Maybe this is your true calling. I've always thought editing was beneath you."

"Really?"

"No."

He shook himself. "Got to get used to this. Take it in stride. I could be doing this for the rest of my life."

"I hope not. I'm too tired to hire your replacement. Besides, you probably wouldn't like being famous. People are always interrupting your dinner in restaurants, begging for autographs and selfies."

He nodded. "Yeah, I know. Shouldn't quit my day job."

"At least not for a month or so."

"Wouldn't be fair to all the other actors who'd have to compete with me for parts."

"Right."

"I'm supposed to join the Screen Actors Guild. I don't know anything about it."

"I'm sure the Internet does."

Just as he took out his phone, Leilani walked up with her clipboard. "Nice work, Stephen."

He gazed at her as if she'd just asked him to marry her. "I owe it all to you."

She chuckled. "I don't think so." She paused. "I thought maybe you two would like a tour of the building."

"Absolutely," I said.

She pointed down the hall with her clipboard. "Let's start with the prop room."

"Bet I know why," I said.

She gave a shy smile. "I don't know what you're talking about."

"Neither do I," Stephen said.

I rolled my eyes. He really *was* out of it.

"Her boyfriend is the property master, remember?"

Stephen blinked. "Motorcycle guy?"

Leilani nodded. "What can I say?"

I stood up and patted her on the shoulder. "That's all right. He's always like this. Lately, at least."

We followed her to a room as big as a basketball court. At least I guessed it was. I couldn't see the walls. There were shelves and workbenches everywhere, cabinets and cartons and signs and teakettles and mannequins, everything from lifeboats to space suits to antique globes to Blessed Virgin statues to machetes, most of them dusty and labeled with index cards.

I shook my head. "What, no hot air balloons? Grandfather clocks? Flying saucers?"

"I'm sure we have some around here," our guide said.

Stephen gasped. "Is that the barber pole from Floyd's in Mayberry?"

"I don't think so. That was Desilu Studios. But it's a barber pole, all right."

Suddenly there was a *BAM* behind us, followed by a string of curses. We turned to face Motorcycle Guy himself, who apparently had dropped a power drill on his shoe.

Leilani ran to him and put her hand on his bicep, half-covering what looked like a rattlesnake tattoo. "Axel, are you—"

He slammed the drill on a workbench. "Broke the freakin' bit."

"Did it go in your foot?"

"Nope. But it hurts like a son of a—"

"Let's take your shoe off."

"No, it's just gonna be bruised."

"But—"

"Back off. I said I'm okay." He raised his gaze to us. "What are you two doing here?"

Leilani did her best to smile. "I'm giving them a tour. Carolyn and Stephen. He got added to the cast today."

"Yeah, I saw that."

"He was good, wasn't he?"

Her boyfriend shrugged. "You tell me. I'm not the freakin' director."

"Well, I thought he was great. Especially for a guy who more or less walked in off the street."

His eyes narrowed. "Maybe you'd like to help him out. Give him some private lessons. Run some lines over a drink or two. Be my guest."

She backed up a step. "I didn't mean—"

He pointed a finger at Stephen. "You up for that, man?"

Stephen stood there, speechless.

I swallowed. "How about we continue with the tour?"

"Sounds good to me," Axel mumbled.

Stephen nodded, his face pale.

Leilani led us to the door. I turned to take a last look.

Axel had his back to us.

I could only imagine what he was thinking.

* * *

I'd seen the phrase CRAFT SERVICES on the ending credits of plenty of movies and had always imagined long, steel tables laden with lobster ravioli, caviar, and vitamin water. For the cast and crew of *Winchester County Homecoming*, though, nothing but the best would do. In this case, the best was greasy sacks of Arby's Beef 'n' Cheddar sandwiches, fried mozzarella sticks, and caffeine-free Diet Coke.

"All my favorites!" Stephen exclaimed when we sat down for lunch next to the set. "Only thing missing is strawberry shakes. At least I *think* they're strawberry. They're pink."

Silently asking the blessing and praying that God would somehow neutralize the calories and sodium, I made a mental note to bring a few granola bars and Skinny Cow chocolates in my purse tomorrow.

Stephen tucked into the repast with no such reservations, then slid his copy of the script perilously close to his drink. I think he asked me whether I'd help him work on his lines. It was hard to tell, given the fact that his mouth was so full.

After wiping my fingers with a napkin, I took a script from my purse. "What page?"

"Seventeen." He licked his fingers and cleared his throat.

No sooner had he begun to read when someone sat down beside me. I turned to see the stunt guy holding a plastic tray of food. His jaw was strong, the slight crookedness of his nose suggesting it had been broken more than once. "Mind if I join you folks?" he asked, and touched the brim of his Texas Rangers baseball cap, its blue matching his eyes. He stuck out a calloused hand. His grip was firm, and his smile made me wonder why he hadn't taken up acting himself. Or maybe he had.

"We're running lines," Stephen said.

"Oh. Well, I don't want to interrupt anything."

"You're not," I said, staring into those eyes.

Stephen frowned. "But—"

"We can rehearse later," I said. "People have to eat. And they don't have to talk at the same time, by the way."

"Jim Oakley," the stuntman said, sitting down.

I reintroduced us, then watched as he took off his cap, closed his eyes for about 15 seconds, and returned it to his head. Was he praying, or what?

"Where you folks from?" he asked, sliding his sandwich from its wrapper.

"New York," I said.

"Ah. Just like our esteemed director. How long you here for?"

I shrugged. "As long as it takes, I guess. We're looking out for the author's interests."

He bit into a mozzarella stick, then took a swig of soda. "I thought *my* job was tough. You've got some real work ahead of you."

"So we've been told."

Stephen kept chewing, watching Oakley suspiciously.

"Back in my rodeo days, my mom used to tell me it was too dangerous. Wanted me to get a *real* job. Didn't listen to her, of course, 'til I'd broken about forty bones, some of them twice. Figured it was time to cut my losses."

"Are you saying we should give up and go home?"

He took another sip of his drink. "Not at all. Just that you need to be careful. Pretty lady like you doesn't deserve to get hurt. This business can be a snake pit."

Stephen finished his food and folded his arms. "Kind of melodramatic, wouldn't you say?"

Oakley tilted his head to one side. "Maybe. I've just seen a little too much not to mention it."

Just then Leilani called from the craft services table. "Hey, people. Break's over in ten minutes."

"Thank you, Mr. Oakley," I said, putting the script back in my purse.

"Oh, call me Jim."

"Jim."

He took a final bite, gathered up the remains, touched the brim of his cap again, and left. I watched, the lanky figure and loping walk making it hard to look away.

Stephen grunted. "It's none of my business, but—"

"You're absolutely right. It's none of your business." I stood up.

"We can't trust these people. Especially if they seem trustworthy."

"I appreciate your concern. Really."

Picking up my script, I headed toward the set. I knew the risks of trusting the wrong person. But surely nothing would happen between us, no matter how blue his eyes were or whether he'd actually been saying grace over his lunch.

But I couldn't help hoping something would.

CHAPTER 5

THAT NIGHT, HAVING HAD ENOUGH OF FAST FOOD, I MADE THE executive decision that we'd eat at what may have been the slowest Chinese restaurant in the greater Los Angeles area. The Bamboo Dragon was one of those places with lots of gold paint, dusty Burgundy curtains, and paper lanterns. The jolly Buddha statue just inside the entrance wore a glittery green St. Patrick's Day derby.

"Obviously not orthodox Buddhist," Stephen said as we waited for a seat.

"Not to mention the fact that March 17 was, what, a month ago?"

A harried-looking Asian gentleman guided us to a booth. We looked the menus over.

"You sure we can afford this?" Stephen asked.

"Harrison can. Just don't order the Pu Pu Platter. Or the Happy Family."

"I'd be fine with a Happy *Meal.*"

I shuddered. "What do the insides of your arteries look like?"

He thought for a moment. "I've never seen them, actually."

Our server stepped up. "Can I get you something to drink?"

I raised my gaze from the menu. To my surprise, he looked more like Vin Diesel than Jackie Chan. Shaved head, a towel over his shoulder, too blunt-fingered to handle those little Chinese teacups.

We stuck with water. Stephen chose Cashew Chicken; I picked Moo Shu Pork.

After the waiter left, Stephen looked doubtful. "What's Moo Shu Pork?"

"Spiced meat wrapped in a pancake."

"Like an IHOP pancake?"

I shook my head. "More like a flour tortilla."

He made a face. "So, what did you think of this afternoon?"

"Other than the time you blew your lines, it went pretty well."

He drummed his fingers on the table, next to the soy sauce. "If you hadn't spent lunchtime flirting with the stunt guy, I would have had more practice."

"I wasn't flirting."

"No, I guess it was more like a mating dance."

"Have I ever told you how irritating you can be?"

"Several times."

"There's always a last straw."

He folded his hands in front of him. "I see I've touched a nerve. Let's talk about something else. Like my costume."

"Do you have one yet?"

He nodded. "Overalls, suspenders, shirt, one of those driving caps. The costumer has to adjust it but I got measured."

Suddenly the sound of the *1812 Overture* clanged from my purse. I fished out my phone.

"It's Mikki!" said the voice in my ear.

"Hey! Hi."

"I want to know every detail."

"Of what?"

"Of what's going *on*. Have you met any movie stars yet?"

"Does Jackson Dunn count?"

She gasped. "You met *Jackson Dunn?*"

"Well, I guess we haven't been introduced yet. But I watched him read the script. He's pretty good."

"*Pretty* good? Who are you, Katie Walsh?"

"Who's that?"

"A movie critic." She paused. "So, is there a part for me in the movie?"

"Doesn't work that way. Although Stephen got one."

"You're kidding."

"I'll put him on. I'm sure he's itching to tell the whole story."

I handed over the phone just as Vin Diesel arrived with our food. I was disappointed that he wasn't balancing our plates on his Mount Rushmore shoulders.

After sending up a quick blessing, I started stuffing a pancake with barbecued pork. The aroma made my mouth water. Plummy hoisin sauce, onions, mushrooms, oysters . . .

I tried not to listen to Stephen recount his brush with fame. Mikki was probably hanging on every word. My only consolation was that the Cashew Chicken must be getting cold.

"But enough about me," Stephen was saying. "The real news here is Carolyn's boyfriend."

I gagged, then coughed, then reached for water to wash things down. I tried to say something but my voice was out of commission.

"So he's a stunt guy," Stephen said. "Name's Jim. Dreamy. But weatherbeaten. Yet self-deprecating. And probably a con man."

I grabbed the phone and cleared my throat.

"He got the occupation and name right," I croaked. "The rest is baloney."

"I bet it's not," she said.

"Depends on your point of view."

"You're not going to tell me about this guy, are you?"

I coughed. "Not at this point."

"I get it. Can I come out and visit the set?"

"I . . . don't think I'm supposed to invite anybody else. I don't have any clout."

She made a frustrated noise. "Well, can you at least get me Jackson Dunn's autograph?"

"I can try."

"And maybe a selfie of you with him?"

"Maybe."

"And one of you with the stunt guy?"

"I don't know."

"Then pray about it."

"I don't think that's at the top of God's to-do list."

"What makes you think He has one?" she asked.

"Speaking of prayer, you said you'd pray for me while I'm out here."

"Um . . . I forgot."

"You do your part, I'll do mine."

"Remember the autograph and the selfies."

"Don't expect miracles."

"Bye."

I put the phone back in my purse and turned to Stephen.

"Thanks, genius."

"Always glad to be the bearer of good tidings."

Our waiter returned with leftover containers. "Can I get you anything else?"

"Yeah," I said. "A muzzle for my friend here."

"Make that two," said Stephen.

Vin Diesel looked at me, then at Stephen. "You're kidding, right?"

"Sort of," I said.

* * *

I'd never been to Appalachia, but I could tell this wasn't it.

The southern California sun had just risen over Barstow when the bus rattled into the desert just out of town. It was the first day of shooting on location. Still half-asleep, I eased gingerly down the steps and put on my sunglasses.

Brown, low-slung mountains in the distance. Grass dry as straw. Tumbleweeds. I wondered how many Westerns had been filmed here. I could imagine the ghosts of Roy Rogers and Ronald Reagan hunkered down on their horses, cresting the nearest hill.

But I couldn't see the Ozarks.

The cinematographer was setting up his cameras next to a large cactus. I expected the Road Runner and Wile E. Coyote to appear at any moment.

"It's getting hot already," Stephen muttered. "Were we supposed to bring our own canteens?"

"I'm sure they have water. Somewhere."

He pointed into the distance. "Joshua Tree. Over there, Beavertail Prickly Pear. The one with the big leaves is Mojave Yucca. And to your right—"

"Thank you, Luther Burbank."

Larry Shapiro was last off the bus. "Okay, people," he said, raising his arms as if to part the Red Sea. "Let's set this up before we lose that morning light." He pulled the brim of his baseball cap lower and marched over to confer with the cameraman.

I shook my head. "This isn't going to work. Appalachia doesn't look this way. It's not a rain forest, but it's not the Serengeti, either."

"What are you going to do?" Stephen asked.

"Lodge a protest."

"With who?"

"You mean *whom*." I licked my lips. It really *was* dry out here. "The director."

"What do you want him to do, water the plants? Spray-paint the grass? Move the mountains? Although I guess you're supposed to be able to do that last one if you've got enough faith, right?"

"Maybe they could do lots of closeups so you can't see the background."

"Good luck with that."

"Well, I've got to do *something*."

"What would Jesus do?"

I frowned. "That's not fair. He could change the climate if He wanted to. But I doubt He'd be wasting His time being a set designer or art director or whatever they call it."

"Go ahead. I'm going to look for something to drink."

I headed for the director. He was waving his arms at the cinematographer, agitated about something. It was obviously the best time to approach him with my list of demands.

"Excuse me," I said, trying to look charming.

The director dropped his arms and turned toward me. "Yes?"

"I was wondering if you'd consider a suggestion."

"About what?"

"The scenery. The story takes place in West Virginia. It's a very different climate there. Lots of trees. With leaves. Rivers."

"What's your point?"

"I thought maybe it would be distracting to see cactus and tumbleweeds. The audience might think it was strange that this background doesn't match the one on the sound stage."

"You want me to make it rain forty days and forty nights? Or bring in a forest?"

I looked at the cameraman. "What if you stayed close to the actors and kept the scenery out of focus? Then people couldn't—"

The director squeezed his eyes shut and massaged his temples with his fingers. "That's the greatest idea I've ever heard." He turned to the cinematographer. "What do you think, Ansel?"

"Larry, I'm not sure I can—"

The director's eyes popped open. "Ms. Nevin, is it?"

"Neville. Carolyn."

"Ms. Neville, how much have you invested in this picture?"

"You mean money?"

He nodded.

"Well, none."

"Can you raise about three million dollars in the next twenty minutes? Because if you can, I'll have the art director buy a gigantic scrim to cover up the northern half of the state of California. It'll have more autumn hues than a Thanksgiving tablecloth."

"What's a scrim?"

"If you have to ask, perhaps this isn't your area of expertise."

"I'm just trying to—"

"Hold that thought. Preferably until the picture is finished and you're back in . . . wherever you came from."

"New York."

"Now, if you'll excuse me, we have a film to make. Ansel, please set up the first shot."

The cameraman gave me an enigmatic smile and started extending the legs of a tripod.

I turned and headed for what looked like the craft services table. Stephen was upending a plastic water bottle into his mouth. Sweating, he put it down and wiped his chin with the back of his hand.

"How'd it go?" he asked.

"He's thinking about it."

"Really?"

"No."

I picked up a bottle of my own.

Sorry, Harrison, I thought.

* * *

The first shot was actually in the middle of the script, opening a scene in which Harmon wanders in the woods behind the Winchester house, wracked with guilt over having argued with his father—the last conversation they'd had before his death.

Since there were no forests in Barstow, and Shapiro had refused to compensate, the audience would just have to suspend its disbelief.

Stephen and I stood near the cinematographer, behind the camera.

"Now, here's the deal," the director told the young actor playing Harmon, gripping the boy's shoulders. "You loved your father. Even though he treated you like a cockroach, you wanted his approval."

The young man, sweaty and nervous, stared up at him. "Okay."

The director smiled crookedly. "Are you sure you're not Jewish?"

Laughter drifted from a knot of actors behind us, breaking the tension.

The boy smiled back. "Yeah, I'm sure."

"Good. I don't need the competition. Now show us how much you miss your old man." He nodded toward the cinematographer. "Let's do it."

A young African-American woman wearing what looked like a tennis outfit stepped in front of the camera with one of those black-and-white clapboards. WINCHESTER COUNTY was written on it with a marking pen. "Scene seventeen, take one," she called out, and the top of the board scissored with a loud *CLACK*.

I glanced down at the script. There were no lines in the whole scene.

"He'll have to do it all with his face," Stephen whispered.

"Shhhh," hissed the sound man.

The young actor's eyes were wide. He swallowed, his Adam's apple bobbing up and down. His lip quivered. He picked up a rock and threw it out of frame, where it hit a cactus the size of a street sign.

"Cut!" yelled the director.

"What's wrong?" The young man asked.

"You're grief-stricken, not angry."

"Right. Of course."

"Do it again."

"Scene seventeen, take two," the girl with the board said.

"This could be a long morning," Stephen mumbled.

The sound man swore. "Will you shut up?"

"Action," said the director.

The boy sank to his knees. He looked around as if he'd lost something—not his father, but perhaps his car keys.

"Cut!"

The actor sat down and closed his eyes.

"Kid, what are you feeling?"

"Confused."

"So is the audience. What are you *supposed* to be feeling?"

"Sad."

The director buried his head in his hands. "No. You're devastated. Sad is missing a sale on paper towels."

The young man nodded.

Somewhere behind us a car was pulling up the gravel road. A dust cloud floated over our heads.

"Everybody take five!" the director shouted.

I turned around. Oskar Pulaski was getting out of a black Mercedes.

Most of the cast and crew drifted over to the craft services table. Stephen was first in line.

I hung back, pretending to study my script, wanting to see what the producer wanted. Even I knew the big shots didn't drive to the middle of nowhere without a good reason.

"Oskar," the director said. "Didn't expect you."

"Didn't *want* you to."

The two of them stepped behind the big cactus.

"Larry, you're killing me."

"What are you talking about?"

"I've got one bill for $5,000 and another for $8,000. That's just in the last two days. He pulled two pieces of paper from his black jacket and waved them around. "Costumes? This isn't *Sense and Sensibility*. You ought to be able to find most of this stuff at the Salvation Army. And safety harnesses? Is Oakley behind this? Does he think this is *Fast and Furious?*"

The director threw up his hands. "Haven't you read the script? There's a car stunt in scene fifty-three."

"If you shoot it right, there won't be any risk. He's not jumping the Grand Canyon."

"Oskar, we're already cutting corners. The makeup woman is getting her eyeliner from Walgreens."

The producer stuffed the bills back in his pocket. "What's your next project, Larry?"

The director cleared his throat. "I don't have one lined up yet."

"Doesn't surprise me. I'm the only person dumb enough to work with you."

"Now, just a—"

"You've spent more time in rehab than Charlie Sheen. I wouldn't be surprised if you're using now."

Shapiro kicked the cactus. "You know I'm not."

"I don't know any such thing."

"I've never gone over budget. I'm not going to start now."

Pulaski leaned in. His voice dropped. "One of my investors is getting antsy. If he pulls out, I pull the plug."

"Who is it?"

"Doesn't matter. Shoot the stunt my way and I may actually not fire you."

"I can't have that on my conscience."

Pulaski laughed. "Conscience? You?"

"I'm not the man I was ten years ago, Oskar."

"You'd better hope not. I'd be so disappointed if this were our last picture together. Not to mention your last picture, period. And it will be if you don't do the smart thing here."

He turned to go. "Break's over. Get rolling. You're losing the morning light."

The director watched as Pulaski got into his car and left another cloud of dust behind him. He looked over at me and frowned, but said nothing.

After grinding the toe of his right sneaker in the dirt, he put his hands on his hips and looked toward the cast and crew. "Let's go! Time is money!"

The small crowd meandered toward us. Stephen brought

up the rear, half a Twinkie in one hand and a small plastic bottle of Sunny Delight in the other.

"Did I miss anything?" he asked.

"Yeah," I said.

"What?"

"Maybe nothing. But we'd better find out."

CHAPTER 6

I WASN'T SURE WHAT TO DO NEXT. CONFRONT LARRY SHAPIRO? Warn Jim Oakley not to do any stunts? I decided to have a cold cup of coffee and wait. Stephen and I took our seats while the crew tried to get Scene 17 down on celluloid—or whatever they used in movie cameras these days.

The director patted Young Harmon on the shoulder. "I know you'll nail it this time, kid."

The boy nodded and hit his mark.

CLACK, went the clapboard.

"Action."

The young man sat down on a rock, then hugged his legs and lowered his forehead to his knees. Finally he raised his head and reached for a nearby yucca plant. He tugged at it, snapped off a leaf, and rubbed it between his fingers. Then he threw it into the brush and put his head back down. His shoulders shook.

"Cut," the director said. "Beautiful."

There was a general sigh of relief. A few people clapped.

"Scene eighteen." The director rose to his feet and looked around. "Where are our extras?"

Leilani stepped forward. "We've got three."

Shapiro shook his head. "I need at least four."

The script supervisor shaded her eyes with her hand and looked in my direction. "Carolyn, can you help us out?"

I gulped. "You mean *act?*"

"Not exactly. Just mill around in the background."

Stephen leaned toward me. "Finally, your big break."

Leilani waved at the costumer. "Can you find something for her?"

The woman frowned. "We're in the middle of the desert. I don't have more than a couple of things, and they probably don't fit." Mumbling, she headed toward a trailer.

A few minutes later she was back, holding what looked like a pioneer dress. Tan, with an apron. "Try this on," she said.

The trailer was even smaller than a room at Motel 6. I wriggled into the dress, then tried the zipper. It stuck halfway up my back and not because it was defective. If only I hadn't eaten those daily doughnuts for the last six months.

Inhaling mightily, I tiptoed back to the set.

"Nice," Stephen said. "You look like you belong on a wagon train about fifty years before this story takes place, but maybe nobody will notice."

"Thanks," I said, trying not to take a deep breath.

The costume lady sighed. "Turn around," she said. "Well, at least it's long enough to cover your shoes. You'll have to take off those glasses, though."

I did so, then tottered over to join the trio of extras—two men, one woman. I was sure we had little in common, especially since I had no idea what I was doing.

"Places, everybody," the director called.

I ducked my head and whispered to the other female extra, who was older and chubbier, much to my satisfaction. "Where do we go?"

"Follow me," she said.

We walked to a spot behind Young Harmon and his cousin. Except it wasn't his cousin. Jim Oakley was standing in for him, wearing overalls, suspenders, shirt, and cap.

He turned to me. "Welcome to showbiz," he said, grinning.

I sucked in my gut. "This wasn't my idea."

"I know. But at least you don't have to do your own stunts."

The prop guy handed me a washboard. The other extras got big clay jugs with corks in them, the kind they always used in movies to hold moonshine.

Jim raised an eyebrow. "If things get tough, maybe you can hide behind your washboard."

"Thanks." I hitched up my dress again.

Shapiro raised his hand. "Harmon, you and Cousin What-shisname aren't getting along. You're both after the same girl. Stunt guy, did you rehearse the fight?"

"Yes, sir," Jim said.

"I can't afford to have Harmon in a cast for the next six weeks."

"He'll be fine."

"Everybody ready?"

We all nodded.

The director folded his arms. "Extras, don't look at me. Action."

Young Harmon reached out and grabbed Jim by the wrist. Jim had his back to the camera.

"What makes you think you can move in on her?" the young man growled.

The actor playing his cousin called from the sidelines. "What makes you think I can't?"

Young Harmon threw the first punch, or pretended to. Jim flew backward in my direction. I tried to get out of his way but stepped on the hem of my dress and toppled forward.

The washboard slipped from my hands, hitting Jim in the head. I hit the dirt.

"Oh, crap," I said.

"Cut!" the director yelled.

Jim lay face down, unmoving. Before I could gasp, he was struggling to his feet, panting.

"No problem," he said, but his ear was bleeding.

I picked up the washboard but there was no point in trying to hide behind it. I needed something much bigger.

"I'm so sorry," I said. "Are you all right?

He managed a smile. "Right as rain. How about yourself?"

"Just mortified, that's all."

"Well, don't be. Happens all the time."

The makeup lady approached with a first aid kit.

The director shook his head. "Let's do it again. Well, not again. This time let's do it *right*."

I brushed the dirt from my dress and looked over at Stephen. He gave me a thumbs up, the most insincere one I'd ever seen.

Jim winced as the makeup lady wiped his wound with alcohol. "Carolyn," he said, "would you care to have dinner with me this evening?"

I stood there for a moment, wondering what to say.

"Consider it your punishment for injuring me. I can tell you feel the need for contrition."

"Um . . . okay."

"Places, everybody!" the director shouted.

"Pick you up at eight," Jim whispered.

I backed up about ten paces, gripped the washboard, and vowed not to get too close.

Not yet, anyway.

* * *

"What's all this about?" Jim asked.

Pushing the door open for me at the Maine Street Bistro at 8:10 the following evening, he squinted at the lights in the lobby. A camera and crew loitered by the front desk. A slightly disheveled but tuxedoed head waiter fumbled a handful of menus and dropped them at our feet.

"Be with you in a moment," he said, his forehead glistening under the lights.

Jim adjusted his bolo tie and looked around. "They're not usually this busy," he said. "And they hardly ever have a camera crew."

Suddenly a woman in a white chef's hat burst through the inner doors. "I quit!" she yelled. "That man is impossible!" Throwing down a towel stained with either blood or marinara sauce, she marched out.

"What man?" I asked.

The head waiter finished gathering his menus. "Wolfgang Maddox."

"The guy with the restaurant makeover show?"

He nodded. "They're shooting an episode here tonight."

Jim sagged. "Can we still get a table?"

"If you don't mind a little . . . chaos."

He turned to me. "What do you think?"

I looked down at the dirty towel. "Are they done with the makeover yet?"

The waiter shook his head. "Sort of in the middle of it."

Jim cleared his throat. "Carolyn, we can try someplace else, or—"

"It's okay. Just showbiz, right? Maybe I'll learn something."

He shrugged. "Table for two, then."

As soon as we cleared the inner doors a shell-shocked

server careened past us, nearly dropping a tray of loaded plates. We made our way to a corner table, where the noise was a few decibels lower than a freight train.

There was another crew about 20 feet from us, pointing its camera at the kitchen door.

"Your server will be with you in a moment," the head waiter said, handing over our menus. He tried to smile but looked like this might be his last meal.

"YOU CALL THIS A LOBSTER BISQUE?" someone bellowed from the kitchen.

"Sounds like Maddox, all right," I said. "I'd recognize that voice anywhere."

"So you watch his show," Jim said, unwrapping his silverware.

"A guilty pleasure."

"How do these makeovers work?"

I scanned the room for our server, but in vain. "He finds a restaurant that's in big trouble, takes over like the Nazis invading Paris, and tries to whip everybody into shape. More or less literally."

"THIS IS ABSOLUTELY THE WORST FREAKING CRAB CAKE I HAVE EVER HAD THE MISFORTUNE OF SMELLING!"

It was Maddox again, only he didn't say "freaking."

"He's known for his colorful language," I said.

Suddenly the great man himself flung open the kitchen door and raised his arms. "LADIES AND GENTLEMEN, I MUST APOLOGIZE FOR THE UNFORGIVABLE INCOMPETENCE OF THE OWNERS AND STAFF OF THIS HELLHOLE!" The veins stood out on his neck. His gray crewcut and goatee complemented his beet-red complexion nicely.

The patrons didn't seem to know whether to applaud, throw their steak knives at him, or ask for refunds.

"Good evening," said a pale young woman who suddenly appeared next to me. She kept glancing over her shoulder as if she were being followed. "Have you folks been here before?"

Jim folded his hands in front of him. "I have, honey. But that was before World War Three started."

Using her pencil, she pushed a damp strand of blond hair out of her eyes. "We're a little short-handed. Mr. Maddox fired most of the staff." She gulped. "I'm sure he knows what he's doing."

Jim drew little circles on the menu with his finger. "What's good tonight?"

"Everything. Really. I'm not saying that just because I need this job."

"I'll have the scallops and a house salad. And a beer. You got Corona?"

"I think so."

I looked up. "Is there a special tonight?"

"Surf and turf, but we ran out of surf."

"Then I'll have the turf. With potatoes au gratin, green beans, and a merlot."

She scribbled on her pad, took our menus, and left. The closer she got to the kitchen, the more reluctant she seemed to go further.

"Sorry about this," Jim said. "If I'd known—"

"No problem. It's dinner *and* a show."

He smiled that crinkly smile. "And divine punishment for nearly breaking my neck."

I insisted on reliving the accident. I was just about to apologize when the kitchen door burst open.

"THIS HADDOCK IS A ROTTING PIECE OF REFUSE! YOU WILL NEVER WORK IN THIS TOWN AGAIN!"

Only he didn't say "refuse."

When our food finally came, our drinks were fine. The rest was pretty much refuse.

"I think these are scallops," Jim said, poking at them with his fork. "Or they might be those rubber things they put on the ends of chair legs."

I tried to saw through my beef with the steak knife. "Not turf. Maybe Astroturf."

Our server passed by, pausing to give us a look that said *Please don't hurt me.*

"How is everything?" she asked.

"Fine," Jim said.

"Dandy," I said.

When she left, Jim shook his head. "I hope she can find another job quick. 'Cause this makeover ain't very pretty."

Somewhere behind us, a woman mumbled something about feeling sick.

"RATS? ARE YOU FREAKING KIDDING ME?" came the voice from the kitchen. To his credit, Maddox actually said "freaking."

But it didn't help. Within moments, patrons were calling for their checks, heading for the exit—or, in the case of the woman behind us, proving she really wasn't feeling all that well.

Jim finished his beer. "I'll have to make this up to you. Can I get a raincheck?"

"If we survive tonight's food poisoning."

He scratched his chin. "I wonder whether we'll be on TV."

"We didn't sign any releases."

"Well, I guess we'll have to settle for the movies."

I frowned, remembering something. "We forgot to ask the blessing for this dinner."

"We'll do it next time. The good Lord doesn't expect us to be thankful *for* all things. Just *in* all things."

Something that sounded like a fist hit the kitchen door

from the inside. "LADIES AND GENTLEMEN, THIS ESTABLISHMENT WILL BE CLOSED FOR ETERNITY!"

"It's been a memorable evening," I said.

"And not the last, I hope."

He smiled that smile, and I smiled back.

* * *

Next morning we were back on the set. The air conditioning wasn't working, but it was better than being roasted alive in Barstow.

Having retired from acting, I was sitting with Stephen in the cheap seats again. I'd just finished telling him about the man-made disaster at the Maine Street Bistro. "You saw Wolfgang Maddox?" he cried.

"Yeah."

"That is *so* cool." He paused. "Did you get food poisoning?"

"Not me." I looked around. Jim was nowhere to be found. "I hope Mr. Oakley didn't sample those scallops."

"What's this 'Mr. Oakley' stuff? It's obvious you two are a thing."

"What kind of thing?"

"You know what I mean. You practically broke his arm to get his attention."

I was about to try my hand at fracturing his femur when there was a commotion at the sound stage entrance. Jackson Dunn was walking in, swinging a big grocery bag. He kept reaching into it and tossing handfuls of something at other members of the cast and crew.

Stephen stood up. "*Free* something! Count me in." He headed toward the crowd.

The director and cinematographer were the only ones who seemed interested in working, putting their heads together and gesturing toward the lights. With a sigh I got up and joined Dunn's fan club.

"How are your kids?" he was asking the costumer.

"One's in jail. The other's a lawyer. Not sure which is worse."

"Hang in there," he said earnestly.

When he got to me, he pulled something out of his bag and placed it in my palm.

"A Pez dispenser," I said. "Um . . . thanks."

"Not just *any* PEZ dispenser. Part of a set. Characters from *Seinfeld*. Jerry loved PEZ dispensers, you know."

Stephen was suddenly at my elbow. "I got George Costanza," he said. "How about you?"

"A guy with crazy-looking hair."

"Kramer. Didn't you watch the show?"

"Not much."

"I'll trade you."

I handed mine over. "Take them both."

"Wow, thanks."

"Now you can never ask me for a raise."

"I wouldn't anyway. Just getting to work with the world's greatest editor is its own reward."

Jackson looked into his bag. "That was the last one." He paused. "There was a whole episode about PEZ dispensers, you know."

"Aired January 15, 1992," Stephen said.

Jackson folded the bag and slipped it under his arm. "PEZ comes from the German word for peppermint."

I looked around for an escape route. This was starting to sound like an endless conversation I'd once heard Stephen have with a fellow Pop-Tarts aficionado. The suicidal thoughts were flooding back.

There was a great crinkling of cellophane as the multitude unwrapped its dispensers. The prop guy, not bothering to load his with the little yellow tablets, simply popped them into his mouth.

"Mr. Dunn," Leilani said, waving her clipboard. "Is it true that you worked with Kirk Douglas?"

The group fell silent.

"It was after his stroke. I was in awe of him. He sat in a wheelchair and could barely speak. There was a nurse with him the whole time. But here he was in this TV movie. Talk about courage." He paused. "One day, between takes, he gave me some advice."

More silence. If Jackson Dunn knew anything, it was how to work a crowd.

"He leaned forward and said, 'When you have a stroke, you gotta talk slowly to be understood. When I do that, people listen. They think I'm going to say something important!' He also told me, 'Son, the learning process continues until the day you die.'"

There was a general murmur and a few sniffles. Leilani wiped her eyes with the back of her hand.

"Okay, people!" Larry Shapiro yelled. "We're trying to make a movie here, remember?"

Amid a chorus of sighs the group began the trek to the set. Stephen slid a PEZ candy into his mouth from George Costanza's balding head. "What a great day," he said.

Someone took hold of my elbow. "Looks like I missed the feeding of the five thousand," he said.

I turned. "Jim! You didn't die of food poisoning."

"Death, no. Food poisoning, maybe. All right now, though."

We took our places on the sidelines. "Jackson, I need you in makeup," the director called.

With a last wave to his admirers, the star went down the hall.

The rest of the PEZ had been consumed by the time Mr.

Dunn returned, aged a couple of decades and dressed in the same overalls he'd worn in every scene so far. If the costume budget was being overspent, I couldn't tell where the money was going.

Lights, clapboard, action, camera rolling. The scene began with Jackson alone, carrying a milk pail. He set it down on the porch, looked up at an unseen sky, and whistled.

In walked a girl about six years old, blonde pigtails, cradling a cornhusk doll in her arms. Her lip trembled.

"My dolly lost her eye," she said. "It was a button."

Dunn stepped forward and went down on one knee. "Happens to the best of us, Jamie. It's gonna be all right. What's your dolly's name?"

"Jamie Junior."

"Now that's sensible." He reached down, chose the lowest button on his shirt, and tugged it off. Then he stood up and searched the ground.

"What you looking for?" the girl asked.

"Horsehair." He bent down and picked something up. "Here we go." Threading the unseen horsehair through the button, he addressed the little girl's toy. "This won't hurt a bit, Jamie Junior."

A few knots later, he handed the doll back. "Good as new."

The girl smiled. "Thanks, Mr. Winchester."

"Thank *you*. Don't let her run with any scissors, you hear?"

"I promise."

"And . . . cut!" the director said. "Loved the business with the horsehair. You nailed it in one take. You, too, kid." The girl beamed and ran to a woman who stood on the sidelines who patted her on the head.

"Let's set up the next shot," Shapiro said, looking at the script.

A sliding door rolled open behind us. Oskar Pulaski stood there for a moment, silhouetted against the sun. I missed the lack of air conditioning more than ever.

The producer strode to the cameraman's side, looking no happier than when I'd last seen him.

Jackson Dunn picked up the milk pail and crossed the set in front of Oskar as the latter took off his jacket. He glanced at the producer, a strange expression on his face. He looked the most unhappy I'd ever seen him.

Stephen stuck his PEZ dispensers in his pocket. "Is it just me, or did our star lose his luster for a second?"

"It's just you," I said.

"And me," Jim said.

"Okay, it's me, too."

I watched Dunn take his pail down the hall. I didn't like Oskar Pulaski, either. But there was something about that look that went beyond dislike.

"Artists are sensitive," Stephen said.

"That must be it," I said.

CHAPTER 7

WHEN IT COMES TO SELF-DEFENSE, MY WEAPON OF CHOICE IS pepper spray. My Mennonite aunt has called me on this, but I've made up my mind not to feel guilty until I've actually sprayed someone with it.

As for firearms, I grew up in Idaho. That should tell you where I stand on guns, except that it doesn't. Most of my friends couldn't wait to go hunting, but I never shot anything bigger than a potato that was rotting in a field near Highway 32. That wasn't exactly self-defense, the spud having expired some time before.

So when the crew set up a hunting scene after lunch, I didn't offer my services as a technical advisor. Stephen, who'd just devoured a Jimmy John's sub and a Creamsicle, sauntered over to my chair on the sidelines.

"I'm in this scene," he announced.

"That explains why you're in costume. But shouldn't you be wearing a coonskin hat?"

"You're thinking of Daniel Boone."

"Nice makeup. That *is* makeup, isn't it? Or did you find a tanning salon near the motel?"

"You're just jealous. You had your chance, but you couldn't help being the center of attention. Extras aren't supposed to do that."

He sat next to me. "I get to carry a rifle. So does the other guy."

"What are you hunting?"

"I don't know."

"Doesn't sound like you're doing much preparation. You're no Christian Bale."

He pulled his phone from the pocket of his baggy hillbilly pants, which was an anachronism if I ever saw one. "Let's see what they hunt in Appalachia."

Larry Shapiro picked up a battery-powered bullhorn, probably because he'd been shouting himself hoarse all day. "Everybody in scene twenty-seven, get your butt over here!"

Stephen tickled the screen of his phone. "Grouse, wild hogs, wild turkeys, coyotes."

"Huh?"

"Things they hunt in Appalachia."

"Okay, you're ready. I think you should lose ten pounds for this role, though."

He stuck his phone in his pocket. "I'm not the one who couldn't zip up her costume." He didn't stick out his tongue, but he may as well have.

"Butts over here! Now!" The director pointed the bullhorn at the camera.

I watched as the prop guy, Axel, walked in with two rifles —one under each arm. I had no idea what kind they were, but they looked real. He handed one to each actor, then pointed at various parts of the guns and seemed to be explaining how to use them. The two men kept nodding. I wondered whether Stephen had any idea what he was talking about.

The actors took their places amid the fake trees. With a

CLACK three banks of lights came on overhead. The cameraman took out a meter and got a reading.

"Are we good on the guns?" the director asked.

"Yeah," Axel called.

"Now, the two of you are out hunting, and—"

"Excuse me," Stephen said. "*What* are we hunting?"

Shapiro looked puzzled. "How should I know?"

"Could be a grouse, a wild boar, a deer . . ."

"What difference does it make? Whatever it is, you're trying to kill it."

"Gotcha."

"You crouch down by this tree. You're looking into the distance. You see something. You raise the gun and aim."

The director stepped over to the other actor, an older man in a plaid shirt and one of those floppy hillbilly hats. "You aim, too." He squinted into the rafters and pointed. "Up there. When I say, 'Now,' you fire."

"They're blanks, right?" Stephen asked, sounding nervous.

The director covered his eyes with his hands. "What am I, a *merder*?" He retreated behind the camera. "Also, I can't afford to shoot the lights out."

"Did you say *murder*?"

Shapiro shook his head. "It's Yiddish. Means *murderer*."

"Oh."

"Scene twenty-seven, take one," said Leilani. The clapboard clacked.

"Action."

Stephen crouched down and aimed. The other actor remained standing and took a bead on the rafters. He seemed a little unsteady, as if there were something slippery on the floor.

"Cut!" Shapiro shouted. "What's the problem?"

"My shoes are sliding."

"Oh, for God's sake. Somebody put down a towel. Cat litter. Whatever."

A young man ran in with a towel. Maybe he was a grip. Maybe even a *key* grip. One could learn only so much by watching the closing credits of movies. He put down the towel and ran off.

"Scene twenty-seven, take two." *CLACK.*

"Action."

Stephen did his thing. The other actor did his.

"Now!" the director yelled.

Stephen squeezed the trigger. An ear-splitting *BAM* reverberated from one end of the sound stage to the other. Blinking, he lurched backward, apparently unprepared for the noise or the rifle's kick.

The other actor aimed, but faltered. His left leg slid out from under him. The rifle's barrel dropped just as the gun went off with a loud *CRACK.*

With a muffled cry, Stephen toppled forward. He lay there, unmoving.

I stood up.

"Oh, my God!" the older actor said, scrambling to his feet. He looked down at the weapon in his hands, then laid it on the floor.

Heart pounding, I ran toward Stephen.

"Dial nine one one!" somebody yelled.

"I thought they were blanks," the shooter said, dazed.

The director swore. "Where's Testaverde?"

I knelt at Stephen's side. I could see blood spattered on the fake bush. He still had a pulse.

"My shoulder," he groaned. "Man, it's on fire."

"I'm *so* sorry," the other actor said.

Leilani appeared at my side. "Stephen, can you turn over?"

"Doesn't seem like a good idea right now," he whispered.

"I just want to see whether you need a tourniquet or something. To stop the bleeding."

With a grunt he eased onto his back. "There."

She pushed the faux foliage aside. "Doesn't look like it hit an artery."

"Where's the ambulance?" he asked weakly.

"I dialed nine one one," said the young man who'd brought the towel.

I heard the approaching clack of dress shoes behind me. "What's going on here?" said a disapproving voice.

Looking up, I saw Oskar Pulaski. He glared at Shapiro.

"So you've got things under control," the producer muttered.

The director put the bullhorn to his lips. "I want the prop guy! *Now!*"

I touched Stephen's hand. "You want some water or anything?"

He shook his head, then winced. "Am I gonna die?"

I could hear an ambulance in the distance.

"Definitely," I said. "But maybe not today."

* * *

Two paramedics lifted Stephen onto a gurney and loaded him into the ambulance. "Can I ride along?" I asked.

Both paramedics shook their heads. "Sorry, Ma'am."

Stephen waved weakly. "I'll be okay." He turned toward the first responders. "Right?"

They looked at each other. "Probably."

I sighed. "Which hospital are you going to?"

"Cedars-Sinai Medical Center."

I watched as they got in, hit the siren, and took off, lights flashing.

My hands were shaking as I fished in my purse for my car

keys. Hearing a door slam down the hall, I looked up to see Axel Testaverde march into the room, scowling.

"What took you so long?" The director whined.

"What's the problem?"

Shapiro pointed in the direction of the fading siren. "They just took one of my actors away. Shot with one of your guns."

Testaverde scoffed. "That's impossible."

"Tell it to Stephen," I mumbled.

He glanced at me, then turned back to face the director. "Those were blanks, I swear. Loaded them myself."

"The hole in his shoulder is real," I said. "You obviously made a mistake."

His jaw clenched. "You're the one making the mistake. You don't know the first thing about guns, or ammo, or how we do things here. So why don't you shut the—"

"Now, that's no way to talk to a lady," said a voice over my shoulder. It was Jim. I'd never heard him sound so cold before. "Whatever happened is no excuse for disregarding manners. And you're not the only one around here who knows something about weapons."

Axel glared. "Stick to stunts, cowboy."

Oskar stepped forward. "We'll straighten this out later. For now, we're shutting down." He raised his chin and addressed the cast and crew. "Go home. Six a.m. call tomorrow."

The director sank into a chair and closed his eyes. The prop guy kicked a cable and walked out.

Finally finding my keys, I headed for the rental car. *Cedars-Sinai.* I had no idea where I was, but I planned to be there in 15 minutes or less.

* * *

I got my visitor's sticker and went straight to Room 402. Cedars-Sinai was a lot fancier than the last hospital I'd been in, where Harrison complained about the cold macaroni and warm apple juice. Most of the nurses and doctors looked as if they'd walked off the set of *The Young and the Restless*, or at least a commercial for the latest bladder control remedy.

I hesitated, then knocked on the door of Stephen's room. There being no response, I pushed it open. "Hello?"

A weary-looking nurse adjusted the IV. "He's right here."

I inched forward. "Okay to come in?"

"Sure. He's awake."

He was sitting up in bed, wearing a light green gown, his left shoulder wrapped in thick bandages. A glass of water with a straw in it sat on his tray.

"Carolyn! We were just talking about you. Well, not really."

"How are you feeling?"

"Better, since they took the bullet out. I wanted to keep it, but they said the police might need it." He paused. "Actually, we were just discussing the celebrities who've stayed here."

The nurse rolled her eyes. "*All* of them."

He picked up his phone and poked it. "Like Patrick Swayze. Kourtney Kardashian."

The nurse wrapped a blood pressure cuff around his good arm and pressed a button on the IV pole. It buzzed to life. "Stay still."

"Jessica Simpson, Victoria Beckham, Kate Hudson, Penelope Cruz. This was where they had their babies."

"You're moving," the nurse said.

"Frank Sinatra, David Geffen, Jeffrey Katzenberg, Liz Taylor and Richard Burton . . ."

"Stop talking."

"Marilyn Monroe . . ."

"What did I just tell you?"

"And my favorite, Peter Sellers. His heart kept stopping."

The nurse took his pulse. "Don't give me any ideas about stopping hearts." She paused. "On a scale of one to ten, how's your pain?"

"Three. Maybe three-point-five."

"If you want it to go higher, give me a buzz." She walked out, shaking her head.

I sat in the chair next to the bed. "You freaked everybody out. Especially me."

"Especially *me*."

"Do you think the prop guy did this?"

He shrugged, then regretted moving. "Ow. Who else?"

"But why? He hardly knows you."

"Are you saying that if he knew me, he'd have a good reason to do it?"

"No comment."

"Maybe he meant to kill the other guy."

"But the prop guy handed out the rifles. He gave the one with the live ammunition to him."

"What if he put live bullets in *both* guns?"

I leaned back in my big chair. "Didn't think of that. I guess the police will check, assuming they get involved."

"It could have been an accident. Maybe the boxes of bullets got mixed up."

"Or someone mixed them up deliberately."

"So who stands to gain by getting you shot? Other than the world at large, I mean."

He looked up at the ceiling. "Let's say somebody wants to shut down the film. Having one of the actors die might do it. Terrible publicity."

"But who'd want to shut it down?

"Uh . . . someone who hates the director? Or the producer?"

I tapped my finger on the arm of the chair. "Or somebody who wanted a part but didn't get one?"

"We could get a list of psychotics who tried out but didn't get called back." We looked at each other. "Nah," he said.

"From what I've seen, the producer's pretty ticked at the director. Money problems. Maybe Oskar's so over his head financially that he needs a way out."

He shook his head. "By killing people? There's an easier way. It's called bankruptcy."

"Or Larry's so mad at Oskar that he's trying to sabotage the movie."

"He'd be sabotaging himself. Nobody else wants to work with him."

We sat there, listening to the beeping of Stephen's monitor. A little motor on his IV, probably pumping antibiotic and pain meds, made an occasional whirring noise.

"I thought it would be hard enough to keep these people from wrecking Harrison's story," I said. "I didn't know we'd have to keep them from killing each other."

"And us."

He picked up the NURSE CALL button. "Think I'll get my drugs cranked up. Anything for you?"

"Make it a double."

* * *

They let Stephen go the next morning. His nurse gave a sigh of relief.

"On a scale of one to ten, how's your pain?" I asked as we squeezed into the rental car.

"Two point five. How's yours?"

"Six. That motel mattress reminds me of Hunter. Thick, dense, and unforgiving."

Our ride to Parthenon Arts was as peaceful as L.A. traffic

can be, mostly because Stephen's phone battery was dead. I had to imagine the species of flora we passed and which stars were buried in which cemeteries.

As soon as we were waved in by the old lady at the guard-house, though, things went south.

"I think we should talk to the prop guy," Stephen said.

"Are you crazy? After what happened?"

"He's our only credible suspect. Maybe we can catch him in a lie."

"I trust you're not hoping for an apology. He's not the type."

He snorted. "Tell me about it."

When I opened the door to the sound stage, a shot was already being set up. Oskar had asked for an early call.

I searched the stage for Axel Testaverde. Absent.

"Let's try his office," Stephen said, protecting his left arm with his right. I wondered whether he was doing it subconsciously.

PROPERTIES, said the sign on the door. The place was old enough that the word was painted on the frosted window.

I tapped on the glass.

"Yeah?"

"It's Carolyn and Stephen."

Long pause.

"Just a minute."

We looked at each other. "He's hiding something," said Stephen. "We should just walk in."

He reached for the doorknob, but I pushed his hand aside. "Wait for it. You're in bad enough shape already."

A few seconds later Axel stood in the open doorway. He was as hostile as ever, but couldn't seem to look us in the eye.

"We'd like to ask you a few questions," Stephen said.

Axel glanced at the bandages, then away. "About what?"

"Well, we—"

"If it's about yesterday, the cops were already here. I can't help it if you guys don't know how to keep from shooting each other."

"Maybe you can give me some tips for next time," Stephen said.

Axel grunted. "Five minutes." He turned and went back inside, leaving the door ajar.

"I'll keep him occupied," Stephen whispered. "You look around."

"For what?"

"A pile of mixed-up bullets. A dart board with Oskar's face on it. I don't know."

"That's one of the dumbest ideas I—"

"Hey, you coming or not?" Axel called.

Stephen pushed past me. I wandered past a couple of Blessed Virgins and a fiberglass dragon.

"This is the safety," Axel said, holding up a pistol and pointing.

"Okay."

"This is on. This is off."

"Got it."

"Anything else?"

"How do you load it?"

Axel shook his head. "Uh-uh. You'd probably shoot off your foot."

"Please?"

The prop man grabbed a box of ammo.

"How do you tell the difference between a fake bullet and a real one?" asked Stephen.

"You mean blanks and live ammunition."

"I guess."

"Live ammo doesn't have a bullet—just a crimp at the top to keep the gunpowder in."

"And you checked before you handed us the rifles?"

"Of course, idiot. They're in different boxes."

Stephen picked up a bullet and rolled it between his fingers. "How do you put them in?"

Axel picked up a black cartridge. "This is a magazine." He dropped the brass bullets in the top, one at a time.

"Can I try it? Never fired a pistol before. These are blanks, right?"

The prop man put the gun down on his desk. "Lesson's over."

"But—"

"You need to learn something else, Stevie." He took a menacing step forward and poked my associate in the chest. "First off, stay away from Leilani."

"Leilani? Your girlfriend?"

"I've seen the way you look at her. She's a little too impressed with you. Maybe she doesn't realize how much you suck."

Stephen just stood there, guarding his left arm with his right hand.

"Second, you've got a lot to learn about weapons in general. Let me give you a few tips about knives."

"But there aren't any in this movie."

Axel yanked out a desk drawer and came up with a serrated stainless steel model about six inches long. "Tactical knife. Used it in Afghanistan."

He raised the weapon over his head, then flung it across the room. With a *CHUK* it lodged in the forehead of a wooden cigar-store Indian.

"Wow," Stephen said, sounding more nervous than awed.

Again Axel reached into the drawer and produced a claw-shaped blade with a short handle. "Karambit knife. Usually used in the desert."

He ambled toward Stephen, then put his arm around him and squeezed.

Stephen flinched. "Hey, man, my shoulder—"

Axel brought the blade to eye level. Stephen stared.

"Now, how are you going to treat my Leilani?"

"Uh . . . *well*," he whispered.

Axel squeezed harder. "Wrong. You're not going to treat her at all. If I see you within ten feet of her, I'll give you some personal experience with this bad boy."

With a grim smile, he held the weapon to Stephen's throat, then pressed.

I gasped.

It looked like the blade was sinking into Stephen's neck, but no blood appeared. His face was ashen but he hadn't passed out yet.

With a derisive laugh Axel pulled the vicious-looking cutlery back, then pushed, then pulled. "Stage knife. On a spring. Can't believe you've never seen one."

"We're editors," I muttered.

He let Stephen go. I watched the latter stumble a few steps, then sink into what looked like an electric chair from an old prison movie, complete with porcelain insulators and leather straps.

Axel looked at Stephen. "You won't forget this little lesson, will you, buddy? I hate to repeat myself."

He turned to me with a crooked smile. "I think your friend may need to change his underwear." Tossing the stage knife on the desk, he proceeded to wrestle the tactical one from the Indian's head.

"Gotta run," he said, and winked.

CHAPTER 8

WE AGREED TO TELL NOBODY WHAT HAD HAPPENED IN THE prop room. Assault with a non-deadly weapon and aggravated shoulder-squeezing weren't exactly crimes. Neither was being a jealous jerk.

Next day, on the set, Stephen and I slumped in our chairs and watched Grandma Winchester singing her heart out, strumming a zither or an autoharp or whatever that thing is. The ballad was plaintive, her voice nasal, unwinding the story of losing a young man to the bottle. The first three takes were awful.

When the director called for a break, Stephen leaned toward me. "I don't get it."

"The song? Her boyfriend was a drunk."

"I don't mean that. I mean the jealousy thing. Why does Axel think I'm after his girlfriend?"

I shrugged. "She's been nice to you. For him, that's crossing the line."

"Then his issue is with Leilani, not me."

"I wouldn't be surprised if he's discussed it with her, too. Maybe worse."

My phone yammered from my pocket. I picked up.

"Carolyn Neville?" It was a woman's voice, husky but unfamiliar.

"Yes."

"This is Carmella Monet."

"Do I know you?"

"We haven't exactly met."

"How did you get my number?"

"From my ex-husband's files. Harrison Yoder."

Uh-oh.

Harrison had mentioned her more than once, but never in a way that made me want to meet her. He'd used words like *money-grubbing* and *vindictive*. And those were just the socially acceptable ones.

"I've been talking with Harrison's lawyer," she continued. There was a slight accent—Jamaican, maybe.

Great, I thought. I couldn't tell whether she was happy or furious.

"I'd like to get together for a drink," she said.

"Why?"

"I'd rather not say on the phone."

"Where are you?"

"I live in San Diego, but I'm staying in downtown L.A. Where are you staying?"

"North Hollywood."

"Do you have a favorite restaurant there?"

"No."

"I like Spumante on Magnolia Boulevard. Think you can find it?"

I took a small legal pad from my purse and wrote it down. "Can I bring a friend?"

"Of course."

"Can you tell me anything about what you—"

"See you at eight?"

I sighed. "Okay."

She hung up.

"Who was that?"

"The last person on earth I expected to hear from."

"Matt Damon?"

"Harrison Yoder's ex-wife. We're about to meet her."

"Is there food involved?"

"Probably Italian."

"I'm in."

The break was over. The director nodded at Grandma Winchester. "Action."

The fourth take sounded like all the rest, but Shapiro apparently had decided to cut his losses. "Darling, that was beautiful," he said unconvincingly. "Next scene."

I got out my phone to find Magnolia Boulevard. It was a mile or so from our motel.

"What does this woman want to talk about?" Stephen asked.

"From what Harrison told me, probably money."

"Is she paying for dinner?"

"I doubt it."

"Then why are we going?"

"Because I can't stand not knowing what she's after," I said, and put the phone away.

* * *

Spumante wasn't hard to find.

That was the last easy thing about the evening.

"Nice place," Stephen said as we stepped inside. Nothing snooty about it; a step above Olive Garden. Dark wood, brass fittings, red-checked tablecloths with candles and vases of breadsticks.

"Do you know what she looks like?"

I shook my head. "Sounded a little Jamaican, if that helps."

He scanned the visible tables and booths. "Not seeing her."

"But I am seeing *you*," said a voice behind us.

We turned to face a tall African-American woman—slender, graceful, high cheekbones. Probably late fifties, but still looked like a model. Hair dyed red. No smile.

"Carmella Monet," she said.

I introduced Stephen, who for some reason felt it necessary to bow.

A gray-haired waiter with a green apron and an unruly waxed mustache stepped up with menus. It was nice to see somebody who didn't seem to be auditioning for anything.

"Party of three?"

"Yes," Carmella replied. "We'd like a table by the window."

We ordered drinks and pasta. The special involved black truffles, which cost almost as much as a trip to Italy. When Stephen said he wanted it, I kicked him under the table.

Carmella handed the menu back, her gold bracelets clacking. Harrison's taste in women had always been impeccable, though it was hard to imagine the two of them together.

"So, what do you do?" I asked.

"I grieve for my ex-husband."

"Of course. I do, too."

"I grieve for his poor judgment. Perhaps it was the result of his illness. As my attorney tells me, I was excluded from his will."

I nodded. "Harrison told me."

Her nostrils flared. "I suppose that should not surprise me. I suspected for some time what was going on."

My eyes widened. "Going on?"

She fiddled with what appeared to be her wedding ring. "Between the two of you."

I opened my mouth to reply but the waiter arrived with our drinks. We looked awkwardly at each other while he passed them out. Stephen stared at me.

"Ms. Monet, we were *friends*," I said.

"I find that hard to believe. Are you saying he never gave you any money?"

"I . . . well, yes, he did. A long time ago, when I was having a financial problem."

She smiled, but without humor. "Exactly what I mean."

"There was nothing romantic about it, ever."

"Have you seen the will?"

"No."

"I have. Harrison made a last-minute change. He left most of his estate to some save-the-whales charity."

"Really?"

"It was because of you, wasn't it? I understand you had some influence on him at the end."

"He didn't tell me he was changing anything."

Her long-lashed eyes narrowed. "My husband wasn't an animal lover. He wasn't even faithful."

"I know."

"Then why would he give your friends my money?"

"I don't even know what charity he gave it to. I never suggested he donate it." I swallowed. "And is it really right to say it was your money?"

She lifted her chin. "Of course it was mine. I was his wife. Not his mistress, like you."

I shook my head. "I was his *editor*. I've never been anybody's mistress."

I was considering getting out the pepper spray when the waiter arrived with our salads. Another awkward pause.

"Almost two million dollars are at stake here," Carmella said, lowering her voice. "After seventeen years with that man, I have been left with nothing."

Stephen raised an eyebrow. "Those bracelets are nice. And that dress. And you're staying in a pretty good hotel, right?"

"Six months from now, I will be evicted from my apartment. I have nowhere to go."

"But you're . . . well . . . beautiful," Stephen said. "I bet you could be a model. Maybe an actress. If you haven't already."

"My, how easy your life must be. Such a wise man. What are you, twenty-five?"

"Twenty-seven," he mumbled.

She looked at me. "Why are the two of you here, anyway?"

"To help the production company make Harrison's book into a movie he'd be proud of."

"Who's paying for that?"

"The rest of his estate."

She took a breadstick from the vase and snapped it in half. "Money down the drain. I may not be an actress, but I know that much about this town."

I looked down at my food, but the knot in my stomach kept me from eating any more.

"I hope this movie is a disaster," she said.

Stephen and I glanced at each other.

"How do you mean that?" I asked warily.

"I hope it never gets made. Or if it does, that nobody goes to see it."

Stephen stared at his food, presumably having lost his appetite as well. "And how far would you go to make that happen?"

"As far as possible."

"Do you know anybody in the cast? On the crew?"

Her frown deepened. "No. Why?"

"Just wondering."

She looked at her Fossil watch. "I've heard enough lies." She stood up.

"Will we be hearing from you again?" I asked.

"Count on it," she said, and left.

* * *

"Charming, isn't she?"

Stephen held the door open for me as we exited. "Can't remember the last time I couldn't finish dinner. Do you have indigestion, too?"

"My gorge isn't rising, but it's not falling, either."

It was dark, a little muggy. We started walking toward our motel, the surroundings getting tackier with every step. A panhandler with a cardboard sign that said MY AGENT SCREWED ME OVER sat slumped on a corner.

"She sure has a motive," Stephen continued.

"But opportunity?"

"She wouldn't have to be on the set. Probably got enough cash left to hire somebody. Or she could string some guy along to do the heavy lifting in return for . . . well, you know. Maybe even Axel."

I felt a drop of water hit my forehead. Then another.

"Oh, great. I thought it never rained in California."

He caught a lamppost with his good hand and swung around it like Gene Kelly. "I'm singin' in the rain!" he cried.

"Let's walk faster. I feel like we're being watched."

He looked around. "I don't see anybody."

"Good. Your Gene Kelly impression is embarrassing."

"You should see my Donald O'Connor. I do the scene where he walks over the couch and up the wall. Except for the wall part."

The sprinkle was becoming a deluge. Stephen started singing "Raindrops Keep Falling on My Head."

"Shut up," I said.

"Remember what movie that was from?"

"No."

"*Butch Cassidy and the Sundance Kid.* Sung by B.J. Thomas. There's this bicycle—"

"Hey," whispered a voice from an alley to our right. "Coke?"

The shadows were too deep to see the speaker.

"Peyote?" he asked.

Stephen stopped. "No, man, we don't have any."

The guy made a disgusted noise. "I'm asking whether you *want* some."

"No!"

"Ecstasy?"

Stephen shook his head. "Who stands in an alley and does this anymore? I thought you guys did everything with texting now."

"My cell's busted."

"Stephen, I'm getting soaked," I said. "You can argue with drug dealers later."

We hustled down the sidewalk.

"If you change your mind," the guy called, "I'm gettin' a new phone tomorrow. You can text me at . . ."

"We don't care," Stephen said.

The storm was reaching biblical proportions. I held my purse over my head, which did absolutely no good. We ran past the tattoo parlor, then paused under a tree.

I looked toward the motel entrance. A figure stood in front of the window, under a dripping canvas awning.

He looked familiar. But not in a good way.

The closer we got, the less I liked what I saw. Beige riding cap, tan London Fog raincoat, khaki slacks, brown driving gloves.

He raised a hand and wiggled the fingers. "Carolyn!" he said. "Surprise!"

It was Hunter Thicke, flashing that clueless grin. "I'm

here!"

"So I see. But *why?*"

He spread his arms wide. "To save the movie! To save *you!*"

"Lucky us," I mumbled, feeling soggier than ever.

CHAPTER 9

"WHO'S *THIS* ONE?"

The old lady in the guardhouse frowned at Hunter, who sat in the back seat of our rental car the next morning. She checked the list on her clipboard and shook her head.

"He's with us," I said wearily. "Hate to admit it, but that's the truth."

"What's he here *for?*"

Hunter leaned forward. "I'd like to direct."

She snorted. "They'd *all* like to direct. Except the directors, who want to produce." She paused. "Go ahead. You clowns all deserve each other."

While I looked for a parking space, Hunter settled back and put his hands behind his head. "Carolyn, is the Oasis Gardens the best motel you could find?"

"On our budget, yes."

"I liked the shower curtain. Very impressive picture of *101 Dalmatians*. But I may look elsewhere, especially if I'm needed for more than a week."

"Oh, I don't think you'll have to worry about that."

We unfolded ourselves from the car. Hunter was still

wearing last night's outfit, even though the storm had passed. The raincoat made him look like Inspector Clouseau. And he hadn't even done anything clumsy yet.

"So this is where it all happens," he said, tugging off his driving gloves. I wasn't sure why he'd bothered to put them on. "Care to introduce me to everyone?"

"*Everyone?*"

"Well, maybe not everyone. Just the movers and shakers."

I looked around. Oskar wasn't here, but Larry Shapiro was setting up the first shot with the cameraman. With a sigh I pointed in their direction. I felt like a 16-year-old having to introduce her uncool mom to the Mean Girls.

When I got to the camera, the two men looked up. Shapiro groaned.

"Excuse me," I said. "Hunter, this is Larry Shapiro, our director. Larry, this is Hunter Thicke, my boss. Hunter is here to check up on me."

Hunter offered a hand. The director didn't lift a finger. "I just had a bagel with cream cheese. You wouldn't like the mess."

"Larry Shapiro. I saw *Vampire Slaygirls of Neptune* three times."

The director closed his eyes. "God help us. Worst picture I ever made." He opened his eyes again. "How long are you going to be here?"

"It depends."

"On what?"

"On how much I can contribute to the success of this movie. I have some ideas I'd like to share with—"

"Ideas? God, no. Talk to our script supervisor. She's got no authority, but it'll feel better than talking to that wall over there."

Hunter blinked. For a moment I thought he'd take the

hint but that was too much to ask. He took a sheet of paper from his inside coat pocket and unfolded it.

"I've got two dozen suggestions. Here's number one." He put a hand on the director's shoulder. "I think the Jackson Dunn character as written is too—"

"Don't touch me."

"Right. Anyway, he's too much of a philosophy guy. You know, going on and on about stuff that'll go right over the audience's head. He needs to be tougher. Man of action. More Liam Neeson, less Mister Roberts."

The director added puzzlement to his look of disdain.

"I think he means Mister Rogers," I said. "The kids' show host."

"I know who he was," Shapiro muttered. "The sweater guy."

Hunter nodded. "So you see my point."

"No. I've got work to do. If you want to sit quietly while we make our movie, okay. And when you leave, which as far as I'm concerned can't happen too soon, please take these two with you." He nodded toward Stephen and me.

Hunter took a deep breath and tried to smile. "Let's talk when you have more time."

"When hell freezes over. Is that good for you?"

"Um . . . perfect."

He backed away, gave the director a little salute, and stuffed the list in his pocket. "Break a leg," he said.

"I think that's for actors," Stephen whispered.

"Everybody knows that," Hunter said.

We picked our way past crew members and cables, then sat in a corner like troublemakers in detention.

Hunter gazed up at the lights. "Carolyn, did I ever tell you the tale of *The Little Engine That Could?*"

"No, but you don't have to. I think everybody's born knowing that story."

He nodded. "I assume you get my point."

"Hardly ever. But let's assume I do."

"I believe Mr. Shapiro and I have more in common than meets the eye."

"You'd both like to see me disappear from the face of the earth?"

He chuckled. "Not just that. We're both men with a vision. We just need to put aside our rose-colored glasses, pick up our binoculars, and train our sights on what matters most."

"Which is?"

"Immortality."

"Whose?"

"His and mine, of course. And, if you like, the rest of you can tag along."

"Thanks," I said.

"Ditto," said Stephen.

"Action!" cried Hunter, but no one was listening.

* * *

A dozen takes later, I felt a tap on the top of my head. I turned to face Jim Oakley, whose boyish grin indicated he hadn't sat through the missed cues and directorial tantrums of the last two hours.

"How's it going?" he asked.

"Slowly."

"Takes time to make great art," he said. He looked at Stephen. "And your shoulder?"

"Won't be doing my own stunts anytime soon."

"Glad to hear it. Like my mom used to tell me, only a fool would take up a career like that."

Hunter leaned in. "Aren't you going to introduce us?"

I considered declining, but it didn't seem worth the effort.

"Jim Oakley, this is my boss, Hunter Thicke. Hunter, Jim is the stunt coordinator."

"Well, on this project I'm the stuntman, too. Got nobody to coordinate."

Hunter's face lit up. "Stuntman! Always wanted to do that."

"I thought you wanted to direct," I said.

He rolled his eyes. "Carolyn, I can walk and chew gum at the same time."

I'd have asked him to prove it, but I was out of Trident.

Jim scratched his chin. "Well, maybe after lunch we can have a little tutorial on dropping and rolling."

Hunter raised an eyebrow. "You mean 'duck and cover'?"

"That's for nuclear attacks," I said. "Not that it works. Dropping and rolling is how you put yourself out when you're on fire."

Jim shook his head. "This is a little different. It's how to fall without really hurting yourself."

"Oh," said Hunter. "I know all about that. Played football in college."

"You can be my teaching assistant," Jim said. He moved to a nearby chair and winked at me.

"Lunch break!"

It was Leilani, calling through Shapiro's bullhorn. I could almost hear the collective sigh of relief.

"Oooh! Lunchables!" Stephen cried when we got to the craft service table.

Hunter stared. "Not quite what I pictured."

I made a face. "Crackers and cheese and scraps of pressed ham?"

"These have Oreos, too," Stephen said, sounding defensive.

"Where's the vegetable?"

Stephen surveyed the repast. "There's a jar of mustard."

"Not a vegetable, even if it's made of seeds."

Jim pointed to a stack of small plastic containers. "Apple-sauce. It's a fruit."

Hunter picked up one of the cracker-and-cheese combinations. "Is this what they serve every day?"

"No," I said. "Sometimes it's worse."

"Well, I'm glad to see they're not wasting money on snails and caviar."

After washing down the banquet with our choice of warm ginger ale or Yoo-Hoo, we followed Jim outside to the edge of the lot. A long, sloping hill lay between us and a chain-link fence. The grass was fairly green but sparse; it was a drought year in most of southern California.

Jim placed his hands on his hips. "Who's up for dropping and rolling?"

Stephen grabbed my elbow and raised my hand for me.

"That's the spirit," Jim said.

I put my arm down. "I'm not dressed for it."

"Oh, come on. You're wearing jeans."

He looked so disappointed. "Okay," I said.

"And of course me," Hunter added, not bothering to wave.

Jim put his hands in his pockets. "Now, you've got your basic side roll, your Arabian rolls, your dive rolls . . . The thing to remember is to tuck your arm under."

He backed up about 30 feet, crouched slightly, then took a run toward the fence. His right arm went under, he spun and did what looked like a sideways somersault, then somehow bounced back up.

"Who's next?" he panted.

Stephen raised my arm again.

"Quit it," I protested.

"Here, I'll help you," Jim said, gently taking my shoulders. He twirled me around, then lowered me toward the ground, tucking my arm under. It was like dancing in slow motion. I couldn't remember the last time I'd felt like this. I hoped I wasn't blushing.

The rolling part I could handle. Couldn't bounce, but came to a halt before I could be shredded by the galvanized steel mesh.

"Perfect," Jim lied.

Picking dry grass and stubble off my denim vest, I wobbled to my feet.

"Bet you're dizzy, but you did it." He turned to Hunter. "I suppose these dives are too simple for you. Maybe you'd like to show us a suicide roll."

Hunter's eyes widened.

"I'm sure you're familiar with it. For more advanced stuntmen like yourself, or course. Looks like you're landing on your head, but you're not . . . exactly. Twists you like a worm. In the end, you're either on your feet or dead."

Hunter fiddled with his fingernails. "I . . . don't want to show off. Maybe just a side roll."

"Suit yourself. I won't insult you by helping like I did with Carolyn. Whenever you're ready."

"Right." He did a couple of deep knee bends to limber up, shook his hands as if they were wet, and touched his toes. Looking worried, he backed up a good 50 feet and sprinted toward the fence.

Halfway there, he tucked his right arm under and spun sideways. Hitting the ground like a motorcycle out of control, he went end over end three times and collapsed.

His face was in the dirt, muffling the most pathetic moan I'd heard since that dolphin documentary I'd watched on *Nova* last year when Netflix wasn't working.

"Oh, *man*," Jim said, wincing. He ran to Hunter and knelt.

"I don't think I can move," Hunter mumbled. It sounded like he wanted to cry but the last management book he'd read wouldn't let him.

"Just stay still," Jim said.

I took out my phone and dialed 911. This was getting to be a bad habit.

"Feels like I broke something," Hunter croaked.

"Anything numb?" Jim asked.

"No."

"Good. It's not your neck, then."

We waited for the paramedics, knowing nobody on the set would miss us. I sat next to Hunter on one side; Jim sat on the other. Stephen took a leftover Oreo from his pocket and munched on it.

After twenty minutes we heard the ambulance howling. I hoped the old lady at the guardhouse wouldn't slow it down.

The paramedics gently turned Hunter over and put him on a stretcher that looked like a board. He spit out bits of grass. I couldn't see any blood.

He blinked at me. "How did I do?"

"You were a ten," I said. "Until you hit the ground."

* * *

When you break your collarbone, there's nothing they can do.

Unless the bone is shattered or literally sticking through the flesh like the spine of an umbrella, the doctor wraps you tightly in those bandages that make you look like you belong in an Egyptian sarcophagus. Then he or she sends you home to sit motionless in front of the TV, watching *Whose Line Is It Anyway?* and sipping the beverage of your choice.

In Hunter's case that was Johnny Walker Red, a fifth of which we picked up on the way back from the hospital the next day.

"Do you think they'll let me put it on my expense report?" he asked from the back seat.

I looked in the rearview mirror. His eyes were shut, his arm guarding his chest. "No."

"You haven't asked how bad the pain is on a scale of one to ten," he whimpered.

"Consider it asked."

"Five. But when you hit a pothole, it goes to eleven."

Stephen, sitting next to me, turned around. "No offense, but it's not like you got shot or anything."

Hunter raised his head. "Shot? When?"

"A few days ago. Didn't you wonder why my shoulder looks like some kind of hunchback thing?"

"Who shot you?"

"One of the other actors."

"You must have really ticked him off."

"It was an accident," I said. "The gun was supposed to be shooting blanks."

"We think maybe the prop guy had something to do with it. He hates me. Thinks I'm fooling around with his girlfriend."

"Are you?"

"You kidding? This guy is a psycho. He pulled a knife on me."

"A fake knife," I said.

"The one he threw was real."

Hunter lowered his head against the seat. "Why am I always the last to know?"

Our motel loomed on the right. I slowed down.

"Do you think there's a connection?" Hunter asked. "Between your getting shot and my getting injured, I mean."

I shook my head. "Stephen's shooting could have been planned. But your accident was a result of . . . human error."

"Yeah," Hunter said. "That stuntman never should have pushed me into doing that."

I tapped the steering wheel with my fingernail. "Uh-huh."

Pulling into the parking lot, I glanced in the mirror. "Jim Oakley isn't out to get anybody."

Stephen snickered. "Other than you."

"What's that supposed to mean?"

"You've gone out with him . . . how many times now?"

Hunter leaned forward. "Is that true?"

"We've gone out once."

"I hope your infatuation won't cloud your judgment. The board is expecting a blockbuster movie and big book sales. Or at least an award-winning movie and big book sales."

I stifled a laugh. "I wonder who led them to believe that was possible."

Hunter just stared out the window.

"Jim's not behind this," I said. "But something's definitely going on. We think someone wants to sabotage the movie."

"Why?"

"We're working on that."

I found a space and stopped the car. "Leave it to us. You go home and recuperate. I'll get you a flight tomorrow."

He sighed. "But I have a whole list of ideas."

"Leave them with me."

"Will you give them to the director?"

"I *think* I can. I *think* I can."

He smiled, then struggled to get out of the car.

"Ow," he said, then added a few colorful terms of impairment.

"Please bring my medication," he begged.

I held up the bottle in the brown paper bag. "Help is on the way."

For a moment I hoped he'd save some for me. But one of us would need a clear head to turn this thing around.

CHAPTER 10

WHEN WE DROPPED HUNTER OFF AT LAX, HE WAS HUNG OVER. After waving weakly at us, he headed into the terminal, rolling his suitcase behind him, raincoat folded under his arm.

"Hope he'll be all right," I told Stephen, pulling into traffic.

"His luggage hardly weighs anything. It's not like his collarbone's going to pop out. Worst that could happen is he'll puke on the plane. Nobody made him drink that whiskey."

"Do you think he finished the bottle?"

Stephen shook his head. "He'd be dead if he did. Stop worrying."

"Are you really gonna give the director his list?"

"I might accidentally misplace it. Depends on whether I want Larry to hate me even more."

"So what are you doing tonight?"

"Jim wants to take me to his church. They have a Saturday night service."

"Wow. Must be serious."

"You don't get it. I know going to church is the last thing you'd want to do, but there's a purpose. It's not a date."

He gave me a skeptical look. "Then you're hunting for celebrities. I hear there are one or two religious types left in Hollywood."

"Is that so?"

"Well, have a great time. If you run into Denzel Washington or Chris Pratt or Patricia Heaton, let me know."

We headed back to the motel. They were shooting today on the set, but nobody really cared whether we showed up. After playing the role of Hunter's nanny, I needed a break.

* * *

Radiant Hills Fellowship looked less like a church than any building I'd ever seen, with the possible exception of Pizza Hut. It was in an old bowling alley. There was still one lane open, and three people were actually playing before the service started. When one of them got a strike, the congregation cheered.

At the concession stand, Jim bought me a coffee and got one for himself. I kept telling myself it wasn't a date.

"I've been going here about three years," he said as we sat. A couple hundred padded purple chairs were arranged in a semicircle, with a platform where the other alleys used to be. An ensemble of guitarists, two singers, a drummer, a keyboard player, and a guy with a mandolin assembled themselves in front of a large projection screen.

I looked around. "I don't see anybody famous."

He laughed. "What did you expect?"

I shrugged. "At least a few people in dark glasses, trying to escape the paparazzi."

"We've got plenty of people from the industry, but they're

mostly crew and studio office workers. And not everybody around here works in showbiz."

"Guess I thought it would be bigger, too."

"Some are. We're not the only church in southern California."

A guy with headphones on the platform adjusted a microphone as the musicians turned on switches, cleared their throats, and gave a few practice strums and cymbal taps. The audience quieted down.

I wondered what song they'd start with. It'd be contemporary, of course. Probably something from those Australian guys. Hillsong. They seemed to have the market cornered these days.

The drummer set the beat, the guitarists joined in, and the rest launched into a number I hadn't heard since Johnny Cash died.

> *I remember when I was a lad,*
> *Times were hard and things were bad*
> *But there's a silver lining behind every cloud . . .*

Country music? On the other hand, what should I expect in a bowling alley?

> *Will the circle be unbroken*
> *By and by, Lord, by and by . . .*

Grinning, Jim leaned toward me. "Don't worry, they're not all like this. Just enough to keep a Texas boy interested."

The rest of the service was pretty conventional. The pastor looked more like a college chaplain than a televangelist. He talked about family. There weren't a lot of kids there, and a few people wiped their eyes as if childhood had left sore spots. Somehow he managed to tie it all up on a hopeful note.

I glanced at Jim. He was smiling at me, then looked away.

It's not a date, I reminded myself.

I'd be crazy to get involved with this guy. Nothing in common. Just faith, sense of humor, and mutual attraction. It'd never work.

Unless I let it.

* * *

Sunday morning started before dawn, thanks to the nagging of my cell phone. Groping in the dark, I knocked it off the nightstand and felt for it on the carpet.

"Carolyn? Mikki!"

I grunted. "Do you know what time it is?"

"You're ahead of us, right? Like at least two hours?"

"Three. The sun's not even up."

"Sorry. But you won't believe this. I can come see you!"

I sank back against the pillow. It was never too early for a headache. "Why would you want to do that?"

"Are you sure this is you? The real Carolyn wouldn't have to ask."

"Look, I know you wanted to be the choreographer. They don't need one."

"No problem. But I've got a chance to fly standby!"

I considered how little the producer and director liked the people I'd already dragged onto the set. "I'm not sure this is the best—"

"Hey, I won't be able to get time off for another six months. This is the chance of a lifetime."

"Yours or mine?"

"Both."

"How is it mine?" I asked.

"Tell me the truth. Things aren't going well, are they?"

"Not strictly speaking."

"You need a friend. Like me."

"Yeah, I suppose."

"And I need you. And I want to meet a movie star."

"I guess the closest thing would be Jackson Dunn."

"You're actually *working* with him now?"

"In the sense that we're sometimes in the same building."

She sighed. "If only you could see me right now. I'm looking dreamily out the window like that girl Frenchie in *Grease* who was always wearing pink poodle dresses. Played by Didi Conn. She's not in this, is she? I think she's still alive."

"Mikki, I've got a headache. If you come out here, will it get worse?"

"What am I, a doctor?"

"Will you . . . try to control yourself?"

"You mean not do anything to embarrass you?"

"Something like that."

"I swear on Didi Conn's grave, in case she's not still alive."

"I don't think we're supposed to swear on people's graves."

"I'll make you a deal. Help me get Jackson Dunn's autograph and that selfie while I'm there and I'll act like one of those boring people in *Downtown Abbey* the rest of the time."

I pulled the covers up to my chin. "I can't promise anything, but I'll try."

"I'll e-mail you my flight information. But remember, it's standby. You have to be ready for anything."

"That's what I'm worried about," I said, and hung up.

* * *

Two mornings later Stephen and I stood in the terminal, staring at the ARRIVALS screen. Flight 2384 was delayed, but Mikki had phoned at the last minute to report that they'd found a place for her. She sounded so breathless I thought she might need her drop-down oxygen mask before takeoff.

"We can catch up with her in Baggage Claim," I said. "Carousel Nine. No need to hurry."

"Good," Stephen said. "Couldn't sleep last night. Kept having flashbacks to that awful scene they shot yesterday."

"Yeah. Jackson seemed a little off, didn't he?"

"The guy is no singer. Reminded me of Clint Eastwood doing 'I Was Born Under a Wandering Star.'"

"Paint Your Wagon?"

He nodded. "They didn't need a song at all. Who sings when he mucks out the barn?"

"The Seven Dwarfs, maybe. They'd sing if they were being marched off a cliff."

I checked my watch. "Let's mosey on down to our rendezvous. With Mikki, you never know. She's so hyper, she could show up before her plane does."

She didn't, of course. Even in California most people were bound by the laws of time and space—if not mathematics.

"Over here!" I called half an hour later, waving. Mikki was easy to spot in her neon green bodysuit and reflective gold sunglasses. Most of the other women wore relatively normal clothing.

She waved back, both arms, and we converged at Carousel Nine. Big hugs, purses swinging and smacking each other. Stephen shook her hand.

"Where are the stars?" Mikki asked, her head pivoting like a lawn sprinkler.

"They've got private jets," Stephen said. "Or they wear bad wigs and really ugly clothes their personal assistants got at rummage sales. Plaid, polyester, stuff like that."

"Wow. I can't believe I'm here." Glancing down at the

moving carousel, she suddenly reached out with both hands and grabbed a huge, black suitcase with a Cinzano sticker on the side.

"Looks like you emptied your closet. Planning to stay for a month or so?"

"You know I can't afford to do that. My boss would kill me, or have his creepy nephew do it. Did you get your boss's old room at the motel for me?"

I nodded. "Hope you like unusual shower curtains."

"Lady, I'm not here for the bathroom decor. Show me the rich and famous. I want to get one of those maps showing where they live. Maybe a tour where they show you the houses and talk about how drunk so-and-so used to get before he was arrested for some big scandal."

"Is that before or after you meet Jackson Dunn?"

"Either way."

Stephen took out his phone and searched. "You can get maps and tours of Beverly Hills. That's where a lot of them live. Or in Malibu."

"Let's go *now*," she said, her eyes a little too bright.

My headache was returning. "Motel first. Then lunch. Then a nap." I yawned. "I mean *map*."

"Then we can—"

"I can't handle more than three things at a time. You just *got* here."

"Sorry. I'm a little wound up."

We turned and followed the signs to PARKING. Mikki chattered until we got to the car, then kept it up all the way to the Oasis Gardens.

I could hardly wait until the jet lag knocked her out.

* * *

Lunch was at a place called Yin and Yang, much to Stephen's dismay. I wasn't too happy about it either. Mikki chose it, going on and on about the virtues of a macrobiotic diet, which was some kind of Zen thing involving unprocessed beans, seaweed, and soy that had gone bad. She informed us that we had to chew each mouthful at least 50 times, as if putting the stuff in your mouth wasn't repulsive enough.

"Now, that wasn't so bad, was it?" she asked when we'd eaten what we couldn't hide in our napkins. "A lot of Hollywood people are into this. And you know how healthy *they* are."

"Physically or mentally?" Stephen asked, still making a face.

"Both."

I waved at the server, a guy who looked like he needed a lot more fat and sugar under his belt, and asked for the check. He got it for me, and when I saw the total I wondered how it could cost so much to dry seaweed and ferment soybeans.

After stopping by the motel, we drove to the Beverly Hills Conference and Visitors Center, a classy glass-and-concrete place, hoping to pick up a map of the stars' homes. No luck, probably because they have to live with all those celebrities who get sick of people like us trying to catch a glimpse of them coming out of the shower.

"I'll try the Internet," Stephen said, whipping out his phone. Within two minutes he'd found a site that offered PDF maps of 42 hot spots for 12 bucks. He swore it was secure. Sending up a prayer that my LifeLock account was paid up, I reluctantly handed him my Discover.

"Download complete," he said a minute later. "Ready?"

"Yes!" Mikki cried.

He cleared his throat and started reading. "Good afternoon, ladies and gentlemen. Welcome to Crimson Carpet

Tours, where you always get your money's worth. No other company can serve up more accurate addresses or shocking secrets. This safari will take you up to three hours if you complete it."

I tried not to groan too loudly.

"On the other hand, feel free to stop anytime. Mortals can absorb only so much star power in a single day."

I'd already reached my limit, but kept my mouth shut.

"If you see a star or get your photo snapped with one," Stephen continued, "let us know. Have fun, don't pester anybody, and enjoy this once-in-a-lifetime peek behind the velvet curtain!"

"I'm in heaven," Mikki breathed.

Stephen gave me the first address and directions. "The Beverly Hills Hotel."

"Skip it," I said. "All we'd see is some doormen and palm trees. Just give us the top twenty or so hot spots."

"Justin Bieber," he said. I navigated to the address. It was hard to see anything because of the trees—which Stephen, thankfully, didn't identify.

"That's okay," Mikki said. "He turned out to be kind of weird."

"Taylor Swift."

More trees, no Taylor. A guard at a gate gave us a dirty look.

"Harrison Ford."

I had to double back to get there. Seems he had a dozen or so houses. This one was a white mansion. Fewer trees, no star.

"But I love him anyway," Mikki said.

"Marilyn Monroe."

White brick wall, dark gray gate, with a square white tower and clay tile roof. Lots of windows. Needless to say, no Marilyn.

"Want to hear the rest of the list?" Stephen asked.

"Just the highlights," I said.

"Jimmy Kimmel, Jeff Bezos—"

Mikki leaned forward. "Who? Kimmel I know, but—"

"Jeff Bezos," I said. "Head of Amazon."

"Not even an actor. Skip him."

"Calvin Klein."

"Nice clothes, but no."

"Johnny Depp, Lady Gaga, John Legend and Chrissy Teigen."

"Okay."

"Queen Latifah and Elton John."

Mikki sat back. "Do they live together?"

"Not likely," I said.

"Keep them on the list."

Stephen continued. "Dr. Phil."

"Nah."

"Walt Disney's house. He doesn't live there anymore, obviously. But maybe his frozen head is in the basement."

Mikki shuddered. "I can live without that if you can."

"Playboy Mansion. Minus Hugh Hefner."

It was my turn to shudder. "I don't want to get within half a mile of that place. Think of the bacteria."

"Jennifer Aniston."

"Oh, I like her," Mikki said.

Stephen tallied up the survivors. Seven, the biblical number of perfection.

We spent the next hour and a half winding our way through Beverly Hills. It was slow going, seeing as how a convoy of tourists was prowling the well-groomed streets with us. At each stop Stephen read related factoids and added his own.

No sightings, no selfies. Once we thought we saw Johnny

Depp through a window, but it turned out to be a reflection of the slowly setting California sun.

Stephen poked his phone a few times. "There's always the Beverly Hills Sign. It's in a park. And Rodeo Drive. We can park and not go in the stores. Unless you're richer than I think."

I waited for Mikki's reaction. When I heard nothing, I looked in the mirror and saw her leaning against her window, conked out. Thank God for jet lag.

Stephen looked, too. "There's always Jackson Dunn," he said.

"Home, James," I said, and turned the car around.

* * *

Next morning Mikki met us in the motel lobby, eye-scorching in her green bodysuit. We all sipped free coffee as I tried to decide how to address the fashion elephant in the room.

"Are you wearing that to the set?"

"Shouldn't I?"

I set my cup down next to a card printed with escape routes in case the place caught on fire. "You want to impress Jackson Dunn, right?"

"Of course."

"Well, he doesn't strike me as a flamboyant guy. Outgoing, yes, but not 'out there.'"

She looked wounded. "You think I look like a freak."

I shifted uncomfortably on the couch. "Not at all. Just a little too . . . colorful." It seemed impolite to point out her similarity to one of those glow-sticks kids carry on Halloween.

Stephen unwrapped a Snickers bar from the vending machine. "Actors want to be the center of attention."

"You should know," I said.

Mikki threw up her hands. "So what do you want me to wear?"

"It's not what *I* want. It's what *you* think is best."

She leaned forward, elbows on knees. "I brought a gray-and-white blouse-vest-pants combination. I can add a nice red necktie. Kind of an Annie Hall look."

"Perfect, if you lose the tie. *Annie Hall* came out when you were in junior high."

"I thought Hollywood was supposed to be wilder." Looking resigned, she stood up. "I'll go change."

When she was gone, I turned to Stephen. "I guess there's no way to keep her off the set."

"What do you think she's going to do? She can't make our relationship with Shapiro and Pulaski any worse."

"You don't know her like I do."

By the time Mikki returned, my coffee was gone and Stephen was halfway through a Butterfinger.

"What do you think?" she asked anxiously, hands on hips.

"Very tasteful," I said.

Stephen nodded. "Kind of an Emily Blunt thing."

Our ride to the studio was uneventful, unless you count the time Mikki thought she saw Alec Baldwin coming out of a Whole Foods and shrieked.

I squeezed the steering wheel. "Do you *have* to do that?"

Stephen squinted at the market. "Alec Baldwin isn't that tall. And I don't think he's into broccoflower and bean sprouts."

The old lady at the guardhouse waved us through, having apparently given up on protecting the place from unarmed, innocent-looking civilians. When we opened the door to the soundstage, Mikki's knees buckled.

"This is where the magic happens," Stephen declared.

"I have to sit down," Mikki said, breathing a little too

quickly.

I led her to our usual economy-class seats. "Let me know when you recover."

"I need a drink," she said.

I got her some bottled water from the otherwise empty craft services table. On the way back I spotted Jackson Dunn huddled with the script supervisor in a corner. The director stood next to the cameraman, gesturing at a bank of lights as if pleading with them to work. I decided not to bring Mikki anywhere near him. This was going to be tricky enough.

"Here," I said, handing her the bottle.

"Gee. Actual Hollywood water."

"Yeah. I think it's from Safeway."

After a few gulps, she settled back in her chair. "I'm okay now."

"See over there, with the girl? That's Jackson Dunn."

She got to her feet, but wobbled and sat down again.

"I can't do this."

"What?"

"I don't know what to say."

Stephen laughed. "Say whatever you want. He's not Bela Lugosi. He's a nice guy. Gives out PEZ dispensers."

"All the time?"

"He's probably out of them right now," I said. "But you didn't come here for a PEZ dispenser, remember?"

"Right." She stood up again and straightened the hem of her vest.

"I'll introduce you," I said.

The closer we got to the corner, the slower she walked. About ten feet away she stopped and signaled me with a nod.

"Hi, Leilani," I said. She put down her script and smiled. "This is my friend Mikki Flaherty. She flew all the way from New York to meet her absolute favorite actor on the planet."

Jackson turned to face us. "You mean Ryan Gosling?

Sorry he's not here. I'm sure he would have been happy to get acquainted."

Mikki opened her mouth, but nothing came out. I elbowed her.

"Mr. Dunn," she said faintly. "I just want to thank you for your entire body of work."

I raised an eyebrow. Had the spirit of some community college assistant media professor taken possession of her?

"I've seen everything you've ever done," she continued.

"My goodness," he said. "I hope not."

She smiled, then pulled her camera from her purse. "Would you mind if—"

"Of course not," he said.

I got a picture of the two of them. He put his arm around her. They actually looked like they could have been a couple. It was eerie.

Leilani consulted her watch. "Jackson, we have to get you into makeup."

He sighed. "Duty calls, Mikki. I don't suppose you'd like an autograph."

"Oh, I would." She rummaged around in her purse. "Rats. Just when I need a—"

He fished a pen from his own pocket. "I can sign anything you want."

Leilani produced a pink sheet of yesterday's script changes. "How about this?"

"Perfect," Jackson said, and scribbled his heart out.

Mikki was wobbling again as she accepted her Holy Grail.

Jackson gave her one last hug. With a little wave he headed down the hall.

"I just had the strangest dream," she said.

I pinched her. She seemed not to notice.

"Time to wake up, Sleeping Beauty."

"Never," she said.

CHAPTER 11

WE WATCHED THE SHOOTING FOR THREE HOURS, THEN WENT to a diner near our motel. After we were seated, I waved my hand in front of her face. She looked like one of those big-eyed Keane paintings. I considered slapping her a few times to make sure she was still alive.

"Have you still got it?" I asked.

She twitched. "Did you say something?"

"The page. Jackson autographed it for you, remember?"

A smile the size of a watermelon slice spread across her face. Figuratively speaking.

I picked up my water glass. "You've got thirty seconds to return to reality. Otherwise I fling this in your general direction."

She looked around the clearly unpopular establishment as if making sure no one from the *National Enquirer* was aiming a camera at us. "Is Jackson married?"

"As far as I know."

"Happily?"

I put the glass down. "I can't believe you're asking this. Have you taken up homewrecking? Not to mention the flakiness of falling for a guy just because you've seen huge blowups of his face in the dark."

"I saw *The SpongeBob Squarepants Movie*, and I've managed to resist *him*. And since when are you a relationship expert?"

"My failures have earned me certain insights when it comes to men."

"Fair enough." She sniffed. "Jackson is charming, but I realize our love isn't meant to be." She started to cry.

I looked down at my soggy English muffin. This couldn't be happening.

Our server, passing by, paused with a coffee carafe in her hand. "Is there a problem?"

"No," Mikki said, picking up her napkin and blowing her nose.

"We'll just have the check," I said.

A minute later she brought it, smiling—probably because she wasn't me.

* * *

Out on the sidewalk, we ran into Stephen. Mikki, her eyes red, put on sunglasses and tried to smile.

"Am I too late?" Stephen asked.

"We just finished," I said, feeling the English muffin reassemble in my stomach.

"Rats. I wanted to tell you about my great movie idea."

"How long will this take?"

"I can do it in sixty seconds. That's how long a Hollywood pitch is. They call it an elevator speech."

"Pitch away. But we're supposed to be on the set in half an hour. Not that anybody actually wants us there."

He leaned against a green recycling can on the sidewalk. "It's called *Watsons*."

"That doesn't tell me anything."

"Okay. High concept. All the actors who've played Sherlock Holmes' sidekick band together to solve a crime. You know, people like Martin Freeman, Jude Law, Edward Hardwicke, Nigel Bruce, John C. Reilly, Robert Duvall, Ben Kingsley, James Mason, Dudley Moore . . ."

"Aren't some of those guys dead?"

"Technically, yes. But we could bring them back with CGI. Deepfaking. Or just stick with the non-dead ones."

"Is the movie supposed to be funny?"

"Either way. I want to pitch it to Oskar or Larry or somebody."

"Well, I wish you luck."

"But do you think it's good?"

I tried to think of a way to say *no* without actually saying it. "Other than you, how many people know these actors played Watson?"

"Probably not a lot."

"What if they were actors who've played *Sherlock?*"

"You mean like Benedict Cumberbatch, Basil Rathbone, Jeremy Brett, Ian McKellen, Michael Caine, Robert Downey Junior, Will Ferrell, Henry Cavill, Peter O'Toole, Ian Richardson, John Barrymore—"

"Of course you'd still have the deadness problem."

Mikki raised a hand. "Maybe you should make them dancers."

"Why?" he asked.

"Then *I* could be in it."

I checked my watch. "Mikki's not herself right now."

"I like the Sherlock idea," Stephen said. "Dancers . . . not so much. Nothing personal."

Mikki shrugged and turned to me. "Tell Jackson goodbye. And that I'll always be his biggest fan."

Swallowing, I reached out and gave her a hug. She couldn't help it. She was just Mikki, that's all.

* * *

Something was wrong when Stephen and I got back to Parthenon Arts.

The gate was closed. The guardhouse was empty, or so it seemed.

We sat in the car, waiting.

"We can't be the first ones here," I said. "How did everybody else get through?"

Finally I got out and walked around the gate. The old lady's clipboard was on the ground. Her pencil lay nearby.

I peered through the window.

She was slumped over the telephone, which was off the hook. No blood on her khaki uniform. Peaked cap on the floor.

I put two fingers on the side of her neck.

No pulse.

I reached for the phone, but stopped. Taking a tissue from my purse, I gently set the receiver back in the cradle.

Sighing, I got back in the car.

"Find anything?" Stephen asked.

"Call 911."

"Why?"

"She's dead."

CHAPTER 12

"So who discovered the body?"

I raised my hand. "That would be me."

Two policemen in dark blue uniforms, looking way too rumpled for Hollywood, squinted in the sun.

"And you would be who?" asked the shorter, tubbier one, pulling a little pad from his pocket.

"Carolyn Neville."

"Who's this guy?" asked the other, skinnier one.

Stephen introduced himself.

The first officer started writing. "Victim's name?"

"I'm embarrassed to say I don't know."

The taller cop nodded toward the building. "These *artistes* too good to come out and get involved? We've got a dead lady here."

"They probably don't know what's going on."

"Then she must have died after they got through the gate."

"Seems logical."

An ambulance pulled up, no siren. The taller policeman went into the guardhouse, poked around, and returned.

"We'll have to wait for the coroner's office, but looks to me like she died of natural causes."

The chubby guy stuck the pad in his pocket. "I'll see whether anybody saw her alive," he muttered, and slipped through the soundstage door.

Slipping a pair of sunglasses from his breast pocket, the remaining cop stepped closer. "You two don't look like you belong here."

"Couldn't agree more," I said.

"I mean you look more or less normal."

"Thanks, I think."

"Not in the movie business, are you?"

"Not exactly."

"Good. Maybe I can trust what you tell me."

Two paramedics, a man and a woman, emerged from the ambulance. "We got a call," the latter said.

"Too late. Waiting for the coroner's office."

Just then the other officer returned, followed by a scowling Oskar Pulaski.

"What's this all about?"

"You know the security guard?" the tall cop asked.

"Of course not. I've seen her many times, but couldn't tell you a thing about her."

"Well, here's one thing. She's dead."

The producer halted. "How unfortunate."

The shorter cop snorted. "Hold on while I call you a grief counselor."

Pulaski folded his arms. "If you have a question for me, ask it. Otherwise, I've got a picture to make."

"When did you get here this morning?" The taller officer asked.

"About . . . seven."

"Was she alive?"

"Yes. Waved me right through."

"See anybody else?"

"No."

"Okay, you can go. We'll be talking with the rest of 'em later. We'll try not to disturb your precious movie."

With a practiced sneer the producer marched back into the building.

A dark sedan that said LOS ANGELES COUNTY CORONER parked beside the ambulance. A man in a gray suit got out.

"Body's in the guardhouse," the shorter policeman called.

A few minutes later the man from the coroner's office ambled over. "We'll need an autopsy, but it's probably a heart attack. No evidence of a struggle, no visible injuries."

"Thanks," said the taller cop.

He turned to us. "You got business cards?"

We handed them over.

"You can go. We'll be in touch if we have to."

After picking up the clipboard and pencil and sealing them in a plastic bag, he got into the squad car with his partner and drove off.

"I should have known her name," I said sadly.

Stephen shrugged. "She never seemed to know ours."

I shivered despite the heat. "Another accident? So far nobody's actually died."

"Carolyn, she was old. Anyway, we'll know after the autopsy."

The paramedics maneuvered a stretcher into the guardhouse.

I turned toward the soundstage door, not wanting to see them take the body away.

* * *

Sitting in our usual seats, we watched the crew set up the next scene. Oskar stood in a dark corner, snarling at anyone who came too close.

"Time to call in the big guns," I said.

Stephen gave me a suspicious glance. "Such as?"

"Marvin."

"You've got to be—"

I held up a cautionary hand. "We have this conversation every time I bring him up. You tell me he's a menace, not a real investigator. Then I say he's the best true crime writer I know, and you claim I'm not objective because he's my friend. Or because he's African American. Then you remind me how old he is and all the times his advice hasn't worked or even made any sense to you, and I end up calling him anyway."

"Well, that saved us a little time."

I dug my phone from my purse. "Even if the guard died of natural causes, too many 'accidents' have happened here. And we're the only ones who seem to care about finding out why."

He shrugged. "Have it your way. And I say that with all due respect as a mere lackey whose financial survival is totally dependent on your approval."

"I hate groveling. Especially in your case, probably because you don't mean it."

I punched in Marvin's speed-dial number and waited. It was three hours earlier in St. Petersburg, Florida, but he'd always been an early riser.

"Cranberry?" said the voice when he picked up. "Got caller ID now. New phone, too. Buttons big as postage stamps. Those are for my lovely bride, of course. I can still read the little paper label on a Hershey's Kiss at fifty paces."

"You're making me hungry."

"And you're making me curious. How much trouble are you in this time?"

"Not sure. You know Harrison Yoder?"

"Met him at an ABA convention once. Girl, I wish I had his royalties."

"He passed away about a month ago. I made the mistake of promising to go to Hollywood and keep the moviemakers from turning his favorite book into a total mess."

"You in Hollywood now?"

"More or less."

He whistled. "Honey, you're in the big time now."

"I wish. Most of the people here wish Stephen and I would get on the next plane to LaGuardia."

"Not much I can do about that, I'm afraid."

"It gets worse. Some strange things have happened on the set. Dangerous stuff. For one thing, Stephen was shot."

"Is he okay?"

"Yeah. But the gun was supposed to be firing blanks. And a security guard died this morning. Could have been a heart attack, though."

"What do the cops have to say about this?"

"Not much. Stephen thinks the prop guy was behind the live ammunition. Can't prove it. It's like somebody wants to shut the movie down."

"Any other suspects?"

"Harrison's ex-wife would love to sabotage the whole thing. The producer and director might have their own reasons, believe it or not."

"Got any friends in the police department?"

"Not this time. They decided the shooting was accidental. And the two clowns they sent out this morning don't seem to take anything the showbiz people do seriously."

"Cranberry, it's not worth getting shot just to ride herd on Brother Yoder's movie."

"I made a promise."

He sighed. "You got a bulletproof vest?"

"No. They clash with my wardrobe. Haven't you got any advice on figuring out who's doing this?"

"If the police won't help, no."

"I guess we'll be stuck with our usual powers of deduction."

There was a long moment of silence.

"In that case, honey, I'll be praying for you."

* * *

When I told Stephen what Marvin had said, he snickered. "A nicer guy wouldn't say, 'I told you so.' But I did, didn't I?"

Ignoring him, I focused on the set. Jackson Dunn was about to play a scene with a big, floppy dog that kept barking. Its trainer, a sixtyish man with a silver ponytail, looked ready to feed the animal a handful of rat poison.

Stephen leaned back in his chair, hands behind his head. "You know what W.C. Fields said about working with animals and children, right? 'Never work with animals or children.'"

"Actually, it was 'Never work with children or animals.'"

"*Actually*, he may never have said it at *all*."

"Thanks for clearing that up."

The director yelled something at the trainer and pointed at the door. The trainer dragged the still-barking canine offstage by his leash. After a minute or so, he carried in a smaller dog with fewer issues.

"I told Marvin we're stuck with our usual powers of deduction," I said.

"Uh-oh."

"So who has the most to gain from disrupting the film?"

"Follow the money," he said.

"That lets Axel off the hook."

"Unless somebody's paying him to cause trouble."

"Who? Carmella?"

"Or Oskar, if he can't afford to finish the picture. Or Shapiro, if he hates Oskar or hates himself so much he can't stand to succeed."

"Strike the second clause of that last sentence. Not believable."

"Hey, I'm an editor, not a psychologist."

"Ready to roll," somebody called from the set.

The clapboard clacked.

"Action!" shouted the director.

The trainer hovered just out of frame as the dog walked to Jackson, who lay on the ground with his elbow propped on an unnaturally shiny rock.

"Good boy," the actor said, smiling that gentle smile. The dog nuzzled his chest. "I can always count on you, can't I, Jesse?"

The dog got closer and licked Jackson's face. A woman near the cameraman let out a thoroughly charmed *Awwww*.

"Get her off the set!" Shapiro bellowed.

The sound man took off his headphones. "We can fix it in post," he said.

"I know," the director said. "But we can't fix *her*."

Leilani took the woman by the arm and led her away.

"From the top," Shapiro muttered.

"He's in a sunny mood," whispered Stephen.

The trainer gave the dog a treat. The animal proceeded to pee on the floor. An assistant something-or-other ran in with a towel while the director took a pill.

"Stephen, do you feel safe here?" I asked.

"Right now? Yes. Generally speaking? No."

"Marvin wanted me to get a bulletproof vest. I said I wouldn't."

"Maybe I should get a gun. The waiting period in California is probably pretty long, though."

"Don't get a weapon. I've got pepper spray."

"Oh, *now* I feel safe. Haven't you ever heard the old saying? 'Don't bring a knife to a gunfight.'"

"I think it's the other way around."

"My point is that pepper spray won't be much use against a gun *or* a knife. Axel's got both."

"But we've got something he doesn't."

"What?"

"Fear."

I turned toward the set, where the dog's lack of self-control apparently had been forgiven. The director seemed to be doing a deep-breathing exercise.

I closed my eyes and tried to do the same.

CHAPTER 13

UNLIKE JOHNNY, STEPHEN DIDN'T GET HIS GUN. I HELD ON TO my pepper spray, just in case.

That was our topic of conversation the next morning as we took our places about ten feet from a fake tree stump on the set. Stephen was trying his hand, or jaw, on some chewing tobacco left over from yesterday's final take.

"I'm glad Marvin's praying," I said. "But as Saint Augustine said, 'Pray as though everything depended on God, and work as though everything depended on you.'"

"I didn't know you were Catholic," he said.

"I'm not."

He continued to chomp, but looked as if he were trying to work the juice from a gob of tar. "If you *were* Catholic, you'd know Saint Ignatius said it. And it went, 'Pray as though everything depended on you, and act as though everything depended on God.'"

"Seems backwards."

"*Backward* is religion's middle name."

"What makes you an expert on early church quotations? You aren't even a theist."

"No, just unusually well-informed."

I was getting queasy just watching him risk mouth cancer or whatever it is those baseball players get.

"Marvin and I will handle the praying. How do we get to work?"

"We talk to anybody who might have seen something. The police aren't going to follow through."

"Does *something* mean anything suspicious that's happened since we got here?"

He shook his head. "Just the guard lady."

"The whole cast and crew?"

"Maybe we could line them all up and ask, 'Did anybody see anything?'"

"They won't let us do that."

He thought for a moment. "They'd let Leilani. Where is she?"

He glanced around, tobacco juice starting to leak from the corner of his mouth. The prop spittoon was gone. He looked desperate.

"Just a minute," he said, and ran toward the restrooms.

Standing up, I searched the soundstage. There she was, standing next to the prop master. He ran his fingers through her hair. She pulled back slightly. He frowned.

Picking up my purse, I headed in their direction.

"Leilani, I have a favor to ask."

She smiled, but looked dubious. It wasn't like she owed us anything, after all.

"Stephen and I are trying to figure out what happened to the lady who died yesterday, and whether anybody saw anything unusual at the entrance. Instead of going from person to person and asking the same question over and over, we'd like to ask the whole group at once."

She bit her lip. "I don't think Oskar and Larry would allow that. Things are a little tense right now, you know?"

I glanced in their direction. The producer was watching the director kick the tree stump.

Just then something bumped my arm. Something smelled awful, a combination of wet cigarettes and stomach acid.

"Sorry," Stephen said weakly. When he belched, the odor got worse.

Axel made a face. "Man, you stink."

"I know."

"Stephen, Leilani doesn't think they'll drop everything and let us pop our question."

He grunted. "Leilani, did *you* see anything when you got here? Was the old lady still alive?"

She nodded. "That was about 6:45 a.m."

"No out-of-place people or cars around?" He burped again, looking pained.

"No."

"Was Axel with you?"

She shook her head. "We come from different directions. Axel rides his motorcycle; I drive my Jetta."

The prop man took a step toward Stephen. "What are you after, moron? I heard the old lady had a heart attack. Who cares whether anybody was around?"

"Maybe it wasn't a heart attack. Or maybe somebody scared her into having one. Like somebody with a knife."

Axel grabbed him by the lapels of his jacket. "God, you're stupid. Why would I give a rat's butt about that old bag? If I wanted to off somebody, it'd be you."

I put an arm between them. "Enough of the alpha male stuff, guys. Save it for somebody who'd be impressed."

Axel shoved Stephen, who stumbled but didn't quite fall. "I had nothing to do with what happened yesterday or you getting shot. Keep getting in my face and I'll beat the crap out of you."

Stephen smoothed his jacket. I reminded myself which

part of my purse the pepper spray was in. Didn't look like I was going to need it this time, though.

I patted his shoulder. "Let's return to our seats."

For a moment he looked like he needed a spittoon again. Finally, he gave a little cough and followed me to our safe, if not happy, place.

* * *

Somehow Stephen's stomach regained its cast-iron constitution by lunch.

Wandering over to the craft services table, we kept a respectful distance from cast and crew. The usual gaunt fellow with a week's growth of whiskers played the part of a chef, complete with white mushroom hat and sauce-spotted apron. He labored over a crockpot full of pasta.

Peeking under the hem of the paper tablecloth, I saw about a dozen opened cans of SpaghettiOs in the garbage.

"My favorite," Stephen said. The cook ladled a pint or so onto a styrofoam plate.

Stephen grabbed a plastic spoon and tasted the pinkish mass. "Needs a little more parmesan," he whispered to me.

The chef rolled his eyes. "All I've got is Velveeta. White bread on the side. Bring your own garlic."

"Perfect," Stephen said.

"Anything for you?" the cook asked me.

"I'm . . . on a diet."

Stephen grinned. "All the more for me."

I turned to the man with the ladle. "By the way . . . when did you get here yesterday?"

"Gee, I'm not sure. About quarter to seven, I guess."

"Did you see the old lady in the guardhouse?"

"Sure. She always waves me through."

"See anything else?"

He gave the sound man a second helping, then stopped to think.

"The prop guy and his girlfriend."

"What were they doing?"

"I'd call it arguing."

"About what?"

"Don't know. They just had that look."

"What look?" Stephen asked.

"Like a Rottweiler and a chihuahua."

Stephen looked around. "Carolyn, do you see where they're sitting?"

"No."

"Let's find Leilani after lunch."

"Are you sure that's—"

"The best thing to do? Yeah."

He walked off to find a table. I found a single stalk of celery in a glass dish, spread it with cheese, and wondered whether it was crazy to follow him.

Which, of course, I did.

* * *

Leilani, it turned out, had an office of her own. Well, more of a cubicle.

It was next to Axel's lair. Binders were stacked higher than her head on an old wooden desk. A six-inch plastic, grass-skirted hula girl posed next to a framed photo of what must have been her family standing under a palm tree.

"A hula girl?" I asked. "Isn't that sort of . . . politically incorrect?"

"Little joke," she said. "Brother gave it to me."

"Can we sit down?" Stephen asked.

"Sure, if you can find a spot. Hand me the clipboard on that chair."

Stephen cleared his throat. "We heard that you and Axel were arguing before the old lady died."

Her eyebrows went up. "Who told you that?"

"Somebody who was there."

She tapped the hula girl with her index finger and it bobbled. "People don't always get along."

He leaned forward. "Leilani, is that a bruise on your cheek?"

Her hand went to her face. She swallowed. "Must have wiped it with a napkin at lunch. That pasta was terrible, wasn't it?"

"You were hiding a bruise with makeup?" I asked.

"Sure," she said, trying to smile. "I got it when I opened a cabinet door. At home."

I put my hand on her arm. "Axel's hitting you, isn't he?"

She looked away. "Like I said, people don't always get along."

"You don't have to put up with that."

There was an awkward silence.

"How long have you two been together?"

"Couple of years."

"Do you love him?"

The pause was too long. "Of course."

"I realize we hardly know each other, but I'm worried about you."

"Thanks, I guess."

Stephen sat motionless in his chair. His nostrils flared.

I took out a business card and gave it to her. "Give me a call if I can help, okay?"

She nodded, turning it over and over with her fingers but not looking up.

Stephen stood. "Some people don't deserve some other people."

He stuck his hands in his pockets and walked out. I followed.

We passed the door of Axel's office.

"That's it," Stephen said, sounding a little hoarse.

"What?"

"I'm going to the cops. Can't let him hurt her anymore. Whether or not he's behind all the other stuff."

"It doesn't work that way. She has to take the initiative. Get a restraining order or something."

He shook his head. "You know she's not gonna do that. They *work* together. It would just push him over the edge. They'd find her body over a cliff somewhere."

I grabbed his arm and brought him to a halt. "You're not just ticked off, are you? You've got . . . feelings for her."

He stepped away. "And if I do?"

"That's not necessarily bad, but it's not smart."

"Are you sure you should be giving advice on this subject? You haven't exactly—"

"Let's not go down that road. Just promise me you won't do anything drastic for at least three days. No police, no duels to defend her honor, no getting within ten feet of him. Cool off."

He looked up at the ceiling.

"Okay. Promise."

I sagged. Three days? What then?

I had 72 hours to find out.

CHAPTER 14

"THAT'S A WRAP!"

Larry Shapiro dropped into his director's chair and closed his eyes. Meditating, probably. Or having a psychotic break.

Stephen was still sitting next to me. Hadn't said a word since his promise.

"I have an idea," I said.

He raised an eyebrow, but said nothing.

"Oskar Pulaski. I want to talk to him."

"About what?" he asked.

"About who stands to benefit if this thing shuts down."

"If *he* does, why would he tell you?"

"He'd rat out somebody else."

"Did you say *rat out*? You sound like Jimmy Cagney."

"If I had a grapefruit, I'd grind it in your face. Like he did to that girl in *The Public Enemy*."

"Very mature." He paused. "I'll go with you."

I shook my head. "Maybe after your next anger management class. See you later."

When I peeked through the doorway of Oskar's office,

the Iguana Lady stared at me. The stale cigar smell drifted into the hallway like halitosis.

"You want something?" she asked, her big glasses sliding down her nose.

"Is Oskar around?"

"Yeah, why?"

"I'd like to ask him a couple of questions."

She looked at her watch. "I don't think he's had his martini yet. Enter at your own risk."

He was pouring the drink as I entered. Smoke and Lysol were still fighting in the air, and the Lysol was losing.

"If you're hoping to join me," he said, "don't bother. I'm running out of vermouth."

"No, thank you."

"I wasn't making an offer. I never drink with people who complicate my life."

"Have I complicated yours?"

He sipped the martini. "You certainly haven't simplified it. Since you and your partner showed up on my set, we've had nothing but problems."

"That's what I wanted to talk to you about."

"A confession? Apology?"

"No. I'm wondering who stands to benefit if this production shuts down."

He sat behind his desk. "Ms. Neville, is it?"

"Carolyn."

"I've made my share of enemies over the years. But I can't imagine any of them going to these lengths to put me out of business."

"Can you name any of them?"

He swirled the last of the liquor in his glass. "Haven't got that kind of time, I'm afraid. If I knew who was behind all this, I would have gone to the police by now."

Eyes narrowing, he downed the last of his drink. The way

he looked at me started to change, and one corner of his mouth turned up.

"I could use another," he said. "Perhaps you'd care to join me after all."

I backed away and sat on the leather sofa. "I thought I was complicating your life."

He shrugged. "That was before I truly noticed you. I like what I see."

I pulled my purse—and the pepper spray—closer.

"I've been in this business a long time. You've got a certain look, Carolyn. Do you have an agent?"

"You mean . . . for publishing?"

"Acting. Or modeling."

I swallowed. Flattering, but obviously as sincere as Harvey Weinstein.

"No agent," I said.

He got up and poured himself another drink. "No problem. I could get you a small part in another film, perhaps a TV commercial or two to start."

"And in return?"

He smiled and took a sip. "I'm sure we could think of something."

He put down the drink and stepped toward me.

I stood up, zipped the purse open, and found the pepper spray, then brandished it like a can of Raid. My heart was hammering. Maybe I should have let Stephen come along.

Oskar clenched his jaw, but backed off.

"If it weren't for that clause in the contract that allows you and your friend to be here, I'd put you both on the next plane to New York," he said. "At your own expense, of course."

I tried to keep my hand from trembling as I put the spray back in my purse. "Glad we could have this little talk."

"Let me know if you change your mind," he said with a charmless grin.

Turning, I passed the Iguana Lady on the way out.

Happy hour was over.

* * *

My heart was still pounding when I sat back down next to Stephen.

"How'd it go?"

"Should have sent you. I don't think he would have tried to fling you onto the casting couch."

His mouth dropped open. "You mean he—"

"Hey, do you have be *that* surprised?"

His blush almost matched his cinnamon hair. "It's not that I think nobody would be interested in—"

"This guy would be interested in anything that didn't fight back."

"Did you?"

"Mr. Pepper Spray could barely contain himself, but lived to fight another day."

He shook his head. "Want me to go straighten him out?"

"Can't be done. He's the original crooked man who walked a crooked mile. Besides, he's already on the verge of hiring somebody to chain us to the bottom of Hollywood Reservoir."

Suddenly a volley of cannons sounded from my purse. Tchaikovsky. I pulled out my phone.

It was Marvin's number.

"Blackberry!" he said.

I put him on speaker. "*Black*berry?"

"I'm promoting you, sister." He paused. "Been doing a little research into the folks you told me about."

"Thanks."

"I know somebody who knows somebody who works in the L.A. County Sheriff's office."

"Networking is your middle name. Right after Ainsley."

"So . . . prop man. Axel Testaverde. Dude has a police record. Mainly speeding tickets and one assault charge. Hasn't served time. Yet."

"He will someday," Stephen muttered.

"Oskar Pulaski. No arrests. But he's been keeping a low profile since the #MeToo movement got him in his sights."

"After what just happened, I can't say I'm surprised."

"What just happened?"

"Nothing. It *almost* did, though."

"Girl, I'm about to jump on a plane and come out there to dispense a little divine justice."

I looked at Stephen. "What is it with you guys? I'm perfectly able to defend myself. I got a free month of karate school when I was in sixth grade. Made it all the way to white belt."

He rolled his eyes. "Congratulations. That's the lowest level."

Marvin sighed. "I'm demoting you back to Cranberry, honey. Now, about the director. Shapiro."

"Larry."

"He's actually done time. Mostly drug charges."

"I know."

"Nothing violent. But you never know, right?"

"Anything else?"

"Not so far."

"Could you look into Harrison Yoder's ex-wife? Carmella?"

"A woman scorned?"

"Mostly a woman cut out of the will. Is she capable of engineering this stuff to get revenge?"

Stephen nodded. "Maybe she's got her *yellow* belt."

"Cranberry, *all* women are capable of revenge. But only a few go into engineering."

"Just tell me you'll look into it."

"Right after I ask permission from my lovely bride."

"Why do you need her permission?" Stephen asked.

"She's got her *black* belt."

* * *

That night I parked in my usual spot near the Oasis Gardens motel, hoping the rental car wouldn't get stolen. I squinted at the sunset, then steeled myself at the gauntlet I was about to run.

A long-haired, surfer-shorted panhandler wielding an aluminum pie plate was the first to cross my path.

"Hey, Babe, I can't afford . . . to wax my board."

Great. He was a poet, too.

Waving him off, I leaned into the sun and kept going. I could see the tattoo parlor and the vaping shop in the distance.

More independent fundraisers positioned themselves like hurdles in my way.

"Care to crowdfund? I can make kidneys with a 3D printer."

"I'm the next Robert Mapplethorpe, only with a glittery pink touch of Lisa Frank."

"Okay, I just want to get stoned."

I kept my head down. Just when I thought I'd eluded every opportunity for philanthropy, I ran smack into something that felt like a beanbag chair and smelled like an old canvas pup tent.

"You're going to hell!" it declared.

I looked up. A bearish, bearded monolith in a gray wool

suit glared down at me, a Bible in one hand and a sweating bottle of Crystal Geyser water in the other.

"No, I'm not," I said.

"'Believe on the Lord Jesus Christ and thou shalt be saved,'" he said. "Acts 16:31."

"Been there, done that."

"Are you sure?"

"Yep. I was five years old."

"Woman, what are you doing in a place like this? It's Sodom and Gomorrah."

"Same thing you're doing—making a spectacle of myself. Now, if you'll excuse me, I'm late."

My stomach growled. I pressed on, seeing the Oasis Gardens sign, hoping I wouldn't have to go to Stephen's room and pound on his door. He was supposed to be waiting in the lobby.

I passed Fleshtones and Fog of War, then came to an abrupt halt.

There, under a palm tree, stood Stephen. He was not alone.

He didn't see me.

He was too busy kissing Leilani.

CHAPTER 15

I'M NOT SURE HOW LONG I STOOD THERE, STUNNED, ABOUT 20 feet away.

They weren't exactly making out—at least not by my definition, which involves a certain amount of lip and jaw torque, along with the visible smearing of lipstick. It was more of a gentle gesture, with Stephen's right hand on her left shoulder. He had to bend down since Leilani was a head shorter.

I'd never seen Stephen kiss anybody. I'd assumed he didn't know how.

He moved his hand to her cheek. She bent her head against his chest. I felt like I should look away, but they'd chosen to make this a public event. A steady stream of people passed by but I was the only one paying attention.

Venturing closer, I tried to come up with something appropriate to say. "Get a room" didn't sound right. Neither did "What the [expletive deleted] do you think you're doing?"

About ten feet away I stopped and cleared my throat.

Stephen turned in my direction. He froze.

"Imagine my surprise," I said.

"Imagine *mine*," he croaked.

Leilani lifted her head. "Carolyn? We were just . . ."

"I noticed. Aren't you afraid Axel's going to see you?"

She shook her head. "He's still at the studio, working on an old car or something."

"It's not what it looks like," Stephen said.

I stepped closer. "It looks like you were trying to comfort her or protect her, and things got out of hand."

"Well, then, it *is* what it looks like."

"I'd better go," Leilani said.

"I'll see you later," Stephen murmured.

"Maybe."

She headed for the nearest crosswalk. I could see her car parked across the street.

"So," I said.

"So." He leaned against the palm tree, looking at the ground.

"I'm impressed. It takes a special person to see the wisdom of getting involved with the girlfriend of a jealous weapons expert with a criminal record."

"It's not like we're getting married or anything."

"My gosh, I should hope not. You've known her for what, a whole week?"

"She needs help."

I nodded. "She might get some from a therapist. Or a lawyer. Or a woman's shelter. What she doesn't need is to get romantically involved with a guy who's going to fly away to the opposite side of the country in less than a month."

"I didn't plan to kiss her. We were just going to talk."

"And you ran out of things to say?"

"Something like that."

I hoisted my purse higher on my shoulder. The sun was beginning to cast long shadows.

"I'm going to get some dinner. I'd invite you to join me,

but I don't think either of us would be good at small talk right now."

"Yeah, I get it."

He peeled himself away from the tree trunk. "Guess I'll see you tomorrow."

"Probably."

Hands in his pockets, he slouched toward the motel entrance.

I didn't feel like driving anywhere, but remembered a cheap-looking seafood place about half a dozen blocks back. There was a crab painted on the window.

The panhandlers were still making their pitches, which I ignored. The street preacher gave me a wide berth as I passed.

Frowning, I replayed the mental image of the star-crossed lovers beneath the palm fronds. If only it had been a movie.

I thought of Axel and what he might do if he found out. The man was psychotic.

But maybe he wasn't the only jealous one in this equation.

It wasn't just shock I'd felt at the sight of Stephen locking lips with that girl. Something maternal, maybe.

Or something else I didn't want to contemplate.

* * *

Wanting to spend dinnertime with a man more my age, I decided to call Jim Oakley.

"Have you got plans?" I asked.

"Sure do."

I sagged. "Oh. Maybe another time."

He laughed. "My plans involve a Domino's Pizza. Just ordered it. You like anchovies?"

"No, but—"

"Good. I hate 'em." He paused. "My place or yours?"

"I'd be embarrassed to let you see the dump we're staying in."

He gave me directions to his townhouse. "Go slow. Give me time to scrape the fungus out of the kitchen sink."

Twenty minutes later I was ringing the doorbell. For some reason I thought it might whinny like a stallion, but it just rang. The knocker, which should have resembled a cow skull, or at least a horseshoe, was also a disappointment. There wasn't any.

Jim opened the door. "Hey! Thought maybe you were the delivery guy. Isn't Domino's supposed to get here extra pronto?"

"Don't know. Now that I think about it, I've never ordered a pizza."

He ushered me in. "Somehow that doesn't surprise me."

Darting around the living room, he picked up a couple of magazines and snapped on a lamp that looked like a cactus. "You got here too early. Now you know what a slob I am."

I looked around at the mostly Southwestern decor. Indian blankets, a big one on the sofa and two small ones on the wall. Shadow boxes housing spurs and silver belt buckles. A Frederick Remington bronco-buster bronze statue replica.

"Pretty much what you expected?" he asked.

"In a good way."

The bell rang again. Delivery guy. The pepperoni smell made me hungrier.

Jim placed the box in the middle of the kitchen table. "If I'd known you were coming, I would've ordered salad or something."

"This is fine. Thanks for sharing."

He found a couple of Coronas in the fridge. After asking the blessing, he let me pick the first slice.

"Everything okay?" he asked. "You look a little . . . distracted."

I stalled by chewing a lot longer than necessary. Finally I took a swallow of beer. "Got a problem."

"Business or personal?"

"Both." I paused. "Axel Testaverde has been abusing his girlfriend, Leilani."

He shook his head. "She seems like a real sweetheart. Puts up with a lot from the director."

"Axel also has it in for Stephen, who'd like to swoop down and rescue her. He tried to 'comfort' her, and they ended up in each other's arms."

"Oh, crap."

"If Axel finds out, Stephen will end up in a full body cast —or worse. If he *doesn't* find out, Leilani will be a mess when he has to go back to New York."

Jim took a long drink. "I wouldn't mind getting into it with Axel if I thought it would do any good. But I couldn't call myself much of a peacemaker if I did."

"The weird things that keep happening at the studio . . . do you think Axel could be behind them?"

"He certainly has the temperament. But I don't see a motive. And even *he* isn't dumb enough to do something that obvious." He paused. "Probably."

"If you were me, what would you do?"

He picked a pepperoni slice from his pizza. "Besides pray?"

I nodded.

"Keep Stephen away from the girl. Keep the girl away from Axel."

"How?"

"Don't know. I'm a broken-down cowboy, not a psychologist."

We sat there in silence. Talk about awkward.

"Can I interest you in a little dessert? My mom sent me

some of her thumbprint raspberry cookies. Pretty sad, a grown man still getting care packages from his mother."

"Yeah, it's pathetic."

He went to the pantry, pulled out a cardboard box, and put six cookies on a plate.

"These may not solve your problem, but they're all I've got."

Each of us had three. They were gems, of course, though they didn't go that well with beer.

We cleared the table, then sat on the couch and listened to a couple of tracks from an old Charley Pride CD. Jim pointed out a few family photos on the living room wall and explained who was who.

It was just after 9:00 when I told him I had to go.

"Want a couple cookies to take home?" he asked.

"Yeah, I guess."

He wrapped them in foil. Our hands touched. His were warm.

That smile crinkled his eyes, which looked into mine for a long moment.

I swallowed.

He bent slightly, closed his eyes, and kissed me on the lips.

Softly. Just touching. Not making out. Really.

I held my breath.

"Good night," he whispered.

I started breathing again when I was outside. It was getting chilly. Lightheaded, I dropped the cookies in my purse.

Was this how Stephen had felt with Leilani?

And could I keep from making the same mistake?

* * *

Still feeling dizzy, I parked in my usual spot near the Oasis Gardens. I'd never walked this stretch after dark alone, but didn't have much choice.

No panhandlers, no street preachers. Nothing but feeble street lighting and the occasional *hrrrretch* of spitting in the alley.

I could hear a car approaching behind me, but at least a block away. Turning, I watched the headlights grow bigger. The make, color, and model were a mystery, even when I squinted.

The engine revved. There was a thump as the vehicle jumped the curb and starting riding the sidewalk.

I started running.

The thumps came faster as the car sped up. No time to look over my shoulder.

My breath came in gasps. Somebody was trying to run me down.

A park opened up on my right. Grass, trees, a garbage can, swings.

I could hear the unseen driver bearing down on me, only a few yards between us. Thought I smelled gasoline, but it could have been my imagination.

I looked around for help. Nobody.

The street was deserted, or seemed to be.

The beams of the headlights lit the sidewalk at my feet. I cut to the right, into the dark.

God, get me out of here.

There was a pain in my side. I hadn't run like this since I was a teenager. Mikki would be so proud. Maybe she'd mention it at my funeral, except she wouldn't know how fast I was going when I died.

I just missed colliding with a streetlamp, then nearly tripped over an abandoned bicycle.

The glowing eyes of a cat or raccoon or something zipped past.

Maybe I can make it.

The headlights lurched to the left. The car couldn't follow this far. I could hear it bumping into the distance.

I kept running, but stumbled and fell headlong into the sand next to a playground slide.

Panting, I hugged the ground and waited for someone to slam a car door and appear with a gun. But there was only silence.

I gripped the pipe that supported the slide and dragged myself up. Hardly any blood. Just a lost shoe and a hole in the knee of my pants.

Squeezing my purse as a child might hug a teddy bear, I hobbled toward what I hoped was safety.

CHAPTER 16

TEN MINUTES LATER, I APPROACHED STEPHEN'S DOOR, limping. God only knew what might be going on inside—and I was probably the last person he wanted to see, other than Axel.

Hesitating, I listened. The theme song of *The Jetsons*. One step above the *Flintstones*.

I heard footsteps, a fumbling with the latch, an opening. There he stood in T-shirt and jeans, his feet bare and his expression a combination of surprise and disgust.

"What happened to *you?* Looks like you got run over by a car."

"Almost. May I come in?"

"I guess."

He grabbed the TV remote and switched it off just as the Jetsons' robot maid appeared.

"You want a drink of water or something?"

Shaking my head, I sat on the chair next to the desk. "Somebody just tried to kill me."

He sat on the edge of the bed. "How?"

"By aiming a car at me and stomping on the accelerator. Just about got me in the park down the street."

"Did you see who—"

"Too dark. Too fast. I definitely smelled gas, but I suppose that doesn't help."

"Are you hurt?"

"Nothing worth going to the hospital for. Going to need some new pants and shoes, though."

"So let's call the police."

"I can't identify the driver or the vehicle. And I didn't actually get hit."

He stood up. "This sucks. There must be something we can do."

I looked around. "I thought maybe Leilani would be here."

"We're not a thing. I was just trying to—"

"I know."

"We can at least talk to the two cops who weren't trying very hard to discover what happened to the old lady. Maybe they could find *something* out. Skid marks. A witness."

I reached down and picked a dandelion leaf out of my stocking. "In the morning."

Slowly, I got up and moved toward the door.

"Sweet dreams," I said, doubting mine would fall into that category.

* * *

Next morning, we stopped by the police station, hoping our friends in law enforcement weren't out apprehending jelly doughnuts.

We found them in the break room, gnawing bear claws.

"We'd like to report an attempted murder," I said.

They kept chewing. The short guy took out a pad.

"Where?"

"The street near our motel."

"Who's the victim?"

"Me."

"Who did it?"

"Somebody in a car tried to run me down."

The tall one looked at the ceiling. "License number?"

"Don't know."

"Can you describe the perpetrator?"

"No."

"The vehicle?"

"No."

They looked at each other.

"Ma'am, do you have any idea who might want to kill you?" the short one asked.

I threw up my hands. "Whoever wants me to stop looking into the old lady guard's death. And the so-called accidents on the movie set."

"Who might that be?" the taller one said, and sipped his coffee.

"Axel Testaverde," Stephen said.

I held up a hand. "Wasn't his vehicle. He drives a motorcycle."

The cops glanced at each other again. "We're making headway," the shorter one said.

The taller one shrugged. "You're not giving us enough to go on."

"Maybe we should hire a psychic," his partner said, rolling his eyes.

I rubbed a sore spot in the middle of my forehead. "Isn't your motto 'To protect and to serve'?"

They nodded.

"Which are you doing right now?"

"We're on a break."

"Never mind. What can you tell us about the old lady?"

"Heart attack," said the taller one. "No foul play."

The shorter one finished his pastry. "She was seventy-nine. Originally from Indiana, wherever that is."

The taller one swallowed the last of his coffee. "But now that you mention it, this isn't the first time an Oskar Pulaski production has had problems."

"Oh, yeah," the other agreed.

"A gaffer got electrocuted once. And I seem to remember something about food poisoning from craft services."

"And there was that time Larry Shapiro got so coked up he broke his hand punching Pulaski in the jaw."

The taller one shook his head. "Why they still work together is a mystery. Unless Shapiro's got something on Pulaski, which is entirely possible."

I looked at Stephen. "Well, that's something."

"We'll let you know if we hear anything else."

"Of course you will."

"Meanwhile, try that psychic. This town's crawling with 'em."

"Good advice."

There was an extra bear claw in the box. "Going to eat that?" I asked.

"You bet," they said in unison.

Sighing, I led the way out.

"They're not gonna do anything about this," Stephen said when we got to the car.

"You think?"

"What now?"

I checked my watch. "Doughnut shop. The sooner the better."

* * *

Shooting was already underway when we reached the set. Nobody noticed our entrance. The director and producer conferred with the cinematographer. Even Leilani kept her eyes on her script.

We tiptoed to our seats as Jackson Dunn took center stage. *Interior, Winchester cabin. A warm light bathes the rustic bed, upon which reclines the family matriarch. A damp cloth covers her brow.*

"Son, is that you?" The actress playing Mother Winchester raised a hand, apparently unseeing.

"It's me, Mama." Dunn knelt at her bedside.

"I think I seen an angel," she whispered.

Dunn adjusted the cloth, his lip trembling.

"So tall he was. Lit up like a campfire. But no wings. Thought angels had wings."

"Maybe some do. Guess yours doesn't need any."

The makeup lady sniffled.

"I know where I'm goin', honey," Mama said. "Gonna see my folks. And Jesus, of course." She paused. "I'm a little scared of Him."

"Why?"

"Never told you this. But you had an older sister. Died before you was born. Her daddy was a boy at school. We were never properly married."

Jackson got up, dragged over a wicker chair, and sat. "I reckon Jesus knows your heart. Lived there for sixty-seven years, hasn't He?"

"Sixty-eight."

He chuckled softly. "You were always better than me with numbers."

The sound man seemed to be wiping his eyes, but it could have been allergies.

"Mama, I've got a confession of my own to make," Dunn said.

The old woman coughed, then waited.

"When I was twelve, I stole two dollars from your purse. Wanted a fountain pen I saw at the general store, the kind Mr. Mark Twain used. Figured it would make me write like him."

"Did it?"

"Nope."

"Then I'd say you learned your lesson."

There was a long silence. The whole crew held its breath, spellbound.

Dunn leaned forward to take her hand. "Don't want you to go," he said, his voice cracking. I could swear he was crying real tears.

She put a hand over his. "The Winchester men don't like to show their feelings. You were always better at that than most of them."

With a sigh she closed her eyes. Her chest still rose and fell, but slowly.

"Cut!" called the director. More sniffles from the crew.

Stephen cleared his throat. I reminded myself it was only a movie, but had to rummage through my purse for a tissue anyway.

The cameraman leaned toward the director and murmured something.

"*What?*" Shapiro shouted.

Looking sheepish, the cinematographer tapped the side of the camera and shrugged.

The director held the sides of his head as if to keep it from exploding. The producer just shook his.

"Technical difficulties," Shapiro announced. "One more time."

Everybody groaned.

Somehow they did it again. Dunn's tears looked genuine as ever.

"Cut!" Shapiro repeated.

The collective sigh of relief that followed turned into a round of applause.

Dunn, still in the spotlight, looked heavenward. "That's for you, Mama," he said.

Stephen leaned toward me. "Have you read about his mother?"

"Not that I recall."

"Died a few years ago. Multiple sclerosis. She'd been an actress once, but never made it big."

"Sad."

"She had mental problems or something, too. He took care of her until the end."

Dunn gave his fictional mother a peck on the cheek and helped her up from her deathbed. With a disapproving glance at Oskar Pulaski he made a most dramatic exit.

CHAPTER 17

WE WERE DINING ON LEFTOVER LUNCHABLES WHEN MARVIN called.

"Cranberry, I've been looking into Harrison Yoder's ex-wife."

"Carmella," I said, putting him on speaker.

"Got a photo of her here. One good-looking sister. Slender, graceful. Pretty as a model, even though she's fifty-nine. Don't tell my lovely bride I said that."

"We know what she looks like. Where'd you get the picture?"

"She's got a website. Not much on it. Got the feeling her best days are behind her. Dyes her hair red. Obviously a cry for attention."

Stephen licked the last bit of cheese from his little plastic Lunchables knife. "Obviously."

"Marvin, what we're really trying to find out is whether she could be sabotaging the movie to get back at her husband," I said.

"Which one?"

"How many husbands has she *had?*"

"Three. The first two were like Brother Yoder—older guys with lots of cash and lawyers who kept her from hitting the jackpot when they divorced."

"I'm thinking you didn't get all this from her website."

"I've got my sources. Anyway, her modeling career was promising at first, but she had something in common with your director, Mr. Shapiro."

"Drugs?"

"That's what they say. No police record, and she probably couldn't afford rehab. Tried to find out what friends say about her, but she doesn't appear to have any."

"I wonder why."

"She's got a brother, Anthony, who played bodyguard when she was a semi-celebrity. He did time for armed robbery and may still live in L.A."

"In which case we should try to talk with him."

"You sure? Sounds like the type who might run somebody off the road."

I paused to shiver.

* * *

We found Anthony in a box.

Our least two favorite cops had reluctantly pointed us in his direction, after the taller one recognized a Google Images photo from Anthony's body-guarding days.

"He's homeless now," the officer said, still sipping coffee at the station. I was beginning to wonder whether he ever did anything else. "Normally bums all look alike to me, but this guy's skinny as a starving cat and twice as nasty."

Stephen and I parked the rental car beneath the North Hollywood Bridge. Three ratty tents and a cardboard carton the size of a refrigerator formed a sort of neighborhood—the kind you wouldn't want to visit, let alone live in.

The box smelled like whiskey, urine, and dirty under-wear. It said SAMSUNG RS267LBSH on the side. Not knowing what else to do, I knocked.

Something grunted inside.

"Anthony?" I called.

He let loose a string of colorful words, none of them printable.

"My friend and I would like to talk to you. It's about your sister, Carmella."

"You got money?"

"Not much," I said.

"Gonna take a crapload of it to get me talkin' on that subject."

Stephen gave the box a tap with his shoe. "All we got is a half a crapload. Take it or leave it."

Another grunt. Slowly a sadly emaciated version of our photo crawled out on hands and knees, dreadlocks wild as snakes, wearing a filthy black peacoat.

He sat on the ground, hugging his knees, rocking back and forth.

"First, we're wondering whether—"

"Money upfront," he muttered.

I looked at Stephen.

"I was using the editorial 'we,'" he said. "I'm a peon."

I found three twenties in my purse and placed them on the box, preferring not to touch the man without rubber gloves. He snatched and counted them, spat, and resumed rocking.

"You know where Carmella is?"

"Oh, she famous. I used to keep the grabby crowds away from her. She don't remember me."

"How do you know?"

"Used to keep her safe. Woman ought to be takin' care of

me now." He coughed. "I'm livin' in a box. She's a criminal. What kind of sister does that?"

"I'm not so sure she's famous anymore," I said.

"She got the power. I got nothing. Except a bunch of FBI after me. Listening, day and night." He pointed at the tents. "I seen them listening."

"Anthony, have you ever been to the Parthenon Arts studio?"

"What's that?"

"A place where they make movies."

He shook his head. "I ain't seen a movie in . . . five, six years."

"Do you remember where you were two weeks ago, in the evening?"

He blinked. "No."

"How about this morning, about ten o'clock?"

"Sleeping, maybe."

I looked at Stephen. He looked at me.

"He's not our guy," I said.

I fished out another twenty.

"Sorry we bothered you," I said.

This time I placed it in his palm. I could wash mine later.

* * *

We decided to see Carmella one more time, to find out whether she had an alibi.

The two-hour drive to San Diego was mostly silent, punctuated only by the occasional billboard for the zoo and Stephen's assault on a bag of Doritos.

"Isn't it wildfire season?" I asked, surveying the parched landscape along the Pacific Coast Highway.

"Guess so. Unless it's earthquake time."

I turned on the radio and found some Billy Joel. "River of

Dreams," my favorite. Dialed down the volume just enough to make out the words.

"Ever been in an earthquake?" Stephen asked.

I shook my head.

"*I* have. Mexico City, when I was ten. My dad was a military advisor in the so-called Drug War. Man, *that* was a waste of time."

"What about the earthquake?"

"Three-point-five on the Richter scale. Stuff fell off the shelves in our hotel, but that was about it. My mom said to stand in a doorframe, then screamed when I ran out in the street. Clouds of dust everywhere. I peed my pants."

I turned up the volume on the radio. "Too much information."

We stared out the window for a few miles, passing a farm stand and watching the surf crash on the other side of the guardrail.

"I keep thinking about Anthony," Stephen said.

"Me, too." I'd washed my hands twice after touching his, feeling guilty as I did.

"I don't think we'll get much out of Carmella."

"Not if she wants money. I'm down to a couple of twenties."

"Maybe she takes credit cards."

* * *

The Appaloosa Canyon Apartments were well-named, their pale green siding spotted by gray areas where the paint had peeled away. Carmella's star had fallen further than we'd thought.

Apartment 4G's exterior looked like all the rest—tired, flecked with dead gnats, decked out with a cheap rubber welcome mat. When I rang the doorbell, the *yap-yap-yap-yap* of some rabid little dog erupted from inside.

The door opened. I could see the mutt's snout trying to nose its way out.

"Pierre!" Carmella, frowning, her latte complexion accented by a milk chocolate lip gloss, pushed the dog away with her foot.

She looked at us suspiciously. "Here to apologize? I'm busy."

"We won't take much of your time."

She reached down, grabbed Pierre's collar, and jerked him back from the door. "Five minutes."

We followed her into the tiny living room, which was decorated with what appeared to be African artifacts—a shield, a dark wooden statue, a framed dashiki.

"I love your outfit," I said. It was a floor-length chiffon scoop dress, dusty rose. Her sense of fashion was perfect, but it was clear she didn't have the financial resources to maintain an impressive collection of jewelry.

We all sat down, Stephen and I on the worn, brown sofa. Pierre, growling and glowering, refused to leave his master's side.

"We met Anthony," I said.

Her frown deepened. "I can only imagine what he said. If he said anything coherent, that is."

"He seems to think you should be taking care of him."

She scoffed. "My brother's always been a loser. Deserves to live under a bridge."

"Carmella, when's the last time you were in North Hollywood? Before our dinner, that is."

"God, I don't know. Probably at least three years."

"Ever been to the Parthenon Arts studio?"

"No."

"Where were you two weeks ago, in the evening?"

"None of your business."

I settled back against the sofa. "Some very strange things have been going on around our movie set. People have gotten hurt, been chased on the street."

"Got nothing to do with me. I don't need no alibi."

"Have you got one?"

She leaned forward. "Yeah. I was with a man."

"Who?"

"Don't care to tell you. But he's a well-known man. Very interested in me."

"Can you say—"

"I don't have to say a thing. You're not cops."

I looked at Stephen. He shrugged.

She stood up. "Get out."

"I had just one more question about your other previous husbands, and how they—"

She nudged the canine with her shoe. "Pierre, attack."

Baring his teeth, the mutt sprang up and flung himself at Stephen's leg.

Stephen yelped. "Son of a—"

"We'll be going now," I said, backing away.

Stephen yanked the door open, banging his head in the process.

"Ow!"

I pulled it shut behind me.

"Don't come back," Carmella yelled.

She didn't have to tell us twice.

CHAPTER 18

STEPHEN WAS FALLING ASLEEP IN THE DINER BOOTH THE NEXT morning, his nose nearly touching the waffle on his plate. Last night had taken its toll.

"How's your head?" I asked. "And your leg?"

He straightened up, eyes still closed. I thought I saw a bit of maple syrup dripping from his nose. "Can we go home now? I don't mean to the motel. I mean Manhattan."

"I thought you wanted to get to the bottom of this. For Leilani. For us."

Opening his eyes, he rubbed the top of his skull. He looked like one of the Three Stooges, but even more pathetic.

"What's the name of that dog from hell?" he asked.

"Cerberus. The Hound of Hades."

"No, I mean the one from last night."

"Pierre."

He nodded. "Promise we won't go back to San Diego."

"I promise *you* won't."

He wiped his nose with a napkin, then got to work.

I dunked a raspberry doughnut in my coffee. "Wonder who Carmella's well-known boyfriend might be. Judging from her marital history, *boyfriend* might not be the most descriptive term."

"Yeah, she likes 'em old and rich." He paused. "We could stake out her apartment. Or *you* could. I'm never going back there."

"Waste of time. We need to talk to our other suspects. Like Larry Shapiro. We haven't said boo to him."

"What's his motive?"

"Passive aggression against Pulaski. Or self-sabotage. Fear of success."

"We've talked plenty with the prop guy. Not that it's done us any good."

I finished the doughnut. "The cinematographer. Ansel Mueller."

"He's a suspect?"

"Could be, but I doubt it. Seems to know Shapiro best. They've got some kind of truce. An understanding."

He poured more syrup on his waffle. The thing was swimming in it. "Like us?"

"Like us *what*?"

"An understanding. You get us into trouble and I get us out."

"That's not the way *I* understand it."

"How do *you* see it?"

"I'm the brains and you want to be the brawn. But you keep getting your brains knocked out."

He sighed. "I'm taking the day off."

"I tell you what. We won't do anything dangerous today. Just talking to the cameraman. He seems harmless."

"He's German."

"They're nice now. No more gas chambers. It's all electric cars and cuckoo clocks."

He rubbed the top of his head again. "You promise?"

"Absolutely. You don't even have to say anything. Starting now."

He looked relieved, then picked up his plate and poured the rest of the syrup into his mouth.

"I can't take you anywhere," I said.

* * *

It took two hours to reach the day's location.

"Not much resemblance between the Ozarks and this patch of scrub brush," I said, and parked near the sound man's van.

"At least there's no cactus," Stephen said, squinting against the sun.

The cinematographer sat at a picnic table, smoking his pipe and reviewing footage from the day before. Judging from the way he kept shaking his head, a lot was going to end up on the cutting room floor. If they even used film anymore.

"Mr. Mueller?" I asked.

He muttered something in German, then looked up.

"Do I know you?"

"Carolyn Neville and Stephen Ames. From New York. On behalf of the author."

Leaning back, he took the pipe from his mouth. "You're here to tell me how to take pictures, is that it?"

I forced a little laugh, trying to sound merry or something. I was out of practice, not to mention the fact that, deep down, I consider merriment to be an offense against nature.

"No, of course not. Just have a few questions about our illustrious director."

He nodded. "Larry is a complicated man."

"In what way?"

"The two of us have never had an argument. But that is only because I've never started one."

"Why do you keep working with him?"

He switched off the camera's monitor. "We share an artistic vision. I suppose that sounds ridiculous if you've seen some of our collaborations. Compared with *Zombies from the Nether Regions*, this one is *Citizen Kane*."

Stephen stepped up. "Hey, I saw that zombie flick. Don't sell yourself short, man."

Ansel looked at him in disbelief. Or pity.

"Please forgive my colleague. He's sustained several blows to the head."

The cameraman tapped a finger on the table. "Larry is his own worst enemy. Nearly killed himself with cocaine, you see."

"So we've heard. This may sound like an odd question, but can you think of any reason Mr. Shapiro might have to sabotage the production? Considering the incidents we've had."

"With the gun?"

"There were a few other things, too. Off the set."

He shrugged. "All I know is that he certainly sabotages himself. And for what it's worth, he is no fan of Oskar Pulaski. At any rate, you'll have to ask Larry."

"He's our next stop."

"Good luck with that." He put the pipe back between his teeth, muttered something else Teutonic, and turned back to something he was better at than conversation.

* * *

Larry Shapiro was sitting cross-legged under a tree, eyes closed, palms pressed together. His baseball cap was pulled low over his forehead.

"I think he's meditating," Stephen whispered.

"Maybe this is a bad time," I said.

The director's eyes popped open. "How could this be a bad time?" he cried. "I finally reached a *samadhi* state. Do you have an idea how difficult that is when you're sober?"

"Sorry," I said.

Stephen put his hands in his pockets. "You're doing yoga, right?"

"Not just any yoga. *Goat* yoga."

"Didn't know there was such a thing," I admitted.

With a grunt Shapiro worked his way to a crouch, then stood shakily. "Would be better if I had an actual goat."

"We were just talking with Mr. Mueller," I said.

"About me?"

"Well, yes."

"What did he say?"

"He wished us good luck."

Leaning against a tree, the director nodded. "Knowing Ansel, that's not all he said. But never mind."

"We've been asking people if they have a theory about who's behind the accidents."

"What accidents?"

"The shooting. And somebody trying to leave tire tracks on my neck."

"The second one doesn't sound accidental to me."

"You've got to admit some pretty strange things have been going on."

He pushed the cap up on his head and sighed. "Bad karma."

"The universe getting back at someone," Stephen said.

"So who's it getting back at?" I asked.

Shapiro looked around as if to make sure he couldn't be overheard. "Oskar."

"You think he deserves it?"

"No comment."

"You keep working with him. Why?"

"Nobody else will work with me. In the eighties I got a reputation for sending my income up my nose. Insurance companies don't like drug addicts. But look what happened to Robert Downey Junior. Not fair, but who said life is?"

I raised an eyebrow. "I'm surprised you're telling us this."

"Old news. Everybody knows about it." He paused. "Oskar employs me because he wants cheap."

"Doesn't cutting corners hurt the cast and crew?"

He shrugged. "I'm delegating that stuff to the prop guy and the stuntman. Now, if you'll excuse me, I'll try to reach *samadhi* again."

Settling down in the dry weeds, he crossed his legs and pushed his palms together. "My kingdom for a goat," he murmured. Closing his eyes, he bowed his head.

We turned to go. A breeze came up—just enough to rustle the leaves overhead.

Suddenly there was a loud *CRRRRAAAACK* behind us.

I whirled just in time to see a tree branch, thick as an elephant's thigh, come crashing to the ground. It missed Shapiro's head by inches.

Screaming, he rolled into the brush.

We jumped back, almost losing our balance.

The director lay there, panting. "You said something about accidents."

"Yeah," Stephen said.

"Maybe it's not you they're out to get."

CHAPTER 19

AT THE SOUND OF LARRY'S SCREAM, EVERYONE CAME RUNNING. Axel Testaverde led the pack, followed by Leilani.

Stephen knelt down and examined the tree trunk. "Doesn't look like anybody sawed it off. If I didn't know better, I'd say it was struck by lightning."

"Maybe it's just old," the prop guy muttered.

I took out my phone. "Should I call for an ambulance?"

The director managed to raise himself to a sitting position. "Too expensive," he groaned.

Leilani stepped forward. "Maybe it's Maui."

"The island in Hawaii?" I asked.

She shook her head. "He's a trickster figure in Samoan tradition. I grew up hearing about him."

Stephen stood up, looking excited. "Like Loki in the *Avengers*. Tom Hiddleston's greatest role, if you ask me."

"The Norse god of mischief," I said. "Or fire. Or war. Depending on which anthropologist you're talking to."

Axel turned to his girlfriend, looking disgusted. "You don't take that crap seriously, do you?"

She looked down at the dry weeds. "I guess not."

"Then why bring it up? God, you are so ridiculous sometimes."

Larry covered his eyes with his hands, then felt the top of his head. "I swear somebody's trying to kill me."

Suddenly, I heard a car approaching behind me. "Oskar," somebody said.

The black Mercedes rolled to a halt 10 feet from the picnic table, covered with dust. The producer emerged in his usual matching outfit, ready to pounce.

"What is it this time, Larry? Directing under the influence?"

Axel folded his arms across his chest. "Thinks the world is out to get him."

"Perhaps it is," Oskar said. "Listen, all of you. I don't pay you to stand around. We have a crucial scene to shoot today, and a fairly complicated stunt. We can only afford to do it once. So get to work."

He marched off to join the cameraman.

I reached out a hand to the director. "Help you up?"

Wincing, he let me pull him to his feet.

"The Emperor of Empathy," I said.

"The Prince of Darkness," he replied.

* * *

Stephen and I were slumped in our usual chairs, wondering why we were still here, when I felt hands on my shoulders.

"Lady, if you'd turn around you'd be a sight for sore eyes."

Being tired of turning around and whirling and pivoting, and knowing who it was, I didn't bother.

"Hi, Jim."

He came around in front of me and got down on his haunches. His vest, jeans, and suspenders matched those I'd seen on the actor playing Harlan Winchester. "You guys look like I did when a bull threw me at the feet of Larry Mahan," he said.

"Who's Larry Mahan?" Stephen asked, not opening his eyes.

"Rodeo reference. Never mind."

I sat up in my chair. "According to Oskar Pulaski, there's a big stunt planned today."

"Depends on how you define 'big.'"

"Is it dangerous?"

He got off his haunches and sat in the chair next to me. "Anything's dangerous if you're not careful. My uncle once busted his shoulder while combing his hair."

Stephen snorted. "That's impossible."

Jim shrugged. "You ain't seen his hair. Like steel wool. And he'd been drinking."

He squinted toward the picnic table. "Is it me, or has our director developed a limp?"

"Had a run-in with a tree," I said.

"Oh." He seemed content to leave it there, having worked with Larry Shapiro before.

I leaned forward. "Now, about this stunt. Are you in it?"

"Yup."

"What are you supposed to do?"

He pulled a slip of paper from his pocket. "Here's a diagram."

I looked it over. Penciled arrows. Numbers. Tiny sketch of a car. I had no idea what it meant.

"This is the scene where young Harlan Winchester borrows Daddy's Ford Model A—one of the first automobiles in the county—to meet a certain young lady. At a fishing hole."

Stephen raised an eyebrow. "To do what?"

"Fish, I guess."

Stephen shook his head. "Are you sure this is based on a

true story?"

"Not everybody has your taste for cheap thrills," I said.

Jim stuck the paper back in his pocket. "Anyway, Harlan has no license. Fishing, maybe, but not driving. Doesn't know the first thing about it. Which he proceeds to prove beyond a shadow of a doubt."

"Takes place in the evening," he continued, examining the sky. "Hope Mr. Mueller can make it look darker. So the car picks up speed going down the mountain road."

Shading his eyes with a hand, Stephen surveyed the landscape. "What mountain?"

Jim stood up and pointed. "It's more of a hill. They can shoot it to look steeper, maybe crank up the speed a little. See the bridge?"

I squinted. Two lanes wide, about 50 feet long. "Looks pretty old."

"Built during the Depression by the WPA. But it's sound. County road. The car picks up speed. Suddenly Harlan realizes the brakes are gone."

"Aha!" Stephen cried. "Somebody cut the brake lines, right?"

"Don't think so," Jim said. "This ain't a mystery. Cars just weren't too dependable in those days. Anyhow, the vehicle goes over the side of the bridge and crashes into the creek."

"So that's why they have to get it on film the first time," Stephen said.

"I don't like the sound of it," I said, fidgeting. "Everything's going wrong around here. You missed Larry getting hit by a tree. What if you get hurt?"

He gave a little laugh. "Carolyn, this ain't James Bond. I'm not drivin' on two wheels or into a helicopter. Don't worry."

He looked at me, waiting for a sign that I was reassured. I couldn't muster one.

"Look. I know Oskar's cutting corners, but there's still

some safety precautions. The old car's got a roll cage. I've got extra padding and seat belts. Body's heavily reinforced with steel."

"Yours?" I asked nervously.

He smiled. "No. A ramp gets me over the side of the bridge, and there's a guy named Tony to get me out of the water. Simple, right?"

"Algebra is simple. This is madness."

Stephen folded his arms. "You know, this reminds me of how Vic Morrow died during the filming of *The Twilight Zone*. The movie, not the series."

I cringed.

"His character was helping two kids escape a helicopter. They blew up some explosives too close, and the helicopter went out of control. Morrow tried to rescue one of the kids but the thing crashed."

"My God," I said.

"I'll leave out the part about how two of them got their heads cut off by—"

"Yeah, leave that part out," Jim said, giving him a *Shut up, moron* look.

I looked up at the clouds. "I suppose you know what you're doing."

"That's what they pay me for."

He gave me a little kiss on the cheek. "Pray if you want to. But it'll work out, believe me."

He winked, started down the road toward the ancient Ford, and gave me a thumbs-up.

* * *

The cinematographer put down his pipe and wheeled the camera over.

"Stopping it down?" Stephen asked, trying to look knowledgeable.

"I beg your pardon?"

"To make it look darker."

Ansel rolled his eyes. "What would I do without your advice?"

Stephen grinned. "Glad to help."

The director came over, started to wave his arms, then grimaced with pain and dropped them to his sides. "Final camera check. Sound. Places, everybody!"

Leilani pulled out her phone. "Tony, you okay in the water?"

I couldn't hear his reply. The clapboard clapped. I prayed.

Jim bent down in front of the Model A and started cranking. The ignition made a whirring sound that revved faster and faster until the old engine caught. Finally he jumped into the driver's seat and slammed the door.

"Action!" Larry shouted.

The car crawled down the road. The cameraman kept it in focus and held it for about a minute.

"Cut," the director said. "Got it?"

"No problem."

"Everybody to the bridge." The car idled as the multitude trudged a dusty quarter mile.

Leilani waved her clipboard. "New setup."

I resisted the urge to run to the car. Jim hopped out just long enough to wave at me again, then got back in.

Suddenly the engine died. With a grunt, he got out and churned it back to life.

At last everything was ready. "Remember, people, we can't do this twice!" Oskar yelled.

Larry clapped his hands. "And . . . action!"

I prayed a second time.

Jim released the brake. The old automobile chugged forward. The guy in the water ducked down.

Ansel, positioned under a tree near the bridge, gave the OK sign.

The car rolled down the road, gathering speed. Five, ten, fifteen miles per hour.

With a *BANG* it backfired, but kept going. Twenty, twenty-five miles per hour.

Jim was nearing the ramp.

The director swore. "Is that the right angle? Seems like . . ."

I swallowed.

"He's not going to make it," Larry said.

Oskar cursed.

The auto rumbled onto the bridge. Jim hit the ramp fast, maybe too fast.

The director turned to Leilani. "Tell him to abort."

"Too late," she said.

The car flew into the air, narrowly clearing the rail, and sailed over the side. My heart was in my throat.

With a splash like the crash of an ocean wave, the Model A hit the water and started to sink.

Larry bit his lip. "Tell Tony to get him out of there."

"We have the shot," Ansel said.

The guy in the water waded toward the car, but the door opened before he could reach it. Out climbed Jim, pumping his fist in victory beneath the bridge's edge.

"Thank God," I whispered.

"Wait a minute," Stephen said. "There's something—"

A creaking sound. The part of the bridge supporting the ramp crumbled, the whole span swaying for a second.

No.

Jim looked up and tried to leap away.

Tony dove in the opposite direction.

Cracking beams and groaning steel plummeted into the water as Jim disappeared.

CHAPTER 20

As we walked through the front door of Cedars-Sinai Medical Center, Stephen shivered despite the heat.

"Brings back wonderful memories," he muttered.

I felt dizzy, stuck in a bad dream. The paramedics had looked grim when they examined Jim and lifted him into the ambulance. One shook his head at the other as if it were all over.

The two of us sat in the waiting area. "I don't know who to ask about his condition," I said.

Stephen nodded toward a lady at a desk, probably a volunteer. "Try her."

Still feeling wobbly, I headed in her direction. Sixtyish, with silver hair and thick glasses, she gave me a sympathetic smile.

"I'm looking for a patient, Jim Oakley," I said.

She picked up the phone. "I'll see what I can find out."

On my way back I paused for a cup of free coffee. There was a little pack of four powdered mini-doughnuts in the vending machine, which I liberated.

"For me?" Stephen asked when I sat down.

"You can have half. Get your own coffee."

"Does the lady know anything?"

"I'm sure she does, but not about Jim. Yet."

When he'd poured his coffee, we sat there sipping and chewing and staring at the phone. Finally I picked up mine.

"Marvin? This is Carolyn."

"Hey, Cranberry. Solved the case yet?"

"Far from it. We're at the hospital."

"Somebody else hurt?"

"The stuntman. Jim Oakley." I wanted to tell him how I felt about Jim, but this wasn't the time. Especially when Stephen was three feet away.

"Looks bad," I said. "Guess I just want you to pray."

"Jim's not just a minor acquaintance, is he?"

I hesitated. "What makes you say that?"

"You wouldn't ask me to pray for somebody you didn't really care about."

"Let's just say he's . . . special. And he's a believer."

"Well, thank God for that. I sometimes wonder about your choice of men."

I closed my eyes. "Marvin, I don't need that right now."

"Sorry, honey. I'll ask my lovely bride to pray, too."

"Thanks." I hung up.

"These doughnuts aren't bad," Stephen said, licking the sugar from his fingers.

The volunteer was talking with two teenage guys who wore football jerseys. Her phone wasn't ringing.

"What if he doesn't make it?" I wondered aloud.

He turned toward me, looking surprised. "I thought you guys didn't worry about things like that."

"What guys?"

"Christian guys. You know where you're going, right?"

"Yes, but . . . we're not always ready to go there."

He finished his coffee. "You've really got it for Jim, don't you?"

I started to protest, but my throat was suddenly tight. I swallowed.

"Sorry," he whispered. "Didn't mean to—"

A middle-aged, red-bearded doctor in blue scrubs wandered into the waiting room. After looking around, he bent to speak with the lady at the desk. She nodded at us.

He wended his way around the other visitors. "You folks here for Mr. Oakley?"

I sat up straight, trying not to show my panic. "Yes."

He sat down across from us and leaned forward. "Family or friends?"

"Friends."

He scratched his cheek, thinking. "Does Mr. Oakley have family in the area?"

I shook my head. "In Texas, maybe."

"Normally I wouldn't be able to tell you anything about his condition because of the Health Insurance Portability and Accountability Act."

"HIPAA," I said.

"But he has extensive internal injuries. I understand a bridge collapsed on him."

I nodded.

"He's sedated in intensive care. There's a piece of rebar in his chest, near the heart."

"Rebar?"

Using his fingers, he measured six inches of air. "About this long. A piece of steel, about the thickness of a pencil. Slightly bent, rusty."

I felt a twinge of pain in my own chest.

The doctor put his hands on his thighs. "I'll be honest with you. Surgery will be risky. He's on heavy antibiotics, but there was nothing clean about that water—or the rebar, of course. We'll do everything we can to prevent sepsis."

"An out-of-control infection," I said, wishing my vocabulary were more limited. "When will the operation be?"

"It's scheduled for tomorrow morning, nine o'clock. I'll be doing it myself. If I were you, I'd go home and come back in the morning. For the time being, he's stable."

He patted my arm and walked down the hall.

Stephen lowered his head. "Sorry. Looks like he's in good hands, though, don't you think? Between the doc and all that praying, his chances must be pretty good."

"Sure," I said.

What else could I say?

* * *

Back at the motel I flopped into a chair, picked up the TV remote, and for a moment couldn't remember how the thing worked.

Sepsis. I knew how *that* worked. Sort of.

Finally I figured out the buttons and cycled through the channels. The Oasis Gardens Motel couldn't afford any interesting ones, so I chose the only one that came in clearly. It was one of those nostalgia stations that ran shows like *Perry Mason*, *The Love Boat*, and *Sergeant Bilko*. I only watched them in an emergency, like when that little red Netflix bar wouldn't budge.

The Three Stooges was on. I'd never understood their appeal but then I'd never liked polio either. I didn't have the energy to turn the set off, so I just closed my eyes and tolerated the sounds of Moe hitting Curly and the *wa-wa* sounds of forced hilarity.

After the seventh or eighth *wa-wa*, I opened my eyes. It had helped a little to talk with Marvin, but not much. Mikki couldn't do anything about Jim's predicament either, but at least she knew better than to bring up my love life in the middle of a medical crisis.

I switched off the remote and switched on my phone. Remembering the time-zone difference, I hesitated. No, she'd be awake. She and I had once stayed up until midnight at what was supposed to be a Christian nightclub but closed after two months due to lack of alcohol.

She answered right away. I, on the other hand, found myself so choked up I couldn't speak.

"Carolyn, what is it?"

I put my phone under my armpit while I cleared my throat repeatedly. Finally I blinked the tears away and put the phone to my ear. It smelled like deodorant.

"Mikki, can you pray with me?"

"About what?"

I explained about Jim.

"Oh, honey, I'm sorry. You find a guy, and now this."

"So will you pray?"

"Sure."

There was a long pause. We'd never actually done this before.

It was her turn to clear her throat. "Dear God, please help Carolyn. And . . . what's his name?"

"Jim Oakley."

"Jim. He's in the hospital, which I guess You know, and he's in pretty bad shape. We know You can do anything, like when You made the entire universe in six days."

I resisted the urge to question her timing, not being quite so certain about the age of the earth.

Another long pause. "I'm tapped out," she said sheepishly. "Any suggestions?"

"No. You've been a big help." It wasn't a lie, not exactly.

"Should have done better."

"You did fine."

"Well, I'll say good-bye. Let me know if he gets better. I mean, *when* he does."

"Thanks," I said, and hung up.

Ten minutes later I crawled into bed, snapped off the light, and tried to sleep. I wanted to call the hospital, but I wasn't family.

I sat up and turned on the TV again. The Three Stooges were gone. Some movie from the seventies was starting. *Make Room for Marty.* I didn't recognize any of the actors in the opening credits.

Except the last one. *And introducing . . . Jackson Dunn.*

I couldn't believe it. He'd been a child actor?

I settled back against the pillow, not really wanting to watch but hoping it would lull me to sleep.

Twenty minutes passed before little Jackson made it onscreen. He looked about five or six, with huge eyes and tousled brown hair and teeth the size of PEZ candies.

The plot was practically nonexistent—something about two socialites adopting a charming but mischievous kid from the Bronx. I dozed off for about 45 minutes in the middle, then roused myself for the unexciting conclusion and closing credits.

Squinting at the small type, I saw that Dancing Girl #3 had been played by a woman whose last name was also Dunn. Beverly.

Blinking, I picked up my phone and went to the IMDb website.

Beverly Dunn was Jackson's mother.

The producer? Oskar Pulaski.

I recalled the way Dunn had looked at him. But why?

Turning off the set, I stared into the darkness.

* * *

Next morning we were back at the hospital. I probably looked like a patient, having slept a total of 45 minutes.

Stephen looked fine, of course, having found another source of coffee and powdered doughnuts he was unwilling to share. To be fair, though, he was somber as a Supreme Court justice when we sat down.

Last night's volunteer had been replaced by a huge, blue teddy bear with a heart on its belly.

"That's helpful," I muttered.

The phone rang. I stumbled over and picked it up.

"Is this the cafeteria?" asked a female voice.

"No," I said, and set the receiver down with a laudable degree of gentleness.

We'd checked in at the nurse's station, where a plumper version of Florence Nightingale with a butterfly tattoo on her forearm said we'd have to get a doctor's okay to visit Jim.

"Cool bear," Stephen said when I retook my seat.

I was about to say something snide about stuffed animals when a very medical-looking fellow in a white lab coat and jeans strode toward us. There was a laptop under his arm. "Here to see Mr. Oakley? The ones who were here last night?"

I stood up. "Yes."

He nodded. "You can do that, but I have to warn you— he's unresponsive."

"Which means?"

"He's in a deep sleep. His body's fighting the infection. Room 303."

When we got there, a nurse was hanging a bag of something yellowish on the IV pole. Jim's face was ashen. The only sign he was still alive was the zigzag trail on the screen of his monitor.

"Ten minutes, okay?" she said. "He's not exactly ready for conversation."

I nodded. She padded out in her bright pink sneakers.

Stephen took out his phone and poked it for a while. "Ouch," he whispered as if observing a one-sided prizefight.

"Here's a dude who was impaled by a large metal object. Four years ago in North Carolina. Fell on his own Civil War sword during one of those reenactments. Entered the right thorax. That's the—"

"Chest. I know." I wanted to roll up a newspaper and hit him with it.

"Poor guy was dead in three hours. Another guy took an arrow in the back. At an archery contest in England."

I started looking around for a spare magazine. "Stephen—"

"He survived. Probably helped that he was wearing chain mail. That's—"

"What knights wore." I shook my head. "No more inspiring stories, all right?"

He shrugged. "Just thought you'd like to know."

He kept searching the Internet, presumably for the Ripley's Believe It or Not Museum. I just stared at Jim's face, wishing I could compose a better prayer than *Help*.

At first I thought I was imagining it, but he did it twice. His eyelids fluttered.

But then they stopped, and he sank back into sleep.

"I saw his eyes move," I said.

Stephen looked up, then put down his phone. With a grunt he got up and took Jim's pulse at the wrist with two fingers.

"Not dead yet," he said, then sat down.

I spotted a copy of *WebMD* magazine on a counter across the room, grabbed it, and rolled it up. It worked great.

"Jeez," Stephen cried, nursing the spot where I'd administered justice.

"Sorry," I said, not meaning it.

The nurse padded back in. "Time's up."

Sighing, I took a last look and moved toward the door.

"We'll let you know if things change," she said.

We got all the way back to the car without speaking. I pressed the remote and listened to the click.

"Back to work," I said.

"Hey, he's still alive. Could be worse, right?"

"Yeah." I left out the *It will be any time now* part.

CHAPTER 21

BACK ON THE SET, NOBODY WAS SMILING. COME TO THINK OF it, though, that wasn't so unusual.

I took it upon myself to make an announcement. The Winchester home's interior was set up; I dragged a kitchen chair center stage, stepped on it, and tried not to lose my balance.

The director's bullhorn lay on the table. Stephen snitched it and handed it to me.

I put it close to my lips and flipped the switch. "Excuse me!" I said.

All heads turned in my direction. I checked the horn for a volume control, wishing I could turn it down enough to avoid sounding like Charlton Heston in *The Ten Commandments*. No such luck.

"I know most of us are concerned about Jim Oakley. We've visited him twice, and the news isn't good. A piece of metal from the bridge went into his chest, near his heart."

There was a chorus of grimaces, groans, and *eeeeews*. Leilani and the makeup lady shook their heads.

"He's unconscious, fighting an infection," I continued. "They haven't quite figured out how to do surgery."

Larry Shapiro held out his hand for the bullhorn. I gave it to him.

"A moment of silence, everybody."

I got down from my perch and bowed my head, then wondered whether others were doing the same. The only sound was a distant radio playing "Fat Bottomed Girls" by Queen.

"That's long enough," declared an imperious voice after about 30 seconds. I opened my eyes. Oskar didn't need the bullhorn.

"I'm sure Tim would want us to keep going," he said.

"*Jim,*" Leilani whispered.

"Exactly. Mr. Oakley was—is—a consummate professional. Let him be our North Star."

Nobody said anything. Everybody went back to work.

"Carolyn," said a voice behind me. Turning, I faced Jackson Dunn. The paper towel protecting his costume from his makeup was still around his neck.

"Terrible thing," he said. "So good that you visited him. Hospitals make me . . . uneasy."

Suddenly I remembered the movie I'd watched at the motel. "I just saw *Make Room for Marty.*"

"You're kidding. That was, what, forty years ago?"

"It was on TV. I couldn't sleep."

"Well, that film was a cure for insomnia." He shook his head. "God, I was awful in that. They wanted me to be the next Jackie Cooper, but I lacked his subtlety."

"I noticed that your mother was in it. Beverly."

He sighed. "It was my first picture, and one of her last."

"And Oskar was the producer."

He looked at the floor. "Yes."

"I hope you don't mind my asking, but what became of your mom?"

"My mother was the finest woman I've ever known. But so fragile. She was mishandled, and she broke."

"What do you—"

"Actors, hit your marks!" the director called through the bullhorn.

Jackson shook himself slightly, as if coming out of a trance. "Sorry. Gotta go." The trademark Tom Hanks smile returned as he pulled out the paper towel and tossed it in a wastebasket near the camera.

"Let's focus, people," the director said.

I joined Stephen as he walked back to our seats.

"So much for moments of silence," he said.

"I was just talking to Jackson Dunn."

"Oh? About what?"

"His mother. Something weird going on there."

"How so?"

"Hollywood did something to her."

"Probably does that to everybody."

We sat, and the scene played out. Oskar sat behind the camera in a folding chair, peering at the actors like Caesar watching a pair of gladiators.

What had made him so unfeeling, and Jackson so wounded?

I thought of Jim, barely breathing.

Caring made you hurt.

* * *

The makeup lady tapped Stephen on the shoulder. "You're up," she said.

His eyes widened. "I am?"

She nodded. "Scene forty-two."

"God, I forgot."

"Not my problem. Go down the hall and get in the chair. They'll want you in about fifteen minutes."

He stood up, unsteady.

"You'll be swell," I said. "You'll be great. Gonna have the whole world on a plate."

"Ethel Merman."

"You should hear my Amy Poehler."

Checking her watch, the makeup lady shook her head. "I hope Wardrobe can get him suited up in time. Patience isn't one of Larry's virtues."

When Stephen returned, he looked positively greasy. "They ran out of powder," he mumbled. The paper towel was around his neck, protecting his simple hillbilly outfit.

"My brain's not working," he said. "Can you run lines with me?"

"Got a script?"

"I'll get one from Leilani."

Before he could reach her, though, the director snapped on the bullhorn. "Scene forty-two. Places, people." He pulled off his cap and wiped his forehead with the back of his hand. Something told me this wasn't the time for Stephen to screw up.

Clapboard.

Larry took a swig from a water bottle and pulled his cap on.

"Kid, take the towel off."

Stephen did so, hastily.

The cameraman turned to the director. "He looks awfully shiny."

The makeup lady shrugged. "We ran out of powder."

"Forget it," Larry said. "Short scene, Ansel. Work around it."

He wearily raised the bullhorn. "Action."

Stephen entered, carrying a wooden bucket. He was meeting a girl who picked fake daisies from a bogus hillside.

"Howdy, Amy," he said, sweating like a matador with no cape.

She smiled. "How'd you know I'd be here?"

He froze, blinking.

Leilani flipped through her script.

"I can follow you like a hummingbird to sugar water," she whispered.

He cleared his throat. "I can follow you like a waterboard—"

The director threw down his cap. "Oh, for God's sake."

"I got this," Stephen said. "Really."

Clapboard. "Take two."

"I can follow you like a hummingbird to sugar water," Stephen declared.

"Is that 'cause you're sweet on me?" the actress asked.

"You're the sweet one, Amy. That's why I . . ."

He blanked out again.

"That's why I came to ask you to the square dance," Leilani said.

"Cut!" Larry cried. "I swear you people are trying to destroy my film."

Stephen raised his hands in surrender. "No more mistakes. I promise."

"Last chance, kid."

The clapboard clacked once more.

"Action."

"That's why I came to ask you to the square dance. Unless Joey Hubbard got here first."

He was sweating so much now I feared his whole face might slide off.

"What do you say, Amy? It's not like you gotta be my girl or anything. Not that I'd mind that."

The young lady stood up, smiled, and arranged her flowers. "See you Saturday night."

"You've made me the happiest guy in Winchester County." He produced a smile that was 10 percent inspiration and 90 percent perspiration.

"And . . . cut!"

"You nailed it!" Leilani said.

The director cleared his throat. "You're fired," he said. "Get off my set."

Stephen sagged. "But I thought—"

"I can't deal with amateurs." He glanced at the cameraman. "I want him edited out of the picture. It's too long, anyway."

Ansel sighed.

Shapiro lifted the bullhorn. "Take five, everybody."

Leilani put her hand on Stephen's shoulder. "Sorry. You were good." She looked around as if to make sure Axel was somewhere else.

"Can somebody fix the freaking air conditioner?" the director yelled.

Eyes glazed, Stephen found his paper towel and started wiping. I could see stains under his armpits.

It had been a short, though not so happy, career.

* * *

Stephen took an Uber back to the motel. I hadn't seen him so despondent since the day *Game of Thrones* was canceled.

He would have liked lunch, though. The Lunchables had something distantly related to nachos in them.

I passed. So did Jackson Dunn. I invited him to join me down the street at a little bistro with outdoor seating. The sun was bright but not infernal as we sat down and studied the menu.

"Full disclosure," I said. "I wanted to follow through on my question about your mother."

"We *were* interrupted, weren't we? Fair enough."

The waiter came by, and I ordered a salad. Jackson went for sushi.

I sipped my ice water. "So, what happened?"

He put his elbows on the table and leaned forward. "She suffered a great deal because the industry chews people up and spits them out."

"Yes, I think we established that."

"She might have become a star if she'd been tough enough. But she was too gentle for that."

"Single mom?"

"My father left when I was six. I remember a lot of yelling before he did. She showed me a picture of him once. Looked like a boxer. I'm sure he must have hit her, though I didn't see him do it."

"Sounds like she attracted abusive men."

"Unfortunately, yes."

"More than one?"

He nodded.

"Long story short. Later, when I was working steadily and she hadn't had a part in twenty years, she was afraid of everything. Couldn't leave the house I bought her. Called me several times a day, claiming somebody was trying to break in or complaining about the neighbor's dog."

He paused. "She got cancer. Eventually she was in hospice. She died at home—alone, since I was stuck in traffic when the nurse called."

A muscle in his jaw contracted. "Three years ago. I'll never forgive myself for not being there."

Not knowing what to say, I listened to the clink of glasses and silverware from other tables.

Finally the waiter brought our food. "Not to change the

subject," I said, "but have you got a theory about what's causing all the 'accidents' on this project?"

He picked up a piece of sushi that looked more decorative than edible. "Human error," he replied.

"Which human?"

He popped the fish in his mouth and chewed slowly. "Couldn't say. But I'd encourage you not to ask too many questions. If somebody's behind all this, he or she won't hesitate to find a way to stop you."

"That's why I'm asking so many questions. He or she's getting a little too close."

He checked his watch. "Wish I could be more helpful, but murder's a bit out of my league. I've never even *played* a policeman."

I moved the salad around on my plate with my fork. "I'm getting tired of playing detective."

"Then don't. Let the professionals do their job."

"They haven't been very interested."

"After what's happened to Mr. Oakley, perhaps they'll pay attention."

He leaned back in his chair, that charming smile spreading across his face. "You deserve a break. Let's talk about something else. Tell me what it's like to be . . . an editor, is it?"

"Too boring."

"Nonsense."

I sighed. It would be nice to set all this aside, take a deep breath, and forget the last couple of weeks.

So I pretended to.

CHAPTER 22

NEXT MORNING I MET STEPHEN IN THE MOTEL LOBBY. "I've got to tell everybody about Jim," I said. "Or at least his church. And his family."

"Better you than me," Stephen said.

"Let's start with the church. Maybe they'll know about his next of kin."

He made a face. "Church? I haven't been in one since—"

I held the door open for him. "Quit whining. Maybe you'll learn something."

The pastor's office was surprisingly small. There was nothing on the walls, either, save for a cross made of two rough cedar fenceposts.

"Please, sit down." The chairs were more or less normal. Unfortunately, I couldn't remember the minister's name and was too embarrassed to ask. I searched the desk for a clue, but in vain.

"You say you're here about Jim Oakley?"

I nodded. Stephen looked around the room, probably for a way of escape.

"He's been seriously injured."

The pastor raised an eyebrow. "Is he in the hospital?"

I gave him the whole story. He kept shaking his head.

When I finished, he rolled back from the desk and put up his Nike-clad feet. "I can't say I know Jim all that well. Came to a couple of our men's retreats. Seems to me he has a mother in Texas but no other family to speak of."

"I don't suppose you have any contact information for her," I said.

"No, I'm afraid not." He paused. "So the doctors aren't telling what his chances are?"

"They really don't seem to know."

He put his feet back down. "I'll visit him as soon as I can. In the meantime, would you mind if I pray for him—and you?"

"Not at all."

He closed his eyes. It was a good prayer. Didn't sound canned. Wasn't too long. When he was done, I blinked back tears.

He turned to Stephen, who looked like a deer in the headlights.

"How can I pray for *you?*"

Stephen held up his hands. "No need, Reverend. I'm good."

The pastor smiled. "I suspect you think prayer would be a waste of time."

"Nothing personal," Stephen said.

"Here's my business card. Anything I can do for you, let me know."

Stephen stuck it in his pocket. "Right."

As soon as we got through the church door, Stephen found a garbage can and pulled out the card. I snatched it before he could toss it.

"Real classy," I said.

He shrugged. "Why would I keep it?"

I examined the card. "So *that's* his name. Byron Campbell. It was driving me crazy."

"Not as crazy as it was driving me."

"Want to go back to the motel? Maybe a shower will wash off those religious cooties."

"I've got some hand sanitizer in the glove compartment."

"As atheists go, you're a big sissy."

"*Now* who's classy?"

"This is one of the dumbest conversations I've ever had," I said.

But at least, for the moment, it kept my mind off Jim.

* * *

I reached for the car door. "We need to track down Jim's mom."

Stephen slid in on the passenger side. "Should be easy. A woman named Oakley who lives somewhere in Texas. Can't be more than a thousand of them."

"Must be a way to narrow it down."

"Do you know how old she is?"

"No."

"What she looks like?"

I started the car. "I envision her as plump, gray-haired, a whiz in the kitchen, but too tough to wear an apron."

"First name?"

"I'd like to say Annie, but that's too obvious."

He pulled out his phone. "Ever hear of the ARRA?"

"You mean AARP?"

"Nope. American Rodeo Riders Association."

I shook my head.

He poked at his phone. "Sort of like a cowboys' union, but not exactly. They promote rodeo and try to fend off all the people who think it's animal abuse."

"Like you."

"Yeah, but it's not as bad as blinding chimpanzees to test eye shadow. Anyway, rodeo used to be Jim's occupation, right?"

"Right."

"Chances are pretty good he is, or has been, a member." After a lot more poking, he found something and smiled. "Actually, he's still enrolled. That doesn't tell us anything about his mom, but there's one other thing I can try."

I waited.

"Ah. The ARRA has associate memberships, too. For fans and supporters and family members and PETA spies." He paused, scrolling. "Thirteen Oakleys. Eleven male. One Jimena, one Darlene."

"I'm guessing Darlene."

"No photos here. But she lives in Houston. I can take it from there."

By the time we got back to the set, Stephen had found a phone number. Stagehands were making a racket, dragging a huge cardboard box of something clattery out of the spotlight, so I found a corner and placed a call.

A woman answered. "Yes?"

Texas drawl, sure. But not too tough to wear an apron.

"Mrs. Oakley, my name's Carolyn Neville. I'm a friend of Jim."

"Is he all right?"

"I . . . there's . . . been an accident."

One, or maybe both of us, took a deep breath.

"What's he broken this time?"

"I'm afraid it's worse than that."

"Lord, I knew this would happen. Just didn't know when."

"He's in the hospital, Darlene. It's very serious. The doctors are doing all they can." I gave her the details, saying as little about the rusty rebar as possible.

There was silence. Finally she said, "I need to sit down, catch my breath."

"Sure."

"Should I come and see him?"

"Um . . . that's up to you." I paused. "If it were me, I would."

"I'll see whether I can get a flight. I'm not sure I can afford it, but I'll try."

"I guess you'd go from Houston to Los Angeles." I paused. "Last-minute trips are expensive. Maybe I can help you out."

"My dear, I can't ask you to do that."

"You didn't. My idea. Call me back when you find out what's available, okay?"

"I will," she said, voice trembling, and hung up.

Stephen's eyes were wide. "You're paying for this?"

I sank back in the chair, feeling my head start to ache. "Maybe she reminds me of my mom. People will do anything for their mothers, won't they?"

He nodded. "Look at Norman Bates in *Psycho* and *Bates Motel*."

I stared at him, too tired to look for another magazine to hit him with.

* * *

The huge cardboard box turned out to contain pieces of Ford Model A. The director was trying to write them into the script somehow. He and Oskar spent most of the afternoon arguing. I just watched, numb.

"Wish I had my laptop," Stephen said. "Seeing as how I've been unjustly terminated, I think it's time to work on my screenplay."

"What screenplay?"

"My great movie idea, remember? *Watsons*. About all the actors who've played Sherlock's sidekick."

"I thought we agreed that wasn't going to work."

"Maybe you and Mikki agreed, but I didn't."

I took a small pad from my purse. "Got a pen?"

"No."

I found one. "Knock yourself out. You're a regular Dalton Trumbo."

He shook his head. "More of a John Mulaney."

"Who's that?"

"Never mind."

The *1812 Overture* beckoned from my pocket. I put the phone to my ear.

"Ms. Neville?"

"Yes."

"This is Breonna, Mr. Oakley's nurse at Cedars-Sinai Medical Center. I'm afraid he's taken a turn for the worse."

I swallowed. "Be right there."

Stephen looked up from the pad. "Problem?"

"It's Jim. You coming with me?"

"Yeah, of course."

If it was time to say goodbye, I wasn't ready.

CHAPTER 23

AT THE HOSPITAL WE FOUND OUR USUAL SPOT IN THE WAITING room. A portly man who looked a lot like Santa in brown suede sat at the volunteer desk. A weary mom tried to distract her crying baby by waving an empty bedpan.

Collapsing into my seat, I closed my eyes. "Wake me if you see a doctor."

Stephen took out his phone. "Will do." I could hear the startup sounds of some video game.

Next thing I knew he was tapping me on the shoulder. I could feel a trickle of drool oozing from the corner of my mouth. Must have fallen asleep.

Blinking, I saw a tall, blonde woman in a white coat whose own eyelids were at half-mast. She bent slightly in my direction. "You're here for Jim Oakley?"

I nodded, still unsure what you were supposed to say under the circumstances.

"I'm Dr. Swanson. I did the surgery. We've removed the piece of rebar, and there's very little bleeding. But I'm afraid infection has set in."

I groaned.

"As you probably know, he's on heavy antibiotics. But we're getting closer to the possibility of sepsis. Are you familiar with—"

"Uh-huh." I rubbed my eyes.

"He's still unconscious. Occasionally he has an irregular heartbeat."

I sat up. "Can we see him?"

"Yes, but he won't be able to communicate."

"Not sure I will either."

After thanking the surgeon, we slipped into Jim's room. He looked paler than ever.

"You want coffee?" Stephen asked.

"Thanks." He headed for the hallway as I sat down.

I watched Jim's eyelids, hoping for the tiniest flutter.

Nothing.

"Wish you could hear me," I said. "I'd tell you how you've made the last month or so almost bearable."

The monitor kept up its steady beeping.

"I've never met anybody quite like you. Totally comfortable in your own skin. Not trying to impress anybody, but doing it anyway. Loving God, apparently, and without being creepy. And when you smile—"

I swallowed, still not knowing what to say and wondering whether it was crazy to talk to yourself out loud. Although technically I was talking to him.

I listened to the beeping until Stephen returned with two plastic cups. The coffee was worse than last time, but holding it made things seem a little more normal.

"The machine was out of doughnuts," he said.

I picked up my phone. "I'd better update Darlene." The last thing I wanted to do.

Unfortunately, she answered right away. "How is he?"

I repeated the doctor's report.

After a long silence, she cleared her throat. "I have a plane ticket for tomorrow. On Frontier Airlines. I'm already packing."

I found a slip of paper and wrote down her flight information. "I'll pick you up at the airport," I said. "It's a big place. Let's meet in baggage claim."

"I have a terrible sense of direction."

"You have a cell phone."

"Not a smart one."

"Don't need one." I gave her my number.

"Carolyn, I couldn't get through this without you."

I sighed. "Bet you could. But we'll help each other."

"See you tomorrow."

"Try to get some sleep tonight," I said, and hung up.

Stephen sipped his coffee. "All squared away?"

I shook my head. "What do *you* think?"

He didn't answer.

Both hands around my drink, I started praying.

* * *

The door opened. Pastor Campbell stuck his head in.

"Are you in the middle of anything?"

"Just my praying."

Stephen looked at me, probably wondering whether interrupting prayer was a mortal sin.

"I can come back."

"Actually, we need you now."

I drank the last of my coffee as the minister took a seat on the other side of the bed.

"How's he doing?"

I filled him in. The more I said, the more dire his condition sounded.

When I was done, the pastor got up and looked through the window. The first orange hints of sunset made his face look warmer.

"I don't want to be nosy, Caroline, but how would you describe your relationship with Jim?"

My own face seemed to get warmer, too. "I'm . . . not sure. Friends. More than friends, I guess."

I could tell without looking that Stephen was turning toward me, hanging on every word.

"Maybe we should change the subject," I said.

The pastor shrugged. "Sure." He returned to his seat. "You know, I remember my first visit to a hospital and what an awful job I did—talking too much, promising too much. The family member was the family patriarch, in his eighties. His diagnosis was awful—late-stage brain cancer. I went on and on about how wonderful heaven is going to be. I learned later that Grandpa was an inveterate gambler who'd lost half his estate to the casinos. Most of his relatives were glad to see him go."

Stephen scratched his chin. "Excuse me, Reverend. I don't know much about how these things work, but is that supposed to be an inspirational story?"

Pastor Campbell chuckled softly. "No. I'm just trying to contrast that old man and this younger one. Jim knows where he's going. I don't have to fill up the silence, and the reality of heaven is infinitely better than anything I can promise."

"Oh."

I was about to add an *amen* when an alarm went off.

I didn't know much about what the numbers on his monitor meant, but the one near the little red valentine seemed to be saying Jim's heart rate had plummeted.

A nurse rushed in, then ran out for a doctor.

A white-coated man I hadn't seen before strode in and asked us to move back.

What happened next was pretty much the way I'd seen it

on TV. The nurse handed the defibrillator paddles to the doctor, who said, "Clear." He didn't yell it, just said it. His expression was like stone.

The pastor was holding my hand.

The numbers on the monitor changed. They dropped to zero. The green line went flat.

"Again," the doctor said. He brought down the paddles and Jim's body seemed to jump.

I held my breath.

Finally the line leapt.

I sank back in my chair.

The nurse turned in our direction. "His vital signs are stabilizing."

She and the doctor hung around for another five minutes.

"Thank God," the pastor said. He checked his watch. "I'm afraid I need to visit another patient. Need anything before I go?"

I shook my head.

"Wow," said Stephen after the pastor left. "You guys are good."

* * *

Back at the motel, I tossed my purse on the floor and toppled directly onto the mattress, not bothering to remove a single article of clothing. It felt like bellyflopping into the field of poppies in *The Wizard of Oz*, only with slightly less dirt.

I waited for its magical effect to overtake me. Nothing. Reaching to shut off the bedside lamp, I took a deep breath and smelled not flowers but the sharp scent of some previous guest's hairspray from the pillow. Good to know Housekeeping was on the job.

Clashing cymbals and *ooomping* tubas, the soundtrack of

19th-century warfare, blasted from somewhere on the floor. With a grunt I rolled over and retrieved my phone.

"Can't sleep?" Stephen asked.

"Not anymore."

"I'm working on the screenplay. Need some feedback."

"Love to. First of all, never call me when you know I must be exhausted. Second, don't ask my opinion when you don't really want it."

"Gotcha. Now, about the story. Do you—"

I sat up. "Is this about *Watsons?*"

"Uh-huh. Do you think one of them needs to be a woman?"

I looked at the ceiling. "Lucy Liu in *Elementary* was quite female, as I recall."

"Man, I can't believe I forgot that."

"Is that all?"

"I've got a plot outline. Sketchy. Not as long as a treatment. Wanna hear it?"

"More than anything else in the world."

"Sherlock Holmes has been kidnapped by Moriarty. A street urchin brings a ransom note to the most recent Watson, played by Martin Freeman. He gathers the members of The Watson Society at Baker Street. They get into an argument about what to do."

He paused.

"And?" I asked.

"The oldest Watson, Nigel Bruce, takes charge and comes up with a plan involving Sherlock's violin and a steam-powered torpedo in the Thames River."

"Isn't Nigel Bruce dead?"

"Of course. We get somebody to play him. I'm thinking John Lithgow."

"Is this a comedy or a drama?"

"Both. More drama than comedy."

I closed my eyes. "Then what?"

"Moriarty gives all the Watsons the Spanish Flu, a virus he's brought back from the future in 1918. But one of them—maybe Lucy Liu—is immune, and she runs into Dr. Who, played by some guy who looks like Tom Baker. He lets her into the Tardis, and they travel to 1972—"

"I think I get the general idea." I pondered telling him how terrible it was, but I knew it wouldn't stop him.

"So my question is, who should play Moriarty?"

I closed my eyes. "How about you? You're . . . between projects."

Short silence, then a gasp. "That never would have occurred to me. Carolyn, you're a genius. I'd have to direct myself, unless Kenneth Branagh's available."

"I'm sure you'd guide yourself to a tour-de-force performance." I yawned. "Got to go. I have an early day tomorrow."

"Have you checked your e-mail?"

"Not since this afternoon."

"Hunter wants a progress report."

"Great. In the morning."

"G'night."

I hung up. If I started now, I could get at least 20 minutes of sleep.

CHAPTER 24

IT TURNED OUT I GOT A WHOLE HOUR OF SLEEP. ALTHOUGH it's hard to tell how long when you're not awake.

Three bitter cups of coffee later, I propped my eyeballs open and got to the airport. Baggage claim was a zoo. Too bad I hadn't told Darlene I'd be wearing a pink ribbon or something.

I stood by Carousel 7, looking for a plump, gray-haired cowgirl with a lost expression. Then my phone rang.

"I'm at the drinking fountain," she said, sounding breathless.

"Which one?"

"The one next to the restroom."

"Which restroom?"

"The one that says 'Women' on it."

I sighed. "Do you have any luggage?"

"Just a carry-on."

"See the numbers on the luggage conveyor belts? I'm at number seven."

"Oh, I see now. I'll be right there."

She looked just as I envisioned, only without the cowboy

hat. Her round, pink face glistened with perspiration. Her carry-on had a small but striking Texas star sticker on the side.

I gave her a hug. She smelled like grapefruit.

"I'm parked in the garage," I said. "I thought we'd go straight to the hospital."

She nodded, gazing around at the roiling, noisy crowd. "Have you . . . heard anything today?"

"Not yet."

She followed me down the corridor. I tried not to go too fast. By the time we reached the elevator, I was only slightly less winded than she was.

"How was your flight?"

"The seats were so close together I could hardly move. But then I haven't been on a plane in about twelve years. And I used to be a bit more . . . petite."

Traffic to Cedars-Sinai was light, considering this was a city of nearly four million people. Our efforts to chat were embarrassing. Maybe when we got to the hospital and got a report on Jim we'd be less preoccupied.

"He's hanging on," the nurse said when we finally tiptoed into his room. "But his temperature is still elevated. They're trying another antibiotic."

Eyes wide, Darlene edged toward the bed. She turned toward the wall for a moment. I couldn't tell for sure whether she was crying.

Finally she turned back, reached down, and touched Jim's hand. His chest rose and fell slowly.

"I'm here, honey," she whispered.

She stood like that for a long time, occasionally brushing the hair back from his forehead.

"Still a little boy to me. What a handful he was. Quiet but stubborn."

I leaned forward. "I can imagine."

"He just idolized his older brother. Jesse was in the rodeo for a while, but had the sense to quit while he was ahead."

I watched the zigzag line on the monitor, willing it to keep moving. "I envision him as a kid wearing chaps and spurs and shooting a cap gun."

She smiled. "That phase didn't last long. He got interested in martial arts and baseball. Had his first broken arm when he was eight."

"Were the girls after him?"

"Too shy 'til he got out of high school." She paused. "He was married once, you know."

I tried not to look too surprised. "Really?"

"Lasted less than a year. They lived in Abilene. The girl took up with a bank vice-president, who made a lot more money than a bull rider."

"When did he start going to church?"

She smoothed his hair again. "We took him when he was little, but he kind of lost his way on the rodeo circuit. Hard drinker."

"That's tough to believe."

"Oh, it got worse. He was a mean drunk. Never said no to a fight. More than once got arrested. When we quit bailing him out, he started listening to a jail chaplain who introduced him to Jesus. An even bigger deal than the time he met Evel Knievel."

"The daredevil in the white suit?"

"Got the man's autograph. He was Jim's inspiration to be a stuntman."

I nodded toward the bed. "At least he didn't try to jump the Grand Canyon on a motorcycle."

"Always told him that kind of thing wasn't worth the risk. He'd claim God made him that way."

She patted her son's hand. "Maybe now he'll change his mind. If he gets the chance."

* * *

I decided not to let Hunter wait. After all, my life was in his hands.

As soon as we got back to the car, I checked his e-mail message.

Carolyn:

   Thanks for leaving me in the dark. Your sending me to the poorhouse. I can accept being rejected by Hollywood, but I can't let you keep fiddling while my reputation here burns.

   You and Stephen have had long enough to play hookie. Time to be leavin' on a jet plane, as the Beatles said. But first give me a heads-up on your progress. Our Friends in Legal need to know how soon to write your termination papers.

"Chilling, huh?" Stephen said.

"The spelling alone is enough to give me palpitations. But ignorance of Peter, Paul, and Mary has no excuse."

I hit the speed dial. He picked up. I put him on speaker.

"I see you can't live without us."

"I'd like to try."

"Our stuntman was in an accident. He may not make it."

"You mean the guy who nearly killed me with that drop-and-roll crap?"

"That's the one."

"Too bad. I was looking forward to a rematch with him someday."

I looked at Stephen.

"Mr. Sensitivity," he whispered.

"Anyway," I continued, "things are sort of on pause. But shooting's almost finished. If I can convince the director to let us sit in on the editing process, we can come back."

"And if not?"

"Then we'll have to come back anyway."

"Remind me again why I haven't fired you yet."

"You have, more than once. But so far you've always returned to your senses and discerned the optimum course."

"Quit trying to confuse me with your abnormal words. What are you, a member of the Tesla Society?"

Stephen snickered. "You mean the Mensa Society?"

"That genius club."

"You flatter me," I said. "But I prefer to work alone."

"If you two aren't back here soon, you won't be working at all." He hung up.

We looked at each other. "You go first," I said.

"I'd give it a seven. He was madder when we got stuck in Atlanta."

"Yes, but he made more grammatical and factual errors this time. I'd give it an eight."

* * *

After dropping Stephen off at the Oasis Gardens, I zipped to the next location. Exterior, nowhere in particular, involving a horse.

The beast seemed docile enough, rust-brown and a little swaybacked, its reins gripped by one of those Hollywood wranglers—a deeply tanned fellow who looked more like a gigolo than a zookeeper. The latter fed the former a carrot.

There being a shortage of chairs, I leaned against my car and watched as the director huddled with the cameraman. Leilani walked up to the wrangler and said something; he nodded. Petting the horse's flank, she leaned her forehead against it.

Larry Shapiro picked up the bullhorn. "Places!"

The horse ambled into camera range and stopped. An

actor, a young man whose name and role I couldn't remember, took up the reins.

The slate went *clack*.

"Sound," said the guy with the headphones.

"Rolling," said the cinematographer.

A loud buzz came from overhead. Squinting at the cobalt sky, I made out a private plane.

The sound man cursed.

Suddenly the aircraft made a dive, almost low enough for crop dusting. The horse panicked, eyes wild, and tore the reins from the startled actor. Rearing back, it proceeded to charge toward Shapiro.

"Cut!" he yelled.

Unfortunately, the stallion didn't understand.

Dropping the bullhorn, the director ran in the opposite direction.

The wrangler chased the horse, but couldn't keep up. Shapiro tripped on something black that looked like a cable, thick as an anaconda, and went flying.

Leilani sprinted over, apparently searching for a way to stop the horse or drag the director back. But it was too late. The horse gave a neigh that was more like a scream, its hooves landing squarely on Shapiro's chest.

I swallowed and stepped forward, grabbing my phone to dial 911. The beast whirled, then bolted, its mane flying. The wrangler did his best to catch up. The plane flew off.

Running toward the spot where the director lay, I saw several others prodding their phones, too. Leilani knelt next to Shapiro, who was unconscious. She took his pulse, then nodded to the cinematographer, who sat shell-shocked on the ground.

I didn't want to look at the director's chest. But blood soaked his denim jacket. His baseball cap was crumpled.

"Ambulance is on its way," somebody called.

I leaned against a tree. It had to be an accident, didn't it?

Not likely someone had hired the pilot, not to mention the horse.

But when it came to results, perhaps it made no difference.

CHAPTER 25

WE ALL WATCHED THE AMBULANCE RECEDE IN THE DISTANCE, kicking up a cloud of dust, siren wailing. Nobody seemed to know what else to do.

Leilani was talking on the phone. After a minute or so, she put it back in her pocket and picked up the bullhorn.

"Oskar says to shut down for the day," she said, looking deflated. No one protested.

My stomach growled. I checked my watch, knowing my stomach often jumped the gun when it came to mealtimes. But it was nearly noon.

I swung by the motel and picked Stephen up. We went to Arby's. He chose it, and I was too tired to argue.

We ate at a table outside. After I'd told him what happened, he pointed a fried mozzarella stick at my face. "Definitely an accident. But you know what? This is Hunter's big chance to direct."

I snorted. "Not even *he* would think that. Besides, Oskar would never let that happen."

"Just sayin'."

"I suppose I'll have to let Hunter know about this. But not

right now." I bit into my Beef 'N Cheddar sandwich, making a face so that he wouldn't know I liked it.

"How's the screenplay going?" I asked, and wiped my lower lip with a napkin.

He shook his head. "I've written myself into a corner."

"Meaning what?"

"I've made Moriarty too sympathetic."

"How? He's one of the great villains in Western literature."

"Well, since I'm playing him, I find myself basing him on me. So he's compassionate. Heroic almost. His backstory is . . . a tearjerker. Taunted by London street urchins when he was little."

"You were taunted by London street urchins?"

"More like two fat guys who stole my thermos when I was in third grade. The point is that he's taking over the story, and not in a good way."

I nodded. "You need to murder your darlings."

He looked around at the other patrons, probably hoping they were out of earshot. "I don't have any. I mean, I like Leilani, but—"

"Surely you've heard that expression. You're an editor."

"Guess I missed that day in Ugly Figures of Speech class."

I took a drink of Zero Sugar lemonade. "Your darlings are passages you've written and love for the wrong reasons. Like showing off your vocabulary or your gift for description. Or using every speck of trivia you dug up when you were researching."

"I have to take out the parts about me?"

"Couldn't hurt."

"But the audience won't like me."

"They're not supposed to. You're the bad guy."

He sighed. "This is more complicated than I thought."

"That's why I'm not doing it."

"Think I'll be allowed on the set now that the director is gone? I was just starting to sink my teeth into that role."

I shook my head. "Stay with the mozzarella sticks."

* * *

Back at the hospital, we gave Darlene a break. The circles under her eyes wouldn't let us do otherwise.

She paused in the doorway on the way out. "His temperature's lower. I've been walking up and down the stairs to get a little exercise. Do you know if the cafeteria's open?"

"No," I said. "Probably plenty of vending machines."

We took our usual places. Jim looked the same—at death's door.

Being a glutton for punishment, I decided to call Hunter with an update.

"Me again," I said when he picked up. I put the phone on speaker.

"Your time's not up."

"I know. But there's been a development. The director was trampled by a horse."

"Is he alive?"

"Yes, but he won't be yelling through his bullhorn anytime soon."

"Far be it for me to speak ill of the deaf, but I think it might be time to step in."

"How?"

"Do they have a replacement for the director?"

"I don't know. The producer has shut things down for the moment."

"Then this is my opportunity. When fate closes a window, open the door. Time to try my hand at directing."

"I think you have to be in the Director's Guild or something."

"I bet they'll make an exception, like when grocery clerks go on strike. They hire anybody who can lift a bag of ice."

I looked at Stephen, who was rolling his eyes. "Directing's a little more complicated."

"Who's the guy in charge of this movie? Looks like a Nazi vampire."

"Oskar Pulaski."

"Right. Give me his number."

"Hunter, the man already hates me."

"Doesn't everybody?"

"No." I sighed. "All right. I've got it here somewhere. But don't tell him I gave it to you."

"Fine."

I read the number from a slip of paper in my purse.

"Your secret is safe with me," he said, and hung up.

Stephen snickered. "Lady, you're toast."

There was a gurgling sound. At first I couldn't tell where it was coming from. "Did you hear that?" I asked.

"Hear what?"

I heard it again, louder. Glancing at Jim, I saw his mouth open and his head lift slightly. I gasped.

Stephen stood. "My God, is he choking?"

Jim's eyes fluttered open, then closed.

We watched him intently. The monitor continued its one-note melody.

Finally his eyes popped open. He blinked and turned toward me.

"Carolyn?" he asked, his voice hoarse. His lips were half-stuck together.

I stood up and gave a little wave.

"You look great," I said.

"Liar," he said, and smiled that crinkly smile.

* * *

I searched the bed for the nurse's call button, then pressed it with my thumb. Jim watched, still smiling but sleepy.

The nurse marched in, sneakers squeaking. "You rang?"

"He's awake," I said.

"Seriously?" She bent over him, peering into his eyeballs and consulting the stats on the monitor.

He tried to sit up.

"Whoa, cowboy," she said, placing a hand lightly on each of his shoulders. "Don't move around." She took the stethoscope from her shoulder and listened to his heart.

"Can I have a drink?" he whispered.

She straightened up. "I'll get you some shaved ice."

Back out the door she went, then returned with a paper cup and plastic spoon and handed them to me. "Do you mind?"

"Of course not." I stirred the ice a little and brought a spoonful to his lips. They were dry, chapped.

"Looks like you need some Chapstick."

He swallowed the melting ice, coughed a little, and gazed up at me. "Who needs Chapstick when I've got you?" he whispered.

"Whoo. Getting hot in here," Stephen said.

"Carolyn, what happened?" Jim asked.

"What's the last thing you remember?"

He cleared his throat. "I was in the water. The pain in my chest—God, it was awful."

"Piece of rebar," Stephen volunteered.

"Ow."

I put the cup down. "Does it hurt?"

"Yeah."

"They took it out," I added. "You've been on antibiotics. They're trying to keep the infection from getting worse."

The door opened. It was Darlene.

"Jimmy, are you awake?"

She practically ran to his bedside, arms outstretched.

"No hugs," the nurse warned.

Darlene saw the ice. "Can I feed him?"

"Be my guest," I said.

"Thanks, Mom, but I think I've had enough for a while."

"Things have shut down on the production for the time being," I said.

"Because of me?"

"Not exactly. Larry Shapiro got trampled by a horse, and—"

"What?"

"Long story. But he's in the hospital, too. For all I know, he could be in the room next door."

The nurse looked toward the door. "Is he a big Hispanic guy who likes to watch *Hoarders?*"

"No."

"Then it's not him."

Jim closed his eyes. "Okay if I rest now?"

The nurse took the cup away. "Good idea. Everybody out except Mom."

I touched his arm. "We'll be back."

He didn't respond.

I hoped he would next time.

CHAPTER 26

NEXT MORNING, BACK ON LOCATION, OSKAR MADE AN announcement.

"Ladies and gentlemen, in light of yesterday's developments, I am stepping in to fulfill the responsibilities of our director, who is incapacitated."

Silence.

Ansel Mueller looked up from his camera and finally started applauding. After that, nobody felt secure enough not to join in. Except Stephen and me, which wasn't really courageous because nobody cared.

I turned to my colleague, who'd allowed himself back in because Larry Shapiro wasn't there to enforce his exile. "I wonder whether Hunter offered his services."

"If so, I can imagine how *that* conversation went." He took out a yellow legal pad and resumed penning his doomed screenplay.

The horse was back, reined in tightly by the wrangler. Everyone else kept his or her distance.

"They shoot crazy horses, don't they?" I asked Stephen.

He shrugged.

"Places!" Oskar bellowed, needing no stinking bullhorn.

Clack.

"Action!"

The actor knew his lines, hit his marks. Not an aircraft was in the sky. Everything went perfectly.

"Cut!" Oskar ordered. "Do it again."

They did it again, without a hitch.

After another three takes, the directing producer gave a disdainful nod to the cinematographer. "Something usable there, I suppose."

Standing up, he rocked back on his heels. "Take five!"

Leilani waved her clipboard. "Mr. Pulaski, do you know how Mr. Shapiro's doing?"

He raised an eyebrow. "I'm afraid I have no idea. I suppose someone would have heard something if he . . . expired."

"Somebody should find out," she said, and looked around.

There being no takers, I waved my hand. "We'll do it."

"Thank you," Leilani called.

Nobody else seemed to notice.

* * *

I dropped Stephen off at the motel, figuring it wouldn't aid Larry Shapiro's recovery to see him.

The director lay in bed, eyes shut. His IV was hung with two bags, one dark red and one pale yellow. The monitor wasn't doing anything scary. Bandages encased him from chin to hip. The blanket covered his nether regions. His baseball cap was gone, no doubt too dirty for hospital standards.

I hadn't realized how bald he was. And without his bullhorn, he just looked like somebody's uncle who ran a furniture store.

"Mr. Shapiro?" I whispered.

He opened one eye. "Who's there?"

"Carolyn Neville."

For a moment he looked like Popeye after battling Bluto. Then the other eye came online.

"You? After all this, Oskar can't spare ten minutes to see what the universe is doing to me?"

"Oskar has taken your place for now."

He lifted his head, winced, and let it flop back on the pillow. "He can't direct. Did you see *Mrs. Doubtfire, Part 2?*"

"I didn't know there was a sequel."

"Never made it into theaters. Robin Williams wasn't in it, rest his soul. You know Ned Beatty?"

"*Deliverance?*"

"He was no Robin Williams. And Oskar couldn't get a decent performance out of Laurence Olivier. Not that he ever got the chance to find out."

"Maybe you can come back soon."

He groaned. "They tell me I've got three broken ribs. Internal injuries. My spleen is like ravioli. They may have to finish the picture without me."

"I volunteered to visit you. Everybody's concerned. Well, practically everybody."

He sighed. "I'm touched that you're here. Bet you didn't have to arm-wrestle anyone for the assignment."

"So, is this karma?"

He chuckled, but it came out, "Ha . . . *ow!*"

"I'll try to stop being so funny."

He shook his head. "When that horse came down on me, I thought it was all over. I wasn't ready to . . ."

He hesitated, clearly unable to say the rest.

"Die?" I asked.

"Some words are better left unspoken."

"Larry, what *do* you think about the afterlife?"

He watched the monitor. "Technically, I'm Jewish. But reincarnation makes sense to me. I'd like to come back as Martin Scorsese. A *young* Martin Scorsese."

I opened my mouth to explain why I think life is a one-time-only prospect, but apologetics isn't my specialty. So I tried the next best thing, which is just blurting out whatever comes into my head.

"I think there's a heaven."

"Most people do."

"I believe God gets to decide who goes there and when."

"Seems reasonable, except for the God part."

A nurse came in, a young one with a ponytail and a butterfly pin on her scrubs. "He needs to rest," she said, unhooking the red bag.

Larry looked at me. "Thank you for coming. I have only one thing to ask."

"Name it."

"Don't tell anybody I got all emotional. I have a reputation to protect, even if that reputation is to get all emotional."

"I promise."

"Must be the painkillers talking. And I intend to get as many of them as possible."

* * *

When I got back to the studio, I couldn't report on the director's condition. It was lunchtime. Stephen and I dined on the usual horrifying fare—which in this case was canned ravioli. I couldn't help remembering Larry's vivid description of his spleen.

I pushed my styrofoam plate away. "Hate to beat a dead

horse, so to speak, but we're back to the question of when an accident isn't an accident. We still don't know whether the Model A or the bridge were tampered with. Now we don't know whether Larry's mauling was instinct or intentional."

"A plane spooked the horse," Stephen said, savoring a slice of white bread. "Or do you think somebody stuck it with a pin?"

I shook my head. "I guess the director should still be considered a suspect, though his motive isn't clear."

"Or maybe Oskar wanted to direct so badly that he had to get Larry out of the way."

"Would have been much easier just to fire him."

Stephen looked at my plate. "Are you going to finish that?"

"No chance."

"You haven't touched it?"

"Uh-uh. And for good reason."

He slid the plate his way and got to work. I looked away, thinking of stopping by a doughnut place on the way back to the Oasis Gardens.

Stephen was done in record time. We stood in unison, but when he backed away from the table he bumped into a brick wall that wore a black leather jacket.

Axel.

The prop man swore. "What are you doing here, moron? Didn't you get fired?"

Leilani stepped out from behind him. "Axel, he didn't mean anything. And Larry was the one who fired him, not Oskar."

Her boyfriend grabbed her arm. "Maybe you two should get a room."

Stephen took a step back, stumbled, and caught himself on the back of his chair. Axel spat on the floor.

The two of us headed back to the cheap seats.

"He's gotta be the guy," Stephen mumbled.

"All we need is proof."

"Yeah. Too bad I've got no idea how to get it."

CHAPTER 27

"Okay, now I've got an idea," Stephen said.

"Does it involve Axel?"

"Of course." He paused. "We—or I—need to look through the prop room for evidence."

"What kind of evidence?"

"To be determined. Your job is to keep him busy."

I looked at the soundstage. The prop guy was ignoring Leilani, stacking apple crates on top of each other.

"Is this one of those deals where I'm supposed to bat my eyelashes to distract him?"

He shook his head. "Not that it wouldn't work."

"So what do I do?"

"Anything you want."

I stared at the ceiling. "I could tell him I want to interview him for a book."

"You're writing a book?"

"No, but he doesn't know that. And I *might* write a book about this someday. Life is research."

"Sweet. Go do your thing. Once you've got his attention, I'll go down the hall."

I gathered up my stuff and worked my way toward Axel, who was examining his tower of boxes as if they were a Marcel Duchamp installation.

"Excuse me," I said.

He straightened up. "I'm busy," he said.

Leilani looked at me and gave a sympathetic shrug. I didn't see any new bruises on her face, but one never knew.

"I'm interviewing people for a book," I said, pulling out a pad and pen.

"Yeah? About what?"

"Hollywood. And I need a chapter about props."

He raised a skeptical eyebrow. "Who else have you talked to?"

"You're the first."

"Wow," Leilani said. "Axel, this could be a big deal."

"How much are you payin' me?"

"Uh . . . I don't have a budget for that. Usually people do this kind of thing for free."

"How long's it gonna take?"

"Maybe . . . fifteen minutes."

He snorted. "There's a lot more to props than that."

"We can take as much time as you want."

He threw up his hands. "Where do we do this?"

"Let's start here."

"There's a lot of stuff to show you in the prop room."

I glanced at the cheap seats to make sure Stephen wasn't there. "We'll get there eventually. First I should take a picture of you here on the set."

I put down the pad and pen and got out my phone. He brushed his hair back with his hand. "How's the light? Get the crates in the background."

I took three shots. He looked like he was posing for the cover of a romance novel.

"Great," I said, and traded the phone for the writing equipment. "What made you want to work with props?"

"I'm good with my hands," he said, and winked. Leilani looked away.

"What's the most unusual prop you ever built?"

He laced his fingers and cracked his knuckles. "A submarine. About half scale. Made it out of silicone rubber left over from the last *Jaws* movie."

"That's *fascinating*."

He checked his watch. "We're gonna start shooting in a few minutes. Let's get to the prop room."

"But—"

"Hey, I'm doin' you a favor." He led the way, and I had no choice but to follow. Leilani stayed behind. I swallowed, picturing what might happen to Stephen if we entered in the middle of his snooping.

The door was ajar. Axel pushed it open.

Biting my lip, I scanned the room. It was as disorganized as ever, a jumble of fantasy machines and centuries of furnishings piled up and hanging from the rafters.

But there was no Stephen.

* * *

Axel held forth on the absolute necessity of props. "People, places, and things. Props are the things. Besides, without props, what would the actors do with their hands?"

I kept peering into the dark corners, hoping to see a tangle of cinnamon-colored hair rising above one of the steam trunks or mummy cases.

Nothing.

"What else you want to know?" Axel asked, checking his watch again.

"Probably better to continue this another time. I know you've got to get back to the set."

"Darn right." He looked around. "Man, the stories I could tell you."

"I can hardly wait."

He made a pistol shape with his thumb and index finger. "Catch you later."

I switched off the light and looked up and down the hallway. Empty.

Stepping outside, I squinted against the sun. At length I saw the rental car in its space. Nobody was near it. The door was locked, and Stephen didn't have a key.

A woman in a generic Tinkerbelle costume walked by.

"Hi," I said. "Have you seen a guy with reddish hair, jeans, and a sort of peach-colored shirt?"

"No, have you?" She frowned and rolled her shoulders. Apparently her wings hurt.

"Never mind."

I proceeded to walk the studio lot, not really knowing where I was going. Two guys pushing an outboard motor in a shopping cart crossed my path. When I asked them the same question, they just shook their heads and kept going.

A guy holding a poodle, a woman with absolutely nothing interesting about her, two old men in top hats—nobody had seen Stephen.

I was about to turn back when I came upon a fake street's worth of brick storefronts. Between two of the shallow buildings was an alley. Sticking out from behind an old-fashioned, dented trashcan was a sneaker.

It looked familiar.

Getting closer, I saw it was on a foot attached to a denim-clad leg.

The leg was connected to a hip, which was joined to a torso, which was dressed in a peach-colored shirt.

I knelt next to Stephen. He was alive, but unmoving.

* * *

I wished I had one of those ampules of ammonia they used to wave under people's noses. It seemed appropriate in a fake Depression-era alley.

Before I could grab my phone to dial 911, Stephen woke up by himself. His hand went to the back of his head.

Blinking, he didn't seem able to focus for a second. "Where am I?"

"In a fake alley."

"How'd I get here? Last thing I remember, I was in the prop room. Somebody must have hit me from behind." He examined his hand. "No blood, but this headache is a bear."

I helped him sit up. "That somebody must have dragged or driven you here. Hard to do without anyone noticing."

"Found something in the prop room. Can't recall what it was."

"Animal, vegetable, or mineral?"

He hesitated. "None of those."

"Bigger than a breadbox?"

He shook his head, then flinched. "Something in a box."

"Shoes?"

"Floppier."

"Clown shoes?"

"Rubber gloves. The kind you might use if you didn't want to get fingerprints on anything. Or if you were a makeup person."

"He's not," I said. "What else might a prop guy use gloves for?"

"Weird thing was, the gloves looked too small for his hands. Kind of an O.J. Simpson thing. The box had an *S* on the side."

"Maybe Leilani used them."

He rubbed the back of his head. "Why would a script girl need gloves?"

I thought for a moment, then shrugged.

"I'm not sure this information was worth the pain."

"Well, I'm sorry I forced you to search the prop room when you had no idea what you were looking for. You remember that, don't you?"

He looked confused. "No, but I accept your apology."

Not having the heart to refresh his memory, I helped him to his feet.

CHAPTER 28

BACK ON THE SET, I SET UP A LITTLE RECOVERY AREA IN A DARK corner. Stephen eased onto the folding chair. I swiped an unused pillow from the Winchester family sofa and stuffed it behind his head.

I checked my script. Scene 97, Jackson Dunn's last in the film. He was sitting on a fake rock. The makeup lady, a cigarette clamped between her teeth, was doing her best to make him look old. It wasn't working.

Jackson coughed, waved away the smoke, and said something. The makeup lady dropped her cigarette and mashed it into the floor with her shoe.

Oskar came over, surveyed the actor's face, and shook his head. "Ansel," he said to the cinematographer, "don't get too close."

Stephen leaned my way. "Hey, she's wearing gloves."

"She always does. But she doesn't seem like the type to hit people over the head and drag them half a mile to an alley."

"I don't know . . . as old broads go, she looks pretty tough."

"*Broads?* If you want to be a misogynist, at least use a more contemporary term."

"You sure? I mean, most of those get pretty nasty. Like—"

"Places!" Oskar barked.

Dunn took center stage. The cameraman backed off.

The actor held a brass music box in his hand, beholding it as if he were Hamlet and it was Yorick's skull.

Clapboard.

"Action!"

Dunn wound up the device. A tinkling version of "Oh, Susannah" tickled the silence. When it ended, he looked into the distance.

"There were many times in Winchester County that I wanted nothing more than to be anywhere else in the world —Paris, Cairo, even Oak Ridge." The aged voice was perfect, nearly overcoming the stiff layers of latex on his face. "I was too young to know that the human heart is the same wherever you go, and there is no better destination than love."

He bowed his head.

"Cut!" Oskar shouted.

As if on cue, cast and crew rose with a standing ovation. Everyone seemed to know another take would be unnecessary.

Oskar, not quite smiling, gave his usual nod. "Ladies and gentlemen, I predict at least a Golden Globe nomination for Best Actor."

Jackson shook his head in that aw-shucks way he was famous for, then stepped off the set to retrieve a shopping bag from his chair. "I have a little remembrance for everybody."

"PEZ dispenser!" somebody yelled.

"No. A commemorative Christmas ornament." He held one up, a flat, silvery circle that glinted under the lights. He went to each cast and crew member to present his gift. He didn't get to us.

"It's been an honor to be part of this production," he said, and blew kisses to everyone. With a final wave he headed toward his trailer. I couldn't be sure but it looked like his makeup was beginning to melt.

* * *

At dinner, the phone rang.

It was Darlene.

"Jim seems worse to me. I hate to be a worrywart, but would you mind coming over? The doctors aren't saying much. Maybe you could—"

"We're on our way," I said.

CHAPTER 29

WE GOT STUCK IN TRAFFIC. I SWITCHED ON THE RADIO AND twiddled the dial until I got a news station. The commercials for Dinovite dog food and LifeLock seemed endless.

Finally a breathy female voice said something about Traffic and Weather Together. I turned up the volume.

"We've got a two-car accident on Beverly Boulevard. Avoid that area if you can. If you can't, good luck."

Stephen must have guessed I was ready to scratch the plastic off the steering wheel.

"Hey, we'll make it. The app on my phone says we're no more than thirty-five minutes away. Unless you want to rent a helicopter or get out and walk, this is the best we can do."

"Do your Human GPS thing."

"Right at the next street, two blocks, left, half a mile, make a U-turn, left, detour for construction, three miles, right, left, and we're there."

"Got it," I said. "Except for the part after 'right at the next street.'"

He shook his head. "Just drive. I'll break it down, like diagramming a sentence."

"Without the diagram."

"Want to trade places?"

"You're not on the rental agreement as a driver."

"Then you're our only hope, Obi-Wan."

I gripped the wheel, looked straight ahead, and started praying.

* * *

Darlene was waiting for us in Jim's room. Her eyes were red-rimmed as she reached out to give me a hug.

"Don't know what I'd do without you folks," she said.

I looked at Jim. His coloring was the same.

Darlene stood by the bed. I sat on one of the visitors' chairs. Stephen hung back by the door, looking uncomfortable.

There was a knock at the door, which was open. A wheelchair slowly rolled over the threshold.

"Excuse me." It was a large African-American man in a gray suit with a clerical collar. "I'm Bill Abernathy, one of the hospital chaplains."

He maneuvered to the center of the room. "How's Mr. Oakley doing?"

"We're not sure," I said.

"Are you all members of the family?"

Darlene raised a hand. "I'm his mother. These are our friends."

The chaplain nodded. "Does Jim have a favorite hymn?"

Darlene thought for a moment. "'Wonderful Grace of Jesus.' Do you know it?"

"I'm afraid not."

"Goes like this," she said, and cleared her throat.

Knowing the first verse and chorus, I joined in—despite

the fact that, under the circumstances, it seemed a little too rollicking:

> *Wonderful grace of Jesus, greater than all my sin,*
> *How shall my tongue describe it, where shall its praise begin . . .*

The chaplain listened closely, trying to pick it up. Stephen stood respectfully in the corner, still looking as if he'd rather be back in that alley, groaning.

We started the refrain:

> *Wonderful the matchless grace of Jesus,*
> *Greater than the mighty rolling sea . . .*

A nurse who looked too young to know such an old hymn came in and added her voice.

> *O magnify the precious name of Jesus,*
> *Praise His name!*

When it was over, we looked around at each other, not knowing what to do. The monitor continued to beep.

Finally Stephen took a step forward. "Anybody want coffee? It's all an agnostic can do at times like this."

We kept watching the numbers as Stephen ran his errand. The nurse adjusted a bag on the IV and walked out.

Five minutes later we were all sipping coffee when the impossible happened. The number next to the little red heart on the monitor began to rise.

Jim stirred. Darlene gasped.

He opened his eyes halfway.

"Sing another one," he whispered.

* * *

Hand trembling, I set down my coffee. "What should we sing? A hymn? A cowboy song?" I knew most of the words to "Bury Me Not on the Lone Prairie," but it was the last thing any of us needed to hear right now.

Jim coughed weakly. "Garth Brooks."

We looked at each other. Darlene shrugged and shook her head.

"I know who he is, but not any of his songs," I said.

Stephen consulted his phone. "How about 'Friends in Low Places'?"

Jim smiled.

"Since none of us knows the words, I'll just play the MP3." He poked the screen and turned up the volume.

> *Well, I guess I was wrong*
> *I just don't belong*
> *But then, I've been there before*
> *Everything's all right*
> *I'll just say goodnight*
> *And I'll show myself to the door . . .*

Darlene covered her eyes with her hands. The chaplain rolled over and put his hand on her shoulder.

Jim tried to prop himself up on his elbow, but had to ease back down. "Now, Mama, I didn't pick that one for the words. I like the tune."

She nodded and pulled a tissue from the box near his bed.

When the song ended, Jim pushed the button to raise the head of his bed. "I got a few things I'd like to say. Just in case."

We waited.

"Mama, I can't thank you enough for letting me make a fool of myself and ignore your good sense. Everything decent I got from you."

He turned to me. "Carolyn, you are unlike any other lady I've ever met. I hope you find a guy who treats you right and knows he's not half as smart as you are."

He looked at Stephen. "We didn't really get acquainted. But you take care of your boss, okay?"

Stephen put the phone away. "I'll try."

Finally noticing the chaplain, Jim raised an eyebrow. "Mama, you got a boyfriend?"

The big man burst into laughter. "Son, she's got better taste than that. I'm the chaplain."

"Oh. Then you can be the witness. I never got around to throwing together a will, but I'd like to make sure some of my belongings get into the right hands. Mama, there's an old Thompson Chain Reference Bible in my dresser. I think you gave it to me. You already got most of my trophies, right?"

She wiped her eyes. "I believe so."

"I'd like my pickup to go to a friend of mine, Jackie Davis, in Burbank. His address is in the little notebook in the kitchen. Carolyn, would you care to have my championship belt buckle?"

I hesitated.

"Girl, it's real silver!"

I nodded, unable to say anything.

"And while you're at it, see to it that my pastor gets my cowboy hat. He'll probably never wear it."

He closed his eyes. I stared at him, making sure he was still alive. The monitor claimed he was.

After saying his goodbyes, the chaplain left his business card and wheeled himself out.

I found my coffee cup and took a sip. Getting cold.

More silence, more beeping.

The room was closing in on me. Had to get out, at least for a while. Grabbing a tissue, I went into the hall.

If not a prophet.

* * *

Six days later there was a celebration at Radiant Hills Fellowship. Stephen and I sat on the front row with Jim and Darlene. Her daughter, Katie, a thirtyish woman with her mother's figure and Jim's crinkly eyes, joined us.

"Are those the movie people?" Katie whispered, looking a little scared.

I turned around. A few of the cast and crew were there, some dressed to the nines and others in their usual jeans. Larry Shapiro was in a wheelchair, staring at the cross behind the pulpit. I wondered what he was thinking.

Those of us who could sang "Wonderful Grace of Jesus." No Garth Brooks, but I doubted most of the guests would have known the words to "Friends in Low Places," either.

The pastor began by reaching inside the pulpit and pulling out Jim's cowboy hat. "Mr. Oakley plans to leave me this." He put it on. "He thinks I'll never wear it." He put it on, and quiet laughter rippled through the sanctuary. He put it back.

"If you know Jim, you know his faith isn't an act. I think he'd want me to talk about that today."

He told how Jim went from reckless drunk to reverent risk-taker, winding up with an invitation to talk with anyone who wanted to know more. Darlene and Katie held hands the whole time, and at the end the daughter leaned her head on her mother's shoulder.

Refreshments were in the basement. Darlene and I had found a caterer who supplied ample amounts of chuckwagon food—barbecued brisket, beans, and bacon-flavored ice cream.

Stephen was first in line to fill his tin plate. "Even better than the craft services table," he said.

A couple of the showbiz people griped about the lack of alcohol, but most managed to shake hands with Darlene or Katie. Larry Shapiro monopolized the vegetable tray, then gave me a little wave and wheeled himself out.

Stephen sidled up to me. "Notice anybody missing?"

"Besides practically everybody?"

"Didn't see Axel. Or the camera guy, Ansel."

"Missing a celebration doesn't make you a suspect."

I sighed, running out of adrenaline. The pastor, sans cowboy hat, was attending to the family. Caterers were cleaning up.

There being no need for my continued presence, I went back upstairs and sat alone in the fourth or fifth pew.

Jim was still downstairs. He'd looked so happy.

I supposed I did, too.

* * *

We were almost last to leave, Stephen and I. He was eyeing the last half-empty tray of canapés. So was a young woman from the catering team, determined to upend it into the garbage.

"Just a second," he said, and held the pocket of his jacket open. Grabbing a relatively clean napkin, he proceeded to scoop up the remainders and dump them inside.

"You are so gross," I whispered.

The young woman picked up the tray and rolled her eyes at me. "Nothing surprises me anymore."

Stephen grinned, apparently taking it as a compliment.

* * *

Two days later *Winchester County Homecoming* went into post-production—anything that happens to the film when shooting's done. Sweetening sound, editing, adding effects. At least that's what Stephen had told me.

We were sitting in a tiny editing bay, Ansel and Larry Shapiro and I, along with the editor. The latter was named Gretchen, a stout woman with stubby fingers who stared at a computer monitor the size of a drive-in movie screen.

I was trying to keep my mouth shut. They'd already cut my brief appearance. Something about the lighting. Thanks to digitizing, it wasn't literally on the floor.

The director, recently liberated from his wheelchair, leaned forward. "No, no. Wrong. Go back to Scene 27."

Gretchen sighed and pushed a key. We watched as the image of Jackson Dunn and a border collie careened backward, fitful and jerky.

"Right there," Larry said.

She stabbed the keyboard. The image froze and so did she.

"Give me a fade," he said.

Another stab.

I bit my lip. "Hmm. Seems to me it needs a dissolve."

The director slowly turned my way. "Are you a member of the Motion Picture Editors Guild?"

"Um . . . no."

"You're just a natural-born genius, then?"

"That's not for me to say."

"I couldn't agree more. Gretchen, what do you think?"

"Are you sure you want to know?"

"Be honest."

"Fade."

He covered his face with his hands. "Why am I even asking? This thing is a mess. We'll never get anything usable out of it, and we've got a premiere in two weeks."

"What's the big rush?" Ansel asked.

"Ask Oskar."

The cameraman sat back in his chair. "What am I, crazy?"

The director took an orange vial of pills from his vest pocket, downed one, and made a face. "My career, and possibly my life, are over."

"Maybe it's not so bad," Ansel said. "You remember *Ishtar?*"

Larry thought for a moment. "Dustin Hoffman and Warren Beatty in the desert."

"Right. Comedy. But they went way over budget. Critics panned it because they expected too much." He pointed at the monitor. "Who's going to expect anything from this?"

The director shrugged. "Certainly not me."

"So is it a fade?" Gretchen asked.

"Of course." He paused.

"Ansel, you're a lifesaver. A little too German, maybe, but a *mensch.*"

Gretchen punched a few more buttons, and the editing resumed.

I thought of asking Ansel why he hadn't come to church, but didn't want to spoil the mood.

* * *

The premiere was held at a small theater in Los Angeles, an art house called Rialto Beach. We used the rental car, no one having offered to pay for a limo. It took half an hour to find a space half a mile away. The red carpet was a bit threadbare, and not much longer than my bath mat at home.

I barely recognized Stephen. He'd rented a tux and shaved more closely than usual. My purple gown was more of a dress I'd found at my local Macy's right before they went out of business.

Two reporters, one TV and one of unknown affiliation, ignored us as we stepped up from the curb. They paid plenty of attention to the celebrity behind us, however; Jackson Dunn and an impossibly skinny blonde I assumed was his wife smiled and sparkled and waved to an imaginary crowd.

Pausing at the entrance, we watched a black stretch limo pull up. Out came Oskar, a vacuous brunette on his arm. No one jumped to interview him, which seemed not to bother him.

Next came a white compact with the UBER logo on the door, ferrying Jim and Darlene and her daughter. In matching pink pantsuits, shocked and awed, the latter two locked elbows and tried not to trip.

"This is the greatest night of my life," Stephen whispered.

"Wow, I hope not."

"Well, my life so far is shorter than yours."

"I can shorten it further if you like."

He stepped into the lobby. "Is there free popcorn?" The butter-and-salt smell was overwhelming, and he wandered toward its source.

Jim and Darlene and her daughter found me standing next to an old life-sized cardboard cutout of Ewan McGregor from *Salmon Fishing in the Yemen*. "May we sit with you?" Jim asked.

"If I can tear my colleague away from the concession stand."

"Never thought I'd be standing in a place like this," Darlene said. "We've got a theater at home, but it smells like bleach and there's a big water stain on the ceiling."

Stephen came over, empty-handed. "Not free," he said, but held up a soft drink the size of one of those orange Home Depot buckets.

We found our seats, old-fashioned burgundy unadjustable velvet. The lights went down. The curtains parted.

Oskar strode to the center. "Ladies and gentlemen, it has been a labor of love to produce the film you are about to see. Of all the Parthenon Arts pictures with which I have been associated, this is perhaps the most moving and unique. I believe great cinema speaks for itself, so without further ado I present . . . *Winchester County Homecoming.*"

The applause was polite. Our row seemed the most enthusiastic.

There were no trailers. The rating was PG. I found myself holding my breath, hoping Harrison would be pleased.

Things started well. It was a real movie. Even though Stephen and I were nowhere to be seen, the audience chuckled and sighed in all the right places. Especially when Jackson Dunn was on the screen.

As we got closer to the bridge scene, I tensed. This couldn't be easy for any of the Oakleys.

Darlene and Katie looked away when the time came. Stephen stopped noisily sucking soda. Jim just shook his head.

At the final fade, a wave of applause slowly built to a crescendo. About half the audience rose to its feet.

The credits rolled. Stephen took out his phone. "I'm gonna try to catch our names."

"If we're in it."

They were there, near the end, but too small and too fast.

Jim looked at me. I swallowed, smiled, and took his hand.

CHAPTER 32

NEXT DAY STEPHEN AND I HIT THE NEAREST NEWSSTAND TO buy all the papers that might have reviews.

The only one that did was *Variety*. We went back to the motel, sat in the lobby, and tried to share it.

WINCHESTER COUNTY BRINGS IT HOME

The latest nostalgia trip from Parthenon Arts, Winchester County Homecoming, shines—thanks largely to veteran Everyman Jackson Dunn.

Helmed by director Larry Shapiro, the film mines familiar ground (think The Waltons *meets Truman Capote). Based on a book by Appalachian-born Harrison Yoder, it rings true without wringing crocodile tears.*

Cinematographer Ansel Mueller brings his trademark palette of muted browns and grays; Dunn brings his A game in scene after scene of youthful yearning and the wisdom of age, despite makeup that requires an industrial-strength suspension of disbelief.

Word has it that producer Oskar Pulaski is creating Golden

Globes buzz, and Dunn is already making the talk-show rounds . .

.

Before I could finish the article, my purse jangled. It was Mikki Flaherty.

I put the paper down and picked up the phone.

"When does the movie come out?"

"It already did. The premiere was last night. Everybody loves Jackson Dunn."

She sighed. "I can relate."

"They're even talking about him as a possible Golden Globes nominee."

"Really? Can you get me a ticket? I've got this outfit that—"

"No."

Silence.

"Maybe I should stop praying for you," she said.

"Don't. Somebody's been trying to kill us out here. But we can't prove it . . . yet."

"Wow. Keep your head down, okay?"

"Right."

"When are the Golden Globes on?"

"Don't know. Soon."

"I'll be watching. Wave if you can." She hung up.

Stephen, who'd been leafing through *Variety*, made a face. "This paper doesn't have any comics."

"It's a trade journal."

He nodded. "Golden Globes, huh? Guess I should buy the tux I rented. Might need it at the Oscars."

"I don't know whether we'll even be invited to either of those ceremonies."

"Maybe we can get in as placeholders. They hire people to sit in for celebrities who need to go to the can."

"Let's not get ahead of ourselves. There's still a killer out there somewhere."

* * *

Three days later, the Golden Globes nominations came out. We read all about it on the *Variety* website, to which Stephen was becoming addicted despite its lack of cartoons.

Sure enough, Jackson Dunn was nominated for Best Actor in a Motion Picture (Drama).

To my surprise, we got invitations a couple of days later—slipped under our doors at the motel. They were gold on white.

I went to Stephen's room and knocked.

When he opened the door, I held up my envelope. "Get yours yet?"

"Yeah. Can you believe it?"

"They must let anybody in," I said.

He grinned. "Now we can take a leak for ourselves. Not easy in a tux, though."

"This is nice, but we still have a job to do."

He looked up and down the hall. "We should set a trap for Axel," he murmured.

"To trap him into doing what?"

"Confessing."

"What sort of trap?"

He paused, thinking. "I got nothin'."

I pushed past him, into the room. "Maybe we can do better than that. When I talked with Jackson, he said a hospice nurse was with his mother when she died. He's always seemed to have this hostility toward Oskar. What if I could find her?"

"What would you ask her if you did?"

"Jackson seemed to think his mom was abused—by

Hollywood in general, but there must have been something more specific. Maybe she told the nurse before she died."

"The *nurse* could be dead by now."

"Wasn't that long ago. I'll bet there are records."

"Okay, you work on that. I'll think about trapping Axel. And buying that tux. Can I borrow a hundred bucks?"

"No," I said.

* * *

When I googled "Los Angeles Hospices" back in my room, about a thousand came up. At least it seemed that way.

I groaned. Then I had an idea.

If I could find Beverly Dunn's obituary, perhaps it mentioned the specifics. I started poking at my phone. Several dozen swipes later, I had my answer.

Jackson's mother had requested that in lieu of flowers, donations be made to the Greater Los Angeles Center for Palliative Care. According to Google Maps, it was still around. I called the number and explained my problem.

"Can you hold?" she asked.

About a minute later she was back. "Sorry. You want the name of the nurse who took care of Ms. Dunn?"

"Very much."

"I can't give out her contact information, but I can tell her you're trying to reach her."

"That would be great."

I gave her my cell number, pushed the END button, and fell back on the bed. At least the woman was alive.

* * *

Agnes Lopez didn't want to talk to me at first.

She called me back around noon the next day, sounding

wary. "Yes, I'm the person you want. But why do you want me?"

"I'm trying to find out who abused Beverly. I thought maybe she said something to you before she passed away."

"She did, but—"

"I have reason to believe that her son knew, or thought he did. He might be trying to do something about it."

She sighed. "Beverly did want to tell somebody before she died. It was weighing on her so heavily."

"Do you think she'd want me to know? Especially if I could help bring that person to justice?"

"Are you from the police?"

"No, but I can get the gears moving."

Silence.

"All right. Have you ever heard of Oskar Pulaski?"

CHAPTER 33

THAT NIGHT STEPHEN AND I SAT IN A DENNY'S. I STARTED TO explain what I'd learned from Nurse Agnes when our server, a fresh-faced country girl who probably churned the butter herself, showed up.

"What can I get you folks?"

"Grand Slam," Stephen said, grinning. "And a large OJ."

"And you, Ma'am?"

"English muffin and tea."

Stephen shook his head. "Is that all?"

"I have to fit into my dress at the Golden Globes."

The server laughed.

"She's not kidding," Stephen said, waggling his eyebrows.

The girl cradled her notepad over her heart. "I'd give *anything* to be there. How did you swing *that*?"

"We were in the wrong place at the wrong time," I said.

"She doesn't mean that," Stephen countered. "It's her life-long dream."

"Is not."

Our server looked at me. Not knowing who to believe, she just nodded and bowed out.

"Now," Stephen said. "About my plan to trap Axel into a confession."

"By all means, let's hear it."

He unrolled the napkin that held his silverware. "So far that's all I have."

"That's not a plan. The invasion of Iraq was a plan."

"We could get Leilani to wear a wire and ask him about it when he's drunk. I bet he drinks like a fish."

"I've got a better idea. I talked to the hospice nurse who took care of Jackson Dunn's mother. She said the abuser was Oskar."

Our server appeared, balancing a tray. "Grand Slam and OJ, English muffin and tea. Anything else?"

"Tabasco sauce and mustard," Stephen said.

I shuddered. "*Mustard?*"

"Goes on the sausage."

"Back in a flash," the girl said, wisely refraining from sharing her thoughts.

Stephen poured maple syrup over everything on his plate. Unable to watch, I shut my eyes and took the opportunity to ask a silent blessing.

"Okay," he said. "Sounds like we need to concentrate on Mr. Dunn."

I picked up my muffin, trying not to compare my austere fare with his cornucopia of cholesterol. "Remember what you found in the prop room the other day?"

"The rubber gloves?"

"You said they were small—too small for Axel, anyway."

He nodded.

I took out my phone. "Have you ever gotten a good look at Jackson's hands?"

"Not really."

"He did a lot of waving at the premiere." I went to YouTube and searched for a video of that night.

There was only one clip, the event having been widely ignored. Whoever took it must have had the shakes. But he or she was close enough to get a good shot of Jackson's hands. They weren't freakish, but they were smaller than his wife's.

"Circumstantial evidence," I mumbled. "Probably not evidence at all."

"But not *absolutely* not evidence." He was alarmingly close to finishing his meal.

I put the phone away. "And enough to keep him in our sights. The question is how to convince the police to have him in theirs."

"Are you going to finish that muffin?" he asked, dabbing at the corner of his mouth with his napkin.

"Yes, if only to keep you from exploding."

"Hey, did you ever see *Monty Python's The Meaning of Life*? There's a scene with this fat guy Mr. Creosote, and he eats this 'waffer-thin' mint after a huge meal, and—"

"Say no more."

"Never saw such a mess."

"*Say. No. More.*"

Wisely, he didn't.

* * *

That night I dreamed of Oskar.

It was definitely not romantic. I was in his office, except that it wasn't really me. It was a young Beverly Dunn, sitting on the edge of her chair, purse clutched with both hands, listening raptly as he painted a rosy picture of her future at Parthenon Arts. Oskar should have had more hair, this being decades ago. But for some reason he looked exactly as he did now.

"A pretty girl like you can go far in this business," he was saying. "But there are hundreds of pretty girls in town and millions more across the country. Are you special?"

I swallowed. "I hope so."

He shook his head. "Here's what makes a girl special: Having the right friends. I think we could be friends, Beverly. Good friends."

"Thank you."

He sat on the front of his desk. "Are you ashamed of your body, young lady?"

I could feel myself blush. "Should I be?"

He laughed. "Not at all. I suppose you have a boyfriend."

"Not now. Once."

"Then you won't mind taking off your dress, will you?"

"Why?"

He shrugged. "The most beautiful people get the most iconic roles. I need to see whether you have what it takes."

I felt in my purse for my pepper spray, but it was gone. Beverly Dunn didn't have any.

"I'll help if you like." He stood up, half-smiling.

I wouldn't have started unbuttoning my dress, but Beverly Dunn was too scared not to.

He stepped forward, his palm reaching for my cheek. "That's right. Let's be friends, shall we?"

I woke up sweating. The bedside clock said it was 3:00 a.m.

I lay there for an hour.

There was no question what I had to do: Confront the man who'd broken Beverly Dunn.

* * *

I didn't tell Stephen where I was going the next morning.

As usual, Oskar's secretary couldn't remember my name. But she didn't pretend he wasn't in.

He was sitting at his desk, comparing two costume drawings. "For my next picture," he said without looking up. "Have you heard of John Green?"

"*The Fault in Our Stars.* Yes."

"This is one of his lesser-known, earlier works. But if *Winchester County* does as well as some are predicting, perhaps the rising tide will lift another boat." He paused. "To what do I owe your visit, Ms. . . ."

"Neville."

He looked me in the eye. "Perhaps you're dissatisfied with your seat at the Golden Globes?"

"Not at all."

If he'd been smiling, it would have faded. But he wasn't.

I sat across from him. "I want to talk to you about Beverly Dunn."

He raised his chin. "Who?"

"Please don't deny knowing her. You'll just be wasting your time and mine."

He folded his arms across his chest. "As far as I'm concerned, I don't have to talk to you about anything anymore. We've fulfilled our contractual obligation. After you and that young bumbler get your chance to play dress-up at the ceremony, I'll be happy to hear you're on a plane back to wherever you came from."

"I talked with the nurse who was with Beverly when she died. She told the nurse who'd assaulted her."

"Really. And who would that be?"

"I believe you know."

"Even if I knew what you were talking about, what you're implying is absurd. I have never done anything non-consensual with anyone. I barely remember Dunn's mother, except that she was a terrible actress. Giving her a role was a matter of charity."

"The nurse has no reason to lie."

"Everyone lies at some point." He pushed the drawings away. "All hearsay. And why didn't this nurse say something years ago? Why didn't Dunn's mother?"

"You're a man with power. Their word against yours. Who would have listened?"

He scoffed. "Oh, they're listening now, aren't they? Guilty until proven innocent. If I had a nickel for every baseless accusation that's ruined the career of a man in this business, I'd be able to finance my next picture alone."

My heart was hammering. The man at the desk was too much like the man in my dream.

I reached for the pepper spray. This time my fingers touched it.

Lightheaded, I withdrew my hand. Bad time to make rash decisions.

"Anything else, Ms. Neville?"

I was too angry to say anything.

"I'm sure you can see yourself out."

He went back to his drawings.

Turning, I headed for the door. He was smiling, I just knew it.

* * *

When I told Stephen what had happened, he reacted with his usual restraint.

"I'm gonna grab him by his black lapels and bash his head against his desk."

"You are *not*."

"We can't let him get away with this crap."

"I'm going to ask the hospice nurse if she'd be willing to testify in court to what Dunn's mother said."

He scratched his chin. "When does the statute of limitations run out for this kind of stuff?"

"I'm not sure. But if she's up to it, we may have some leverage with the police."

"Okay. Want me to go?"

I shook my head. "Not that you're headstrong and scary. But I'm sure you have better things to do, like working on your screenplay."

"It's not going very well."

"All the more reason to work on it."

* * *

Nurse Agnes reluctantly gave me her address over the phone. It was a half-hour away.

Golden State Assisted Living was the kind of place I hoped not to end up in. I'd seen worse, but the quiet gloom in the hallway made me shiver.

I found her sitting on the bed in her tiny apartment, an untouched tray of soup and crackers on the dresser. Frail and dressed in a gray sweatsuit, she looked as though she were in hospice herself.

A classical music station was playing on her radio. She switched it off.

"Excuse the noise," she said.

"I met with Oskar Pulaski. It was like talking to a brick wall."

"Can't say I'm surprised."

"He denies everything. Seems to think he's above the law."

She nodded. "Maybe he is."

"Not if you'd be willing to say in court what you said to me."

She smoothed the rumpled blanket. "Would it really make a difference?"

"It could make a *huge* difference. It could light a fire under the police."

"But it happened so long ago."

"Things have changed. The system listens to women now."

She sighed. "So I've heard."

"Agnes, this is your chance to do for Beverly what you couldn't do then."

"All right. If the Lord sees fit for me to last long enough, I'll do it."

"They might even be able to take a deposition if you couldn't be there." I pulled my purse over my shoulder. "I'll keep in touch. Thank you."

When I closed the door behind me, I heard the radio come to life again.

In the car I dialed Marvin.

"Cranberry? They still after you?"

"Probably. I need your advice on something." I explained what I'd learned about the Pulaski-Dunn connection.

"Congratulations. That nurse is a hero. But I doubt it's enough for the police to act, based on what they haven't done so far."

"Any suggestions?"

"Have you confronted Mr. Dunn?"

"Not yet."

"If you decide to, you might do it in a public place where it's relatively safe. Maybe get somebody with a weapon to keep an eye on you."

It sounded a little crazy, but I didn't tell him that.

"I'll think about it," I said.

"Call me anytime."

"Thanks."

After hanging up, I checked my watch.

The Golden Globes were less than 48 hours away.

CHAPTER 34

THE PARK NEAR THE OASIS GARDENS WAS CROWDED WITH skateboarders, strollers, and frantic moms yanking toddlers from the Olympic-sized puddle surrounding the leaky drinking fountain. Perfect for following Marvin's advice to meet Jackson Dunn in a public place. Stephen swore he hadn't brought a weapon.

To my surprise, Jackson arrived in a Silverado pickup. "Shouldn't he be driving a Mercedes or something?" I asked Stephen, sitting next to him at a picnic table.

"He's a man of the people, right?"

"That's what they'd like us to believe."

To my greater surprise, the actor wasn't alone. He held hands with a pouting girl, maybe five years old, with red braids and a miniature version of the kind of dress you might find on Rodeo Drive.

"His granddaughter, I bet," Stephen said.

Jackson gave us a wave as he approached. "This is Diane. Say hello to my friends, honey."

Ignoring the request, the girl pointed at the swings. "Push me."

Jackson gave us a "what can you do" shrug. "Meet you over there," he said.

"This is a little awkward," I mumbled to Stephen. "We're going to discuss some rather adult subjects."

"Something tells me she won't be paying much attention."

By the time we reached the swings, Diane was barking orders. "Higher!"

Jackson complied. "What can I do for you?" he asked us, keeping his eyes fixed on the Shirley Temple from hell.

I backed away, avoiding the arc described by an older child who seemed bent on catapulting himself to Catalina Island. "I talked with Agnes."

"Who?"

"The hospice nurse who took care of your mother."

He looked at me. "My God, she's still alive? She seemed so old."

"She told me who abused your mom."

"Who?"

"Oskar Pulaski."

"Higher!" the little girl commanded.

Jackson gave her a mighty shove, then stepped toward me. "She's right. And, yes, I have a grudge against Oskar. Can you blame me?"

"Of course not."

"But I can't imagine being violent. No one who knows me would even suggest I'd hurt somebody."

Suddenly, at the zenith of his arc, the older boy let go of the chains and bailed out. He sailed a good 20 feet and landed on his knees in the sand. Scrambling to his feet, he proceeded to strike a *Rocky* pose nobody else seemed to notice.

Stephen shoved his hands in his pockets. "How do you explain the rubber gloves?"

Jackson scratched his head. "What rubber gloves?"

"I found some in the prop room."

"So what? Ask the prop guy why they're there."

"They're size S, for small. Axel has big hands."

"And I don't?"

"Not according to a video shot at the premiere."

The actor laughed and held up his hands. "How big are they supposed to be?"

Impatient with this line of questioning, I broke in. "Circumstantial evidence, I know."

Still smiling, he shook his head. "I don't know the first thing about switching guns that are supposed to fire blanks or ramps that send cars off bridges."

"Hey!" his granddaughter cried. "You can't quit!"

"If you want to pursue a case against Oskar using the nurse's testimony, I'm all for it." He resumed launching the girl toward the clouds. "I'll testify myself if you like. Now, if you'll excuse me, I have some granddaddying to do."

We headed toward the car. "What do you think?" Stephen asked.

"Not sure."

"Maybe he's lying, maybe not. But Axel's the only one who knows how to cause those so-called accidents. We've got to smoke him out."

"How colorful. But vague."

"Okay, how's this? We get Leilani to do it."

I stared. "You mean the Leilani from an alternative universe who isn't scared of him and kicks butt?"

"So it's not a perfect plan. You got a better one?"

"Yeah, but waterboarding's out of fashion."

"We've got to get her somewhere to talk. Away from her dipweed boyfriend. I think she likes the ocean."

"You have her number?"

He nodded and took out his phone. "Don't forget your sunscreen," he said.

* * *

Will Rogers State Beach was practically deserted the next morning, probably since almost nobody went there before 9:00 a.m. It was chilly; the weather report on the car radio had promised Death Valley heat later.

Leilani wasn't hard to spot. Rounded straw hat, sunglasses, one-piece pink bathing suit that made me shiver vicariously. She sat on one of those webbed aluminum lounge chairs, reading.

"Sorry I've only got one chair," she called over the roar of the surf. "Got a blanket if you want."

We sat. I pulled my knees up to my chest, wishing I'd brought a sweater.

"What are you reading?" I asked.

"Script for my next project. Oskar's making a John Green movie."

"So we've heard."

"We'd like to talk to you about Axel," Stephen said.

She put the script down. "I know you don't like him."

"He doesn't deserve you."

"Is that why you're here? To get me to break up with him?"

Stephen shook his head. "He could be behind at least some of the weird stuff that's happened. Like my getting shot. And Jim Oakley's so-called accident."

"Has he got something against Oskar?" I asked.

She looked around as if to make sure nobody important was listening. An elderly man with a metal detector trudged past, his flip-flops churning sand.

"I don't know of anything specific," she said. "But I can't think of anybody who actually *likes* Oskar."

Stephen stretched out on the blanket. "Who else at the studio knows how to sabotage stuff? Like guns and stunts?"

"Nobody, I guess."

She fidgeted. "Is there anything else? I . . . have to read this by the end of the day."

"You're nervous, aren't you?" I asked. "Afraid Axel's going to see you with us."

"No comment."

Stephen sat up. "I can protect you."

I closed my eyes. "Let's not go down that road. You've already been shot and beaten to a pulp, and that's without trying to defend anybody."

I paused. "Leilani, you can do so much better than Axel. You've got to stand up for yourself before it's too late. Beverly Dunn never did that, and look what happened to her."

"Beverly Dunn? Who's that?"

"Jackson's mother. Oskar abused her."

She hugged herself. "I've heard rumors about him for years. But I can't change him, or Axel, or the world."

"But you can change your future," I said.

"I'll think about it."

I hauled myself off the blanket, found a business card in my purse, and handed it to her.

"Call me," I said.

* * *

"Ever feel like you've hit a brick wall?"

I was standing next to the rental car, brushing sand from my feet.

"Yeah," Stephen said. "I was on my bike in fifth grade, got the bottom of my jeans caught in the gears, and went flying at—"

"We're not getting anywhere. The clock's ticking. Never thought I'd say this, but we should go to the police."

"With what?"

"Our suspicions. It's not like we don't have *anything*. Nurse Agnes is willing to testify."

He sighed. "As long as we don't have to deal with those two clowns who wouldn't do anything about the old lady guard person."

"Ask the Internet how to get to the station."

We climbed into the car, and he started directing.

* * *

It goes without saying that we got the same apathetic pair we'd encountered before. I'm sure they had names, but I just thought of them as the tall one and the short one.

Their desks were adjacent. As we laid out our case, they looked bored. When we were done, the tall one pulled some forms from a drawer.

"Too complicated," he said.

"You say the old nurse is willing to be deposed?" the short one asked. He looked at his partner. "*That's* something."

"If we start messing with every guy in Hollywood who can't keep his pants zipped, we won't have time for real crimes."

"I think that came out wrong," the short one said.

"Okay, but we could also find ourselves out of a job. Pulaski's not really a major player, but most of these guys are well-connected."

I took the phone from my purse and aimed the camera at them. "Would you like to repeat that for YouTube?"

They looked at each other. "Oh, *that's* it," said the tall one. "Blame the *good* guys."

Long silence. I put the phone back.

Finally the short one returned the forms to his desk drawer. "We'll make you a deal. If you can find any real evidence linking Dunn with this Axel guy, we'll take a deposition and open an investigation."

I raised an eyebrow. "Really?"

"But these things take time. And don't expect the SWAT team to come crashing through anybody's door."

I nodded. "Consider my expectations lowered."

"If that's possible," Stephen said.

Back in the car, I turned on the ignition. "Something went right."

"Must be a mistake."

"Depends on what real evidence is."

"We'll know it when we see it."

"Then let's start looking," I said.

CHAPTER 35

"YOU SURE THOSE GUYS ARE REAL COPS?" STEPHEN ASKED. WE were halfway back to the studio, looking for a place to stop for lunch.

"Pretty hard to fake it right there at the station, don't you think?"

"Maybe they're all like that around here."

"The flakiness capital of the world, if you don't count Battle Creek, Michigan."

He looked perplexed. "I don't get it."

"Flakes. Like cornflakes, bran flakes. Kellogg's is in Battle Creek."

"Where's General Mills?"

"I have no idea. Let's apply your massive brainpower to finding a way to prove Jackson and Axel were more than passing acquaintances."

The rather unattractive scenery whizzed by as we concentrated. At least I hoped *he* was, since I was coming up empty.

"The old lady at the guardhouse. She could have seen them together. And that got her killed."

"It was a heart attack. And don't tell me they scared her to death. A little too convenient."

He sat up straight. "Hey, there's a Taco Bell."

I shook my head. "I'm boycotting them. They took Pintos 'n' Cheese off the menu."

He slumped in the seat, pouting.

"The obvious solution," I said, "is to check phone records to see whether Jackson and Axel talked."

"And the obvious solution to *that* is for the police to get the records."

I sighed. "Not if it means filling out a form. They put the ball in our court."

A KFC was approaching on the right. "You have anything against Colonel Sanders?" Stephen asked, sounding desperate.

"Other than the fact that he was a privileged white male Southerner who killed thousands with his secret recipe? I guess not."

We did the drive-thru, then got back on the highway. Fried chicken is the worst thing to eat while you're driving, except for practically everything else—but somehow we managed.

"I wonder whether there's a surveillance camera at the studio," I said, looking in vain for more napkins on the floor. Sometimes being finger-lickin' isn't so good.

"How do we find out?"

I looked in the rearview mirror. He had a ring of Extra Crispy crumbs around his lips, which didn't seem to bother him a bit.

"Ask the new guard," I said.

He nodded and wiped his face with the paper bag, trying to look presentable. Amazingly, it didn't work.

The car still smelled of chicken fat and pepper gravy when we arrived at Parthenon Arts. Its parking lot was nearly empty. The new guard, a gym rat in khaki about 30 years younger than his predecessor, was doing something on his phone.

"Hey," I called.

He looked up. Or at least his head moved. I couldn't see his eyes through the dark sunglasses.

"Yep," he said.

"We're trying to figure out what happened to the lady who used to work here."

"Heart attack, I heard."

"Yes, but we wondered if there are surveillance cameras that keep an eye on the place."

"Oh, sure. At least a dozen. One's pointed at me. Another at the entrance to the nearest soundstage."

"I assume it records what it sees."

He nodded again.

"How long do they keep the tapes?"

"I don't think it's tape anymore. Probably on a hard drive. But that's a pretty long time ago."

"Can we look at them?"

"You'd have to do it in the Security office. Take a right after the water tower. Kind of a flat white building with a green door."

When we got there, the door was locked. I knocked.

"Just a minute," a voice called from inside.

A chair squeaked. A latch clicked.

"Yeah?" A woman in more khaki, presumably the gym rat's boss, regarded us suspiciously. She looked like a prize-fighter with a gray-blond ponytail sticking out the back of her Parthenon Arts cap. Not even Larry Shapiro had one of those.

I told her what I'd told Guardhouse Boy. She frowned. Clearly we'd interrupted her reading of the romance novel on her desk.

She shuffled a pack of DVDs, looking at the dates on strips of masking tape. "Can't guarantee you'll see anything useful."

We sat on two old wooden chairs. A grainy black-and-white image time-coded on the lower left swirled into view. Ten seconds later, it vanished.

She shook her head. "That's what I was afraid of. It's been erased."

She repeated the process with one more disk. The same thing happened.

"Who erased them?"

"Usually we wipe them within a couple of weeks. Unless there's been a break-in or something, no reason to keep them around."

"Well, it was worth a try," I said.

She lined up the DVDs and slipped them back into their case.

"How's the book?" I asked, pointing at her paperback.

She blushed. "Ain't mine," she said gruffly.

"Ah. My mistake."

It seemed the wisest answer. Like I almost said, she looked like a pugilist.

* * *

Neither of us said much on our way back to the motel. The car still smelled like KFC.

Finally I broke the silence. "Well, crap."

"Double crap," Stephen echoed.

"Maybe we should just focus on getting ready for the Golden Globes."

"I've got my tux." He paused. "I saw in *Variety* that Jackson Dunn is one of the presenters."

I rolled my eyes. "You know, I pretty much hate awards

shows. Who cares which rich celebrity wins? If I were nominated I might show up. *Might.*"

"Geez. Aren't you missing the point? People watch because they're rooting for somebody, or they want the glamour to rub off on them, or they hope some drunk will fall off the stage."

"Who else from our movie will be there?"

He shrugged. "Everybody, maybe. Or at least Oskar, Larry, Axel, Leilani, the makeup lady, and the costumer. Plus Ansel, naturally. Maybe Jim."

I thought for a moment. "What if Ansel had leftover footage showing Jackson and Axel together in the background? Maybe between takes, or testing the camera?"

"They couldn't just be together. They'd have to spend some real time talking."

"True." I paused. "I don't know Ansel's number. Don't suppose you do, either."

"Nope."

"And I'm not sure he'd cooperate anyway. I can't tell whether he loves Oskar or hates him. Or Larry."

Long silence. We were almost to the motel.

"What about Gretchen?" I asked. "The woman in the editing bay."

"What about her?"

"If anybody has access to leftover footage, she does."

"Yeah, I guess so."

"But how do we get hold of her?"

He took out his phone. "Maybe Leilani knows."

* * *

Leilani knew.

But Gretchen didn't want to meet with us.

Until she learned this could lead to Oskar's undoing.

We sat in the editing bay. "So you're looking for stray shots of Dunn and Testaverde."

I nodded. "*Long* stray shots."

"Like they're discussing something."

She sighed. "Okay." Snapping on the computer monitor, she proceeded to open a folder labeled WINCHESTER HOUSEKEEPING. There must have been a hundred clips.

Her pudgy fingers stroked the keyboard. "I'll play them one at a time."

There were a lot of half-focused shots of clapboards clapping. Stephen and I leaned over her shoulder, watching.

It got later and later. Eventually even the focused shots looked blurry.

"I should file a grievance with the Editor's Guild," she muttered.

I looked at my watch. It was 2:00 a.m.

"Nineteen clips to go," she said. "This had better go somewhere."

Seven files later, we hit pay dirt. Tentatively. The camera was too far away to tell us much.

"Definitely Jackson and Axel," Stephen said.

"Gretchen, can you zoom in?" I asked.

"Yeah, but it'll be pixelated."

"Try."

More stabbing of keys. "How's that?"

I bit my lip. "A little closer?"

She grunted and triple-clicked a button on the screen. "That's as far as I can go."

I squinted. "Can anybody read lips?"

Stephen leaned forward. "Those are lips?"

"Well, at least we've got them having a prolonged conversation."

Gretchen duplicated and renamed the file, then opened

another. We were down to the penultimate clip when our targets reappeared. This time they were closer.

She rolled her wrist around. "Carpal tunnel," she mumbled.

"I think we've got what we need," I said.

She copied and renamed the second file. "I've got a couple of small, portable drives," she said wearily. "Give you one for a hundred bucks."

"Fine," I said, taking out my checkbook.

Thirty seconds later I stowed the drive in my purse.

She powered down the computer.

"Get the son of a—"

"We'll do our best," I said.

CHAPTER 36

THE BIG NIGHT WAS FINALLY HERE. STEPHEN CAME BOUNDING down the stairs into the motel lobby.

"I've got a rip in the crotch of my tux," he whispered.

I pointed at the front desk. "I suggest you fix it with staples. Bet they've got some."

While he tried to charm the clerk into giving him what he needed, I took out my phone. We had to get to the Beverly Hills Hotel in 45 minutes, and I had no idea where it was.

Stephen thanked his benefactor and bent down to mend his pants.

"Maybe you should do that in the bathroom."

"How come?"

"If you have to ask, never mind." I looked away.

* * *

Not surprisingly, no one had reserved a parking space for us near the hotel. We had to pay $25 to squeeze in on the top floor of a garage that couldn't reasonably be called "nearby."

"My crotch seems to be holding," Stephen said as we

hustled down Sunset Boulevard. He was just loud enough that passersby raised their eyebrows and kept their distance.

I was wearing heels, which I never do, and which I vowed never to do again. Ankles aching, I led the way toward the police barricades, limos, and spotlights pointed skyward.

"Red carpet," Stephen said, panting. The paparazzi were facing the other direction.

"Is that Ryan Reynolds?" I asked.

"Ryan Gosling. People get them mixed up all the time."

Inside the lobby we handed over our tickets, kept the stubs, and joined the surge of superior genes and glitter that washed us into the auditorium. The seats were a sea of red velvet; the din sounded like a United Nations assembly, but with fewer languages and more plastic surgery.

Winchester County Homecoming had two tables reserved for a total of 16 people. Nine seats were still empty. Oskar was there, and Larry, along with Axel and Leilani and Ansel. And Jim, who smiled and waved at me from the other table.

"Jackson must be backstage getting ready to be a presenter," I said. "That leaves makeup, sound, editing—"

"Ladies and gentlemen, please take your seats," said an unseen announcer. The giant screen over the stage displayed the start of a five-minute countdown.

We sat down three seats from Oskar, who ignored us. "Hey," Stephen whispered. "Do you think they have any swag?"

I looked at our table. There was bottled water and a limited selection of booze. Nothing said SWAG on it.

He felt under his chair. "Jackpot!" he said, and hauled up a canvas bag with the Dolce & Gabbana logo on it. Taking the contents out one at a time and placing them on the table, he proceeded to sniff the cologne and make a face. Into his pocket went a miniature replica of the Golden Globes trophy, which resembled an upside-down doorknob.

"Ah, now we're talking," he said, and began to devour the edibles. A bar of Dove chocolate, a tiny flask of champagne, a mini-carton of oat milk, a gold-wrapped stick of biscotti. When it came to the package of organic dried green bean chips, he shuddered and offered them to me.

"Trying to cut down," I said.

The rest of our seats were filled just as the orchestra struck up the Golden Globes theme. Jackson and his wife beamed at life in general, not acknowledging anyone in particular.

The countdown hit 00:00. "Ladies and gentlemen," declared the announcer, "welcome to the annual Golden Globe Awards, sponsored by the Hollywood Foreign Press Association."

Cue the ovation. The music faded.

Stephen leaned in my direction. "There's no host, just presenters. They didn't want a repeat of last year."

I wanted to ask what had happened then, but the house lights went down and some guy from the foreign reporters strode onstage and made a dull but mercifully short speech about how much the arts contributed to society in these challenging times—and how selfless artists were when they questioned those who would condemn us all to a diet of cartoons and football.

"Spare me," I muttered, and downed the contents of my complimentary flask in one swallow.

Jackson got up. "Excuse me. Time to go backstage." He kissed his wife on top of her perfectly coiffed head and headed toward the rear exits.

The orchestra played off the foreign reporters guy. "Ladies and gentlemen," said the announcer, who sounded the same no matter what he was saying, "Robert Pattinson and Scarlett Johansson."

They came out and did their thing, with the usual

awkward attempts at humor and the mispronunciation of names. From then on things went smoothly enough, including Jackson's appearance with Sally Field to introduce clips of the nominees for Best Screenplay.

They started by joking that they'd never worked together before. "Why is that?" Ms. Field asked, trying not to look like she was reading from the teleprompter.

"My wife knew I liked you—I really *really* liked you."

The laughter was muted, the applause empathetic.

"It all begins with the written word," he intoned. "Without writers, we humble players would have nothing to say."

"Since the days of ancient Greece, playwrights have explored the human condition," his co-presenter added. "The inheritors of their mantle are the screenwriters. And that is why wordsmiths are so highly respected in our industry."

"Oh, *please*," I muttered.

I didn't like her. I really *really* didn't like her.

On the other hand, I knew she hadn't written the script. Some writer who knew it was all baloney had inserted his particular message from the Department of Wishful Thinking.

Not long after Jackson returned triumphantly to our table, it was time for a clip from *Winchester County Homecoming*. Jackson was in it, of course, doing a monologue about his mother. A startlingly loud cheer went up when it was done.

His wife made the fingers-crossed sign.

Finally Daniel Day-Lewis and Emily Blunt came to the podium for Best Motion Picture (Drama). Both actors, whose work I have greatly admired, earned my further admiration by not participating in the awkward humor sweepstakes. With great dignity they repeated the names of the nominees.

Ms. Blunt opened the envelope and handed it to Mr. Day-Lewis. "And the Golden Globe Award goes to . . ."

Some film about a lighthouse keeper.

Not *Winchester County Homecoming.*

"How many movies do we need about lighthouses?" I asked Stephen over the pandemonium.

A delegation of tuxes and gowns marched, waving, to the stage to accept the award. After the speeches, Jackson did his best to outsmile them.

"It's an honor just to be nominated," he said. I could almost see his halo.

* * *

When the credits rolled and the band stopped playing, Jackson stood up. "Who's going to the after party?"

"*Which* after party?" the director said. That's the question." He stood up, too, with the aid of his cane.

Jackson put his hands on the back of his chair. "There's a new club about six blocks from here. Built in the basement of a renovated warehouse. Camelot Seven."

"Oh, I've heard of that," Leilani said.

"And I'm not just recommending it because I own an interest."

"What do you think?" I asked Stephen.

He pumped his fist in the air. "Let's *after party!*"

I, of course, loved parties as much as the next hermit. But this chance would never come again—thank God.

Jim made his way over and touched my shoulder. "Honey, wish I could go with you. But I'm still running out of steam by ten o'clock."

"I'll miss you."

"Have fun anyway."

Stephen and I left our car in the parking garage and walked. So did most of the others.

With Jackson in the lead, we made it past the velvet rope and into a glass-walled labyrinth that echoed with a THUMP

THUMP THUMP THUMP that sounded like a whale's heartbeat. I carried my purse and the bag of swag.

"Are you going to eat the food parts?" Stephen asked.

I handed him the whole thing. "Enjoy," I said.

Eventually about half the cast and crew were there, getting drinks at the bar and lounging at glass tables. I thought I saw George Clooney and Jerry Seinfeld, though not together.

Oskar sipped a martini and kept looking at his watch. Axel, having already overindulged, pinched a passing server in a French maid outfit. Jackson held court, telling stories. Larry stuck with the nonalcoholic punch.

Finally Jackson got up, freshened his drink, and came over to me, looking smug.

I looked him in the eye. "I know what you did."

He frowned.

I fished in my purse for the hard drive and held it up. "You and Axel. You had a lot to talk about, didn't you?"

He backed off and threaded his way to Axel's table. They conferred. I couldn't read their lips, but I could tell plenty from their expressions.

Suddenly Axel glared at me and started moving through the crowd in my direction.

I leaned toward Stephen.

"I think I just made a mistake," I whispered.

* * *

We slipped out of the club and spotted a security guard, a beefy guy with a blue uniform and badge. And gun.

"Call 911," I said. "We're being followed."

"By who?"

"You'll see."

Stephen looked over his shoulder. "Axel's on our trail. Leilani, too."

We took the stairs. Before we could reach street level, Axel was about 10 yards behind us.

Ducking into a landing, we found ourselves facing Jackson.

He smiled.

"Took the elevator," he said.

CHAPTER 37

JACKSON REACHED OUT, HIS HAND PALM-UP.

"I'll take that hard drive."

Pushing me aside, Stephen charged our opponent. There was a whiff of liquor behind me as Axel shoved me in the opposite direction and grabbed Stephen by the shoulders.

Locking his arm around Stephen's neck, Axel proceeded to whirl and fling him down the stairs. Stephen flailed as his shoulder hit the metal rail and the bag of swag went flying, the remaining loot clanging into the abyss.

I backed away, the concrete wall cold behind me. Stephen tried to snag the rail but lost his balance and went headfirst over the side. With both hands I caught the hem of his pants, breaking a nail, and held on for dear life.

"Can you find something to grab? I can't do this forever." I could feel the fabric slipping from my sweaty grip. I hoped the staples wouldn't give way.

Axel, his jaw clenched, wobbled slightly as he turned to confront me. Fumbling under the jacket of his tux, he withdrew a pistol, black and squarish. I didn't know much about guns, but I figured this one wasn't shooting blanks.

He pointed it at my head.

"The hard drive," he said.

I swallowed.

"Can't get it out of my purse while I'm holding my friend's leg."

He came closer. "Well, I can fix that. Let him go."

I shook my head.

Leilani, still behind her toxic boyfriend, stamped her foot. "*No!*"

To my astonishment, she raised her leg and kicked him in the middle of his spine. She wasn't wearing heels, but didn't need them.

With an *ooof*, the wind knocked out of him, he stumbled forward and tumbled down the stairs. All I heard when he hit the bottom was a grunt. The usual string of expletives would have to wait until he found his breath.

Leilani joined me at the rail and snatched Stephen's other leg. "On three, *pull!*" she yelled. "One . . . two . . ."

The muscles in my arms and sides burned as we hauled up our remarkably weighty catch. Leilani latched onto his elbow, braced her knees against the side of the staircase, and dragged him over the rail.

He was panting. So were we.

"Pretty strong staples," he said, looking down at his pants.

I sagged against the rail. "Leilani," I said. "You were great."

"Sometimes you just can't take it anymore."

There was a rustling at the bottom of the stairway. "Oh, you'll take it, all right," Axel muttered, getting to his feet. Having found sufficient oxygen, he let loose with a hurricane of curses.

The gun was in his hand. I couldn't tell which of us it was pointed at.

What mattered was that none of us was pointing back.

* * *

Ducking down, I grabbed the tarnished brass knob on the EXIT door. Unlocked.

Axel fired. The bullet grazed my ear, stinging, and ricocheted somewhere in the stairwell.

Should be a landing on the other side. If I could just—

Jim would have known what to do. He'd probably do one of those drop-and-roll moves he tried to teach us that day. The basic roll, Arabian roll, suicide roll. Stephen and Hunter had nearly killed themselves in the process.

Another blast of profanity from Axel echoed. Another shot. Leilani cried out.

I wrenched the knob, pushed, and dove into the darkness. Shoulder first, tucking my arm under, gripping my purse.

Unfortunately, I couldn't manage the sideways somersault or the bouncing back, and it didn't look or feel like dancing in slow motion.

I hit the concrete floor like a family pack of raw hamburger. My shoulder met it first, followed by my right cheek.

Fortunately, it was too dark to see whether I was bleeding. A lone fluorescent tube flickered on the verge of burnout. I lay there, stunned.

The door opened behind me. If it was Axel, this was the end.

"Carolyn, you surprise me." It was Jackson.

As far as I knew, he didn't have a gun. But right now he didn't need one.

"So you know what I did, eh? I really doubt you do."

"Were you behind all the accidents and injuries?"

"Depends on what you mean by *behind*."

"Take the incident with the rifle and Stephen's shoulder."

He shrugged. "Guess I was. My idea, but Axel's expertise was indispensable."

"The old lady in the guardhouse."

"Elaine?" He shook his head. "Heart attack. I didn't put on one of Axel's masks and scare her, either."

"Larry and the horse?"

"Pure chance the plane flew over. As for the stallion, I'm not Dr. Doolittle. I can't talk to the animals, much less control them."

"The night I was run off the road in the park?"

He looked behind him to make sure we were alone. "I was the inspiration, but Axel's a better driver."

I rolled over, trying to shield my purse. "Jim Oakley. You tried to kill him, didn't you?"

He sighed. "No. He wasn't supposed to die, just shut production down. Turns out old cars and bridges and ramps are unpredictable."

He checked his watch. "Wish we could continue this conversation, but I'm in a bit of a hurry. Mr. Testaverde will be here any time to tie up loose ends."

He grabbed my purse, yanking it off my arm. I felt a tendon ripping. The pain was sharp enough to warrant some unbridled cussing, but I didn't have the energy.

"Gotta go," he said.

I listened for Stephen or Leilani. Nothing.

But then there were feet clambering up the stairs. The door clicked open again.

Axel's nose and temple were bleeding. His tux was smeared with dirt. That muscle in his cheek quivered.

He had the gun. Raising it, he aimed at me.

"'Bye," he whispered.

BAM! The door flew open. A shot rang out.

It was the security guard. The beefy one in the blue uniform, from the club.

Axel's eyes grew wide. The gun dangled from his trigger finger, then dropped to the floor.

So did he.

* * *

The guard holstered his revolver, then bent down to take Axel's pulse. "He's alive."

He looked at me. "I'd ask whether you're okay, but you obviously aren't."

I managed to get to a sitting position. Everything was throbbing.

Stephen limped in, dazed.

"That shot I heard," I said. "Sounded like it hit Leilani."

"Yeah, but in the leg. Axel was pretty wasted." He squinted at me, the light still flickering. "Speaking of which, your ear is bleeding. So's your cheek."

The guard handcuffed Axel, who was starting to groan. "I called 911 back at the club. Good suggestion."

Again the door opened. Leilani came in and leaned against the wall. She looked down at Axel. "Loser," she said.

Jackson, who'd been lingering in the shadows and holding my purse, edged toward the door. I tried to get up but couldn't.

"Stop that guy," I said. "He's got—"

The door burst open one more time. Two cops, a man and a woman. The woman hit Jackson like a football lineman. He went down like a piñata on Cinco de Mayo.

My purse came to rest a few feet in front of me. After a brief crawl I rummaged around and felt the hard drive.

Seemed like a good thing.

Smiling, I passed out.

* * *

I woke up in the emergency room, lying on a bed, not hooked up to anything. No vital body parts seemed to be missing. Stephen and Leilani sat across from me. We were all black eyes, bruises, and bandages. Curtains separated us from the normal patients.

I looked around. "Where's my purse?"

Leilani held up a large white plastic bag with the Cedars-Sinai logo. "With your other personal belongings."

"Can't lose that drive."

"It's here, I promise."

I told them what Jackson had said in the stairwell.

Stephen shook his head. "So Jim was an accident." He turned to me. "How do you feel?"

"Like crap. Did they give me anything for the pain?"

He shook his head. "We just got here. You've been out for an hour."

Leilani shivered. "I hope Axel can't make bail. I'll need a restraining order."

"They won't let him out," I said. "Jackson, maybe, but just until the trial."

Stephen brushed dirt off his tux. "Oskar better get arrested."

I closed my eyes. "He will if we get that drive to the police."

Just then a woman in scrubs slipped from behind the curtain. She looked at me, then Stephen, then Leilani. "Who's first?"

I raised my hand. "*Ow.* Bad idea."

She consulted her clipboard. "My God, what happened to you guys?"

"Long story," I said.

* * *

They let me out the next morning. After breakfast Stephen and I made reservations to fly home.

"Got to call Jim," I said.

"To say goodbye? Shouldn't you do it in person?"

"Yeah, I guess. I hate goodbyes."

I picked up my phone. Jim picked up on the seventh ring.

"I need to talk to you," I said.

"Okay."

"Are you at home?"

"Yep."

"I'll be there in twenty minutes."

He answered the door wearing his cowboy hat, having apparently retrieved it from the pastor. "I was just on my way out, but I've got plenty of time for you."

We sat on the couch.

"You're leavin'," he said.

I nodded.

"It's not like we didn't know this would happen, Carolyn."

"I want to rewrite this ending. I want to believe it's not really over."

He took off his hat and set it on the coffee table. "Doesn't have to be."

"Why not?"

"I've been thinking. Tinseltown's kind of lost its luster. And I've broken my last bone. Maybe I should hightail it back to Texas and take care of my mom and sister. I'm sure I could find work, maybe at the American Rodeo Riders Association."

"We'd still be a thousand miles apart."

"Yeah, but it wouldn't be forever. And they've got these things called *planes* . . ."

I leaned forward. "Maybe Hunter will fire me. Then I'll have lots of time on my hands."

It was his turn to lean forward. He looked into my eyes.

His lips met mine.

Not making out, of course.

"Just leave the light on," he said, and smiled.

EPILOGUE

Six months later, Jim got that job. Goodwill Ambassador. He didn't mind the cut in pay.

Hunter didn't fire me. So far Jim and I have gotten together twice. I'm leaving the light on and the door open.

Nurse Agnes' deposition led to Oskar's indictment. He's roaming free on his own recognizance. After all the media coverage, nine other women came forward and said he'd assaulted them, too.

Agnes died a week ago.

Jackson Dunn and Axel, who have the same celebrity lawyer, are in jail awaiting trial for attempted murder.

Leilani is working on the John Green movie, now being produced and directed by Larry Shapiro—financed by a settlement with the horse wrangler, who was found to be negligent.

Leilani says this may be her last picture; she'd like to run a shelter for battered women.

Stephen's still working on his screenplay, now titled *Robins* and involving at least a dozen Batman sidekicks, real and imaginary.

Carmella married that well-known man she kept talking about. Turned out to be the mayor of San Diego. Must have reminded her of Harrison Yoder, only 30 years younger.

And Hunter? He still wants to direct.

ACKNOWLEDGMENTS

Thanks to my son the recording artist, Jonathan, for his help with showbiz and Los Angeles locations. And for rushing to order *Murder Most Annoying*, the first book in this series. Thanks also to my niece, Heather Dane, for giving me a nurse's perspective on some medical questions.

A LOOK AT BOOK 5: MURDER MOST UNLUCKY

A WITTY MYSTERY FULL OF SUSPENSE AND ACTION.

Thanks to a children's writer with a gambling addiction, editors Carolyn Neville and Stephen Ames are caught up in a cross-country flight while evading an organized crime family.

Carolyn and Stephen are playing miniature golf with a children's author when an innocent bystander suddenly dies – he has been mistaken for the writer. They scramble to stay one step ahead of the killer on a road trip, all while trying to dodge the crime family's enforcers.

Carolyn has her hands full this time, with trying to survive, protect her colleagues, and take down a seemingly bullet-proof crime lord's daughter.

For fans of Horace Rumpole, Monk and Stephanie Plum, the Carolyn Neville Mysteries are full of witty humor and suspense.

COMING AUGUST 2021

ABOUT THE AUTHOR

John Duckworth is a novelist, editor, playwright, scriptwriter, cartoonist, and father of twins. After earning his bachelor's degree at Linfield College, he spent 35 years in the publishing industry as a curmudgeonly editor, product developer, and author, working with people like Ken Blanchard, Dr. Kevin Leman, Richard Foster, and Calvin Miller, producers like VeggieTales, organizations like Focus on the Family and companies like Random House, Thomas Nelson, NavPress, Group Publishing, Zondervan and Rainfall Toys.

His works include *Joan 'n' the Whale, Just for a Moment I Saw the Light*, four collections of short plays, a ton of curriculum, at least 90 articles and short stories and three videos about a giant chipmunk puppet. He also contributed chapters to several trade books, edited scores of nonfiction and fiction titles, wrote animation and live action scripts for a major video series, several ounces of online content, and co-directed a traveling drama troupe called the Jericho Roadshow. On the radio he's done voice-over work for the popular *Adventures in Odyssey* program and wrote, directed, and performed in *The Semi-Amusing Half-Hour Comedy Show*.

After producing nearly 250 issues of weekly publications *Power for Living* and *FreeWay*, he created seven multi-volume series of youth ministry resources. He's edited or rewritten hundreds of books, articles, and lesson plans.

John's hobbies include figuring out how to promote himself while pretending to be humble, reading stories to children in the hospital, holding tiny babies in the neonatal intensive care unit, and feeding the cat. He and his lovely wife, Liz, live in Colorado Springs.